Red Flo

Donald Thomas is an acclaimed novelist, poet, playwright and biographer. His poems *Point of Contact* won the Eric Gregory Award, his biography *Robert Browning* was runner-up for the Whitbread Award, and *The Victorian Underworld* was shortlisted for a CWA Gold Dagger Award in 1998. Among his documentary drama, he has written two series of *The Detectives* for the BBC.

Donald Thomas is also the author of the Inspector Swain series of Victorian mysteries, including *The Arrest of Scotland Yard* and *The Ripper's Apprentice,* and his most recent crime novel is *Sherlock Holmes and the Running Noose.* Sonny Tarrant first appeared in *Dancing in the Dark,* which was published in 1992.

By the same author:

Donald Thomas

Red Flowers for Lady Blue

PAN BOOKS

First published 2000 by Macmillan

This edition published 2001 by Pan Books
an imprint of Macmillan Publishers Ltd
25 Eccleston Place, London SW1W 9NF,
Basingstoke and Oxford
Associated companies throughout the world
www.macmillan.com

ISBN 0 330 39252 2

1 3 5 7 9 8 6 4 2

A CIP catalogue record for this book is available from
the British Library.

Phototypeset by Intype London Ltd
Printed and bound in Great Britain by
Mackays of Chatham plc, Chatham, Kent

For Alan Quick and Carol Lambard

Author's Note

The action of the following novel is set within
the brief reign of King Edward VIII, later Duke
of Windsor, between January and December 1936.

The crime of 'constructive murder' or 'constructive
malice' was abolished by section 1 of the Homicide
Act 1957.

January

Cat's-Eyes

Chapter One

'Got a match?'

In the driving mirror, the scrape of a Swan Vesta cast a flaring image of the car's interior. Its wavering flame lit three profiles, clean-shaven but for the driver's narrow David Niven moustache. The glow flickered over polished wood on the dashboard, the clock and instrument panels, white figures on black within silver-chrome rims.

Sandboy shook the match out. McGouran took the box and dropped it into his pocket. In the front passenger seat, Gillis sat back against the braided leather and sang with a soft impatience, 'I saw my girl at the pictures . . . Up there on the silver screen . . .'

He stopped singing and glanced at Sandboy, 'You sure Pender'll be alone?'

Sandboy adjusted the angle of his soft felt hat. 'Just him and the old woman. They don't have servants sleeping in. They'll be no trouble. Pelly Pender's well past that.'

The rain began again. It fell from a night sky, as if pouring through holes torn in the clouds by a strong wind, bouncing like glass marbles on the black tarmac of the street. The slate roofs of drab domestic terraces off the arterial roads of south London glinted sleek in the downpour.

Here and there, a light went out behind a curtained window at ground level and another came on upstairs. A nation stirred Ovaltine or Bourn-Vita into its bedtime milk. Despite the tapering bonnet of its black chassis, the expensive chrome lining of its running-boards, spare-wheel boot and headlamps, no one in St Vincent Street had paid the Rover any attention.

Sandboy straightened his hat in the mirror and rested his hands on the wheel. His position in the leather driving seat gave him a new authority. He seemed to himself like the leader of a patrol or a platoon in a trench raid. Behind him, McGouran folded a woollen scarf more closely over his throat and fastened the top button of his raincoat. He said sharply, 'For God's sake let's move, Sandy.'

Sandboy shook his head. 'Ten o'clock the street lights go out down the side roads in Purley and Coulsdon. That's when we'll be at Rooks Lane. The less anyone can see, the better.'

Gillis hummed to himself again, 'I saw my girl at the pictures . . .'

Sandboy smoked without taking the cigarette from his mouth. His hands were busy now with the neat silver shape of a Walden Safety Revolver, checking the twelve chambers for .22 ammunition.

'Christ!' said Gillis plaintively. 'It's only old Pender and his woman. What the fuck you want to bring that thing for?'

Sandboy took the cigarette from his mouth at leisure and blew out smoke. 'Show. Mostly for show. Definitely not noise. Any case, you can't do much damage with something this small. Mac's used one before, if it ever comes to that. Just for show.'

4

'Guns,' Gillis said. He drew on his brown kid gloves.

The whine of a train leaving Streatham Common for Victoria was lost in a shower of sparks as the track divided beyond Greyhound Lane. Across the far end of St Vincent Street, a tram swayed on the curve of Streatham High Road like a fully lit ocean liner riding a night swell. Along its upper deck, the rain shone on a banner advertisement for Jack Buchanan and Elsie Randolph in *This'll Make You Whistle*, at the Streatham Hill Empire. The tram picked up speed, the steel edge of its wheels grinding against iron rails as it whined towards Thornton Heath and Croydon.

McGouran tapped Sandboy's shoulder. 'This friend of yours, Sonny Tarrant. All right, he's big-time now. But how? How come he got so big, in the first place?'

Sandboy took the cigarette from his mouth again. 'Tarrant's not my friend. He's not anyone's friend. I reckon even the women only do it for money or because they have to. Old Manders. Manny, that runs the picture-house. He's the one who knows Tarrant. That's all.'

'So what's between them?'

Sandboy shrugged, frowned at the little revolver and sighted it. 'Manny's about skint, but for what Tarrant gives him. Still, he's a good front. Tarrant's got money he shouldn't have and he needs to put it somewhere. Until he pulls the curtain down on Manny, that's where it is. The Garden Royal Hotel, the Luxor Picturedrome, Brandons Garages. Sorry. Except the hotel. Tarrant fronts that himself.

'But how come he got so big, though?' McGouran insisted, 'If he's pulled out of robbing and rackets? He can't be forty, even now.'

Sandboy looked at the revolver by the reflected

5

yellow-green slant of the street lamps. He wrapped the gun in its cloth and put it away. 'Horses, dog tracks to begin with. He pulled a big stunt out the White City. When he was eighteen or twenty.'

McGouran grunted. 'No one pulls in money like that on the dogs.'

'Tarrant did. Doping, not betting.'

Gillis stopped his nervous humming and interrupted them. 'Someone's having you on, Sandy. Doping greyhounds out the White City? I seen the outfit at Harringay, where they're strictly second division. Even there the racing association got dozens of retired coppers at the stadium to make sure it never happens.'

'I know that.'

'White City, week before the race, you have to leave your dog in their kennels. They have police there, too, even at the kennel yards, and they don't even tell the dog owners where it is. The dogs go to the track in special yellow vans. Two rows of steel boxes with two guards sitting between them. They have vets that examine every dog's saliva every day and the food before it's given to them. Not a chance.'

Sandboy stubbed out his cigarette. 'I know all that. What I heard about Tarrant, White City had twenty sets of kennels in one yard. Different set of kennels for every race. Each dog in a separate run. They had a watch hut at one end. Tarrant got over the perimeter wall before they brought the dogs for the next Wednesday night's racing. No one around just then. He went to the end kennel. Tall enough for him to stand up, like the rest of them. Seeing they don't need all the kennels at once, this one was spare, used as a store. Timber mostly. Sonny went in and fitted a bolt on the inside, so anyone outside would think it was locked or nailed up. Being a store, a watchman wouldn't be bothered about it.'

He paused and sniggered at what was coming next. 'He even took up some boards from the floor and piled them just inside the door so anyone trying to look through the crack would be sure it was a wood store. Then, in the middle of the night, he moved the boards, let himself out and slipped into the next kennel. They had the dogs in there for the last race at White City on Wednesday evening . . .'

'What did he dope them with?'

'Chloretone,' Sandboy said. 'Scraps of fish dipped in chloretone. Not hard to get the stuff. They use it in seasick pills. Can't trace it by tests. No sign of it until the dog's blood pressure goes up. When it does, it knocks 'em back in a few seconds. Anyway, Tarrant puts the fish mixed with chloretone behind every dog's food shutter, except for one dog called Moonbeam. Then he goes back to his hiding place, bolts himself in, piles wood back against the door. While it's still dark, he takes two boards out of the rear of his shed. He can just squeeze out and over the main wall that's a couple of feet behind, and he's away.'

'How much did he win?'

'Thousands,' Sandboy said. 'Wednesday night, in the last race, they reckon Moonbeam was 8–1. In the last few minutes, money piles in at the bookies and on the tote. The odds get shorter, of course, but Tarrant's got his money on by then. When they left the starting traps, all five dogs were doing a good speed. Nothing suspicious. Then they come skidding round the first bend. By that time blood pressure's going off the scale. One dog slows down and three begin dropping back. Moonbeam wins by a dozen lengths. What I hear is, Sonny Tarrant had boys putting money on everywhere. Manchester, Birmingham, all over the place. Only thing the bookies know in Manchester or Birmingham is the wire saying Moonbeam won at White City. No reason not to pay out. He came out twenty grand ahead.'

Gillis put the edge of his thumbnail to his teeth. 'If they couldn't test the dogs, how could they tell they'd had this chloretone?'

'They found it in some of the scraps that were left from the fish.'

'How come all this was never in the papers?'

'It wouldn't be,' Sandboy said. 'The last thing the greyhound racing association wants to do is tell people what's happened and how it's done. Especially when they can't prove who did it.'

'So where'd you get this yarn?' McGouran asked sceptically. 'Tarrant?'

''Course not. Just someone who should know.'

'A tart? A woman of yours, in other words,' Gillis said dispassionately. 'You need your flies sewing with steel wire, my son. Come on, let's go!'

Sandboy turned the key in the ignition and the engine came quietly to life. Full beams from the chromium headlamps cut a path of white down the wet street. The low black car turned right at the shop-lit brilliance of the High Road, past the red and green neon-rimmed façade of the Streatham Ice Rink. Dull Edwardian brick of tall buildings with their ottoman-domed and spired corner towers rose into the rain of the night sky.

'Believe it or not,' Sandboy said indifferently, 'but Sonny Tarrant didn't buy half the Garden Royal Hotel and Brandons Garages without a lot of money from somewhere. He's more or less a businessman now. Pays his taxes. Never was a bogie smart enough to catch him.'

'Like Pender.'

'Pender?' Sandboy glanced at McGouran in the driving mirror and grinned. 'Pender's nothing. Just fiddling the Customs and Excise, same as anyone would.'

Down the drab arterial road, crowds were leaving the last performances of the night at the cinemas of south London, coming out into drizzle. The showcases to either side of the wide steps were placarded with *Charlie Chan in Egypt*, Robert Donat in *The Ghost Goes West*, Ginger Rogers and Fred Astaire in *Top Hat*, Nelson Eddy and Jeanette MacDonald in *Naughty Marietta*.

'You see anywhere round here to take a leak?' Gillis asked suddenly.

McGouran leant forward. 'Tie a knot. Let's get this done.'

Beyond West Croydon station rain had creased the posters on the railway hoardings that promised 'Venos Lightning Cough Cure. Cures Your Cough or Costs You Nothing', 'Amami Shampoo. Friday Night Is Amami Night.' Placards at the street-corner newsstands repeated the same headlines: 'NO CHANGE IN THE KING'S CONDITION. THE EMPIRE PRAYS.' 'GIRL BELIEVED MURDERED BY POISONED TOOTHPASTE.'

'When this lot is over, Mac,' Gillis said tersely, 'I'm going to get so drunk you'll have to bottle me.'

They were coming into Croydon centre, down the long stretch of the London Road. Gillis began murmuring again, 'I saw my girl . . .'

'He is in pictures,' McGouran said, nodding at Sandboy, and laughed sharply. 'He's a bloody rewind boy!'

'Projectionist!' Gillis patted Sandboy on the shoulder.

9

'Your boss's wife danced with Jack Buchanan in some film, Sandy?'

'In the same movie. Not with him. She was Lady Blue.'

'She the one you're screwing?'

'No.'

He slowed for the traffic lights at the long depart-ment-store windows of Allders and Kennards. A strip of lighting shone on another hoarding: 'A Bungalow at Pevensey Bay. £50 deposit. Andereida Limited.' 'Blonde and Brunette Prefer the Same Cigarette. Player's Bach-elor Cork-Tipped.' Crowds filled the pavement outside the brightly lit Dance Hall and Balcony Café of the Lido after the Tango and Quickstep championships.

'And she gave you the nod about Pender smuggling furs without paying duty, I suppose?' Gillis asked.

'No.'

Gillis sat back and gave it up.

'What's it matter?' McGouran said. 'Pender can't run to the law and complain about losing what he shouldn't have in the first place. That's what makes it so cute.'

The more expensive houses of Purley and Coulsdon were above them among the hillside trees.

'You think Pender will do as told?' Gillis asked quietly.

Sandboy slowed the car at a turning. 'Christ knows. Still, he'll be well scared. So long as we remember to act as agreed. I don't suppose he's been hit since he was a kid. He's bound to be frightened.'

'And having the old woman with him . . .' McGouran left the rest unsaid.

The lights were out along the side road, its surface little more than an asphalt track. There was open land to one side, new five-bedroom houses spaced out and set well back on the other. Sandboy touched a switch and the

Rover's headlights died. Inside the car, the engine seemed quiet as a sewing-machine. Rooks Lane had been improved by the local safety council, its verges studded with glass cat's-eyes reflectors. Sandboy drove so that the car's inner wheels bumped rhythmically over the studs.

'That's neat,' Gillis said.

'Manny's last driver got night-blind. Drove for miles bumping along like this. Cat's-eyes Carter, they called him.'

He pulled into the side of the lane, drew on the brake and cut the engine.

'Three houses down,' he said quietly. 'Even if they haven't left a ground-floor window unlocked, it's easy to do one of these.'

Neither of the others spoke. It was the worst part. Gillis and McGouran were now wearing their soft-brimmed trilbies. Sandboy was the first to fold his scarf into a triangle and tie it round his head to cover the lower half of his face. Neither Gillis nor McGouran spoke as they masked themselves. McGouran saw himself in the driving mirror and grinned. 'Bloody Lone Ranger,' he said.

Sandboy reached for the door handle. 'That's all it is, Mac. Just cowboys and Indians. Remember that. Nothing else. Just that.'

Chapter Two

'The rules are easy,' Sandboy said. 'They're simple. They're not hard to understand at all.'

The Penders sat among the overstuffed cushions and gathered velvet curtains of their drawing room. Their electric log fire was grey and dead, the tiled surround an arctic white in the glare of the centre lights. Armchairs and leather chesterfields were empty. The couple sat on upright dining chairs, their wrists tied behind their backs. They were living the householders' nightmare of masked and armed intruders by night.

The first phase was over now, the shock of sudden waking, the torch in the face, the warning against noise, the pinioning. Even Mrs Pender had been too uncomprehending to cry out. Brought downstairs in their dressing gowns, they were only now waking from unbelief to the particular terror of violent crime.

'The rules,' Sandboy said again, as though the repetition made him impatient. The woollen scarf muffled his words and would make his voice harder to identify. Like Gillis and McGouran, he stood in trilby and raincoat, his lower face covered by the folded scarf, kid gloves fitting tight. They were like three interrogators in the coven of a modern inquisition. The man and woman were scared as they gazed at him, Sandboy could see that.

Pender with the rim of grey hair round his wide, shallow-domed head, the horn-rimmed glasses magnifying his staring eyes. Mrs Pender with the face that could have been anyone's, a little bloated from sleep, the grey hair disordered.

The Penders began to come to terms with terror, leaning forward a little to catch the rules, frightened of missing a word, wanting to obey, dreading punishment. They watched Sandboy's eyes. Had it not been for the scarf over his mouth and jaw, they might have been trying to lip-read. Neither of them glanced aside at the silver muzzle of the Walden Safety Revolver which McGouran was holding.

Sandboy's own tension began to ebb. These two would be easy. Despite his self-assurance in the presence of Gillis and McGouran, he had dreaded that Pender would defy him. The three young robbers had come too far to go back. And Sandboy was the leader who must give the proof of his command. But despite the mask and the gun, he had never learnt how to hurt. There was an art to such things which he had never understood. He feared that he would either lack the nerve or go too far, that if Pender called his bluff he might turn and run.

'First rule,' he said again quietly, 'speak when spoken to. Otherwise, keep it shut. Second rule, always answer when asked. Third rule, no noise. Noise, especially, means a smacking. Got that, 'ave you? Both of you?'

They both nodded. Pender first, slowly and dumbly, Mrs Pender in a hasty imitation of her husband.

'For Christ's sake tell us . . .' Pender said.

'First rule!' McGouran shouted, holding the gun at the old man's side, 'You fucking broke the first rule! Speak when spoken to! Got it?'

The unexpected shout terrified Pender far more than the gun. He stared at Sandboy as if for protection from McGouran.

'Got it?' McGouran shouted again. 'You just broke the second rule as well. Answer when spoken to! I asked you if you'd got it! 'ave you?'

'Yes,' Pender said. It was a thick, catarrhal whisper.

Sandboy walked over and stood close in front of Pender again, looking down at the magnified eyes behind the thick lenses. 'Now. See how easy I am to get on with?' he said. 'You think we're bastards, don't you? 'Course you do! But I'm all right really, aren't I? I'll let you off a smack, just this once. My pal over there with the gun, though, he's not all right, is he? He'd put a bullet into an old crook like you as soon as look at you. And don't come the respectable ratepayer with us, Pender. You are a crook. Have been for years. What's happening to you tonight is only what you're well due for.'

'For God's sake, what . . .' Pender said.

'Shut it!' Sandboy said sharply. 'You really are going to get a smack next time, 'f this keeps up. First rule! Speak when spoken to! Remember? I don't want to hear from you otherwise. Understand? But when I do ask, you answer smart. No ifs, no buts. Just answers. My pal's not pointing that gun for a lark. We decided about you two before we come in. It's your missus that gets the first slug, if we don't hear answers to questions. Not to finish her but so's there'd be room for a few more in her until you decide to tell us what we want to know. After her, of course, there's always you. We got enough ammo for the pair of you.'

'Tell us . . .'

Sandboy raised his hand, Mrs Pender gave a whimpering cry of alarm, and the old man fell silent. Sandboy lowered his arm and patted Pender's cheek, as if to reward belated obedience.

'That's better,' he said encouragingly. 'You don't have to be hit, unless you want it. And you wouldn't want to be. My mate's wearing his knuckles. First time he fists you, he'd bust your nose to smithereens. If you can't do as I tell you, I'll let him ask the questions.'

Sandboy walked away slowly, into the dining room with its new electric wall-lighting in semicircular bowls of frosted glass, its drum-shaded standard lamps and new tables of polished Canadian maple.

McGouran crossed the drawing room and stood behind Pender's chair. The old man said suddenly, 'For God's sake tell us what it is you want! Take what you come for and leave us. We could have a deal! That's all I ask! For God's sake show some heart!'

McGouran turned to Gillis. 'Hark at him! He wants a deal! He wants a smack round the head, more like!'

'Show him,' Sandboy said from the other room. 'I don't think he believes us. Just show him what happens if he fancies he can be clever.'

McGouran drew his glove off, stretched his hand forward and showed Pender the brass on his fingers, dulled as if it had been clouded by breath. He touched it to Pender's cheek.

'You never had it from one of these, did you, Mr Pender?' he said amiably. 'You'd be jumping with fright by now if you ever had. A noser from this is something you'd wear the rest of your life. Now on, any time you wanted to breathe, you'd only be able to do it with your gob open.'

He took the box of Swan Vestas from his pocket and put them on a cake stand by Pender's chair.

'And even without bullets,' he said patiently, 'you got any idea what a simple box of matches can do? No? You have a little think about that. Both of you.'

'Leave us alone!' Mrs Pender's was a cry of anger. 'We never did harm to you.'

'Speak when spoken to!' McGouran shouted indignantly. 'You broke the fucking rules!'

There was a dry sound from the silver automatic as he laid its barrel against the old woman's face.

'You think we wouldn't use this, Mrs Pender? Let me show you!'

Pender sobbed in terror. McGouran raised the little revolver and aimed it at the wooden picture rail. It made a report scarcely louder than a Christmas cracker and a tiny splintering of wood. Mrs Pender hung forward in her chair. McGouran straightened her and raised her chin.

'She's all right,' he said for Pender's benefit. 'It never went near her. Don't you worry. She's good as new. Plenty of use in her yet.'

Sandboy heard the thin report of the shot and cursed McGouran to himself. Firing the target revolver was no part of the agreement. But what was done was done. He walked back from the dining room. Though his eyes returned repeatedly to the electric mantelpiece clock in its oak surround, he acted as if he had all the time in the world.

'You want to hear or not?' he asked Pender.

'Yes! For God's sake, yes!'

'You'll only be told once. So listen. We're not here to mess about. You got that well in your head, have you?'

'Yes!'

16

'Right,' Sandboy said. 'This is your first and only chance before the music starts. It's what you must have thought all the time. The keys. The keys to Sheil Street. All four of them. Street door. Alarm. Workroom door. Storeroom door. You'll be looked after here, while I'm up there. Any trouble, the pair of you can go up like a couple of Guy Fawkes.' He nodded at McGouran. 'We'll leave our friend here. He's good on the rules. So let's hear about the keys.'

Pender leant forward earnestly. 'The keys aren't . . .'

'Oh, dear,' McGouran said. 'Don't tell us the keys aren't here. If they are, you'll soon tell us, believe me. If not, you could be starring in your own bonfire night.'

'They're not down here!' Pender shouted. 'Why the fuck don't you listen? They're kept upstairs. Top drawer of the little set inside the wardrobe!'

McGouran stood behind him. 'You want to watch your language,' he said humorously. 'There's a lady present.'

Sandboy went up to the bedroom, the bed itself disordered and the lights now on. The little set of drawers inside the oak wardrobe was unlocked, the keys lying in the first of them. He came downstairs with the keys and showed them to Pender.

'Just four? Right? Street door here? Alarm there? Workroom and storeroom? That the lot?'

The old man nodded.

'Thing is, Mr Pender,' Sandboy said casually, 'you been a bit of a naughty boy. Haven't you? There's a lot of pussies in Sheil Street should never be there. They come to you without paying duty. All accounts, you been working it for years. I'd say someone goes out of the country in a bit of old fox with a receipt for pure mink. Comes back in the real thing. Customs don't look at receipts on the way out. You could use the same bit of paper a dozen times.'

Pender shook his head. Sandboy shrugged. 'Then say there's a jack in the water-guard that takes money off you to look the other way when the stuff comes in. They got one or two bent. However it's done, you got some stuff at Sheil Street that you never should have. We'll be doing you a favour taking it off you. Better us than the law. Right?'

Pender stared at him. 'There's nothing there that shouldn't be.'

'There is now,' Sandboy said, 'but there won't be soon. You're in luck, Mr Pender. We're going to make an honest man of you, mostly. Two of us is going now. We got two more outside that can be called, if needed. But we'll see you later. Might even bring you something nice.' He turned to McGouran. 'If you don't hear from us at the latest two hours from now, or if there's any trouble here, burn them and this whole place! But make sure they go up anyway.'

He turned in the doorway. 'And I don't want another word out of either, especially not them asking for favours. Whichever it is that does it gets a smacked head every time the rules is broken. All right?'

The door closed. Pender looked quickly and furtively at McGouran, then dropped his eyes and stared in terror at his own feet.

Chapter Three

The darkened car followed the lane to its further junction.
Two woollen scarves lay discarded on the ribbed leather
of the rear seat.

Gillis said, 'Almighty Christ! That was strong!'

Sandboy switched on the white beams of the headlamps and turned smoothly on to the arterial road.
Heading fast for North Croydon, he drove with the
instinctive ease of a chauffeur. Pender's keys were in his
pocket, his apprehension had gone. Now that it was over,
he was excited by the memory of the encounter with
the Penders, secretly proud that his gloved hands on the
steering wheel were firm and steady as a Brooklands
racer.

'You never had much to say for yourself,' he said
cheerfully, triumphing a little over Gillis.

Gillis looked the other way, towards the new houses
with their white stucco and mock-Tudor gables. 'You and
Mac said enough between you.'

'Thing is,' Sandboy said, 'if you go in strong, that's all
you have to do. We did it that way, and no one got hit.
Scared, yes. Hurt, no. It's when you don't have them in
your pocket at the start that it can turn heavy.' He talked
now as if terror had been his way of life. 'What I mean,
suppose you let them argue? Then they get cocky and

19

won't talk. What d'you do when that happens? You either quit and run or you half kill them. You have to go in like storm troopers at the start. Best all round.'

'Pender wasn't trouble.'

'Pender would like to be trouble,' Sandboy said. 'Pender would really love to be trouble. Pender would like to see us both hang for what's happening tonight. Eight o'clock jump with a slip knot round the neck. Especially him having to be limp in front of the old woman.'

'McGouran was the real trouble,' Gillis said. 'That stunt with the gun. McGouran makes me nervous. He could be a psycho. I can stand just so much of him.'

Sandboy was threading his way through side roads of unlit houses, through streets bearing the names of Victorian battles, towards Streatham and Balham.

'We'll keep an eye on McGouran,' he said.

But Gillis was still subdued. Sandboy, rehearsing the memory of his triumph, drove in silence. Rain swept in sudden diagonal sheets across the darkness of the common and the tall houses of Clapham that faced it. Beyond Lambeth, the dark river running from Westminster Bridge was streaked by city lights, like multicoloured sequins on black satin.

It was happening quicker than Sandboy had planned but that was to the good. As he turned the Rover from Pall Mall towards Piccadilly, the foyer doors of the Carlton Grill were still open. The theatres of Shaftesbury Avenue and Cambridge Circus spelt out their attractions with white electric brilliance. Emlyn Williams in *Night Must Fall*, Marie Tempest in *Short Story*. High in the Piccadilly sky, the rippling neon on tall metal scaffolds filled the clouds with colour: the Bovril clock, the glass of Guinness filled from a bottle, emptied and immediately refilled, the promise of eternal romance in a diamond-twinkling Bravington Ring.

Sandboy kept north towards Sheil Street. The window displays of the Regent Street stores shone like brilliant stage sets. Patterned silk draped among antique vases, handcrafted silver, imported china etched with gilt, a hat perched on a stand with a necklace and a bottle of perfume. The white-lit square of the clock on Broadcasting House, pillared consulates, Nash terraces facing the black spaces of Regent's Park, then the shabby ill-lit streets of Camden Town.

Down Chalk Farm Road, the vegetable debris and broken boxes of a street-market were scattered on the pavement. Rear lights of parked cars glowed like fireflies as Sandboy drove slowly past. Where the plate-iron trench of a railway bridge carried the track from the Midland Goods Yard across the street, a locomotive and a set of empty carriages shunted and jangled towards the north-western line, short pillars of steam lit by the glow of the engine's furnace. Sandboy drew up by a dark row of lock-up shops. A seller of sheet music, a supplier of surgical appliances, a milk bar, a grill and the usual pawnbroker's which called itself 'Cash Jewellers'.

He stopped the car in a patch of darkness, reached back and took three compactly folded sacks from the rear seat. He gave one to Gillis and stuffed the other two into the breast of his fawn raincoat. They left the car in a distant rumble of thunder and a relentless cascade of rain. A hammering of wind met them as they turned the corner into a waterside cul-de-sac. The space was feebly lit by a single lamp on a swan's neck pillar, high above a lock of the Grand Union Canal. The haze of rain-clouded light formed pools of yellow-green on the cobbles and the rutted paving. Wind and rain were driving downwards the thin drifts of chimney smoke.

Sandboy turned up the collar of his raincoat. Coal grit between his teeth had the taste and smell of a railway terminus. At the far end of the road a pair of high iron gates blocked the way to the canal wharf and the railway goods yard.

'Watch your side, Gilly. There shouldn't be anyone this far down, specially not on a night like this. If there is, we'll stand back until it's clear. Any trouble, the story is we come over on Mr Pender's behalf. Someone thought they heard his alarm go off. We're here to make sure it's set properly. And here's his keys to prove it. Any doubt, they can phone his number and ask. They'll only get McGouran. All you got to remember is old Pender must be keener than we are not to have law, let alone Customs and Excise, nosing round his premises.'

From the pocket of his raincoat, he took a silver pencil torch that a doctor might have used to examine a patient's throat. The wind blew back the flaps of his mackintosh, rain soaking his trouser legs, as he strode past the red-pillared front of a warehouse to a smaller building behind it, arranged on three floors. The access to the top floor was by a metal staircase that might once have been an exterior fire escape. A sign fastened to the railings at the foot of it identified the premises above as 'Pender's Manufacturing Furriers. Est. 1921'.

Sandboy glanced round to make sure that the canal-side yard was still deserted. Nothing short of a major alert would have a watchman in the further goods yard out of his hut in this weather. With Gillis following, he went quickly and silently to the top of the metal stairs. Pender's entrance was a tin-sheathed fire door with barred windows either side of it. The crimson metal box of the alarm had been bolted to the soot-crusted brick of the exterior wall, out of reach of the metal stairs and with a drop of twenty-five feet below it.

'This one for the door,' Sandboy said quietly, choosing the first of the four keys on their metal ring. 'This for the alarm. It's a Crawshaw Bailey. I checked the sign on it. Other words, you can get as far as the alarm panel. If it's not turned off then, there's a pressure mat or something that activates it the minute you go past.'

He slipped the first key into the lock of the fire door and turned it.

'Watch the light,' Gillis said. Sandboy went cautiously into the building by the beam of the little torch. The alarm box was on show, as if to deter an intruder who had got this far, set in a wooden surround on the adjoining wall with the locked door of the workroom beyond it. Sandboy traced the floor ahead of him with his torch beam.

'Bet you there's a pressure mat under the carpet in front of the workroom door. Catch anyone that walks past the dial.'

The wet skirt of his raincoat brushed the wall as he moved to the panel in its wooden case, unfastened its hinged cover and opened it. There was nothing fancy about a device like this. A Crawshaw Bailey would answer to the key or not at all. He chose the second and smallest key on the ring, inserted it and turned it as far as it would go, as though he had been winding a clock.

'If that's not done it,' he said quietly, 'we'll bloody soon know. If it plays up, we got one minute to be down those stairs, out of here and in the car before someone comes nosing. They don't have a special watchman for these places but there's bound to be one down the canal wharf or the railway goods yard. Still, he'll take a good minute to get here. Maybe longer.'

With his hands still sheathed by the kid gloves, he stepped in front of the workroom door and waited. There was no sound except the wind buffeting the barred windows and the rain sweeping the tiles immediately overhead.

'Or they could put an extra alarm contact on this door,' Sandboy said. 'But they won't have. A door is apt to drop or warp in time and the contact goes out of true with the frame.'

Once again, Sandboy the leader spoke as if locks and alarms, like terrorism half an hour before, had been his life's profession. He tried the third key, turned a handle and opened the workroom door. The length of Pender's industrial loft stretched before them in the narrow beam of the torch, heavy tables set at intervals, with high-backed chairs at each. Over each table was a double-branched gas lamp, low on a long brass pipe from the ceiling. The green conical shades had been painted white on the underside, increasing the brilliance of the mantel. There were three skylights set in the slope of the roof, each steel-barred on the inside.

Foxes, racoons, ocelots in various stages of completion lay chalked and pinned. Furs that had been stitched together and dampened were nailed on pine pattern boards, ready to be trimmed and softened when dry. Knives, scissors and thread lay by each chair. Through an archway in a partition was a long bath, in which the grease was washed from the cut patterns.

With its shutters closed for security, the workroom

was still warm and unventilated, an acid smell from the treated pelts stacked by the far wall. Sandboy shone his torch on the tables and the mantels in their coolie-hat shades.

'Just scraps,' he said indifferently. 'The storeroom is where the pussies'll be.'

They walked the length of the workroom to the store-room door at the far end. To one side, the half-clad dummies were hung with sections of coats, like a butch-ered army.

After so much protection to begin with, the steel door of the storeroom was held only by a padlocked bolt. Sandboy felt the lock move at the fourth key. He opened the door inwards and ran the pencil beam along row after row of long coats, short coats, stoles and wraps, in the airless and windowless space.

'Now that's more like pussies,' he said steadily. 'But we're not greedy. We take as agreed. Three pieces each, Gilly. One full-length mink, and something short but nice, and one ocelot or something cheaper. We pop the cheap ones first. Starting with a mink is bound to cause talk. We have to build up trust. Once Samuelson and the others take the first two and sell 'em on, they won't so easy cut up over the mink.'

Gillis ran his hand over the black rippling of silky fur. 'He'd hardly miss a dozen each.'

'Three in each sack,' Sandboy said, walking down the first row. 'That way we can take them in one go and use the torch at the same time. Drop them down the foot of the outside stairs. Bring the car, scoop them up, and away. Enough to keep you out of work for a couple of years.'

Gillis was still staring at the electric sheen of the

25

coats in the torch beam, the gloss of black mink, blue, off-white, canary. 'You know the right ones in this lot, Sandy, the ones he shouldn't have?'

Sandboy turned and stared at him, as if Gillis had misunderstood the plan. 'It doesn't matter which ones,' he said simply. 'Pender can't go to the law. That's all. We take what we want. He can't scream for insurance and risk having his stock sniffed over. Any case, out of nine of them, some have to be bent for certain. Hold the sack open.'

As Gillis held it, Sandboy walked down the nearest row of coats. Then he stopped, realizing for the first time that they might be on security hangers. But the sleek and slithering length of the nearest black mink came free. It slid through his gloved fingers to the floor. The plan was in perfect order.

Three black minks, three short blues and three leopard-pattern ocelots. As Gillis held the sack, the elusive coats slipped and twisted like the living creatures they had lately been.

'That's it,' Sandboy said presently. 'Let's get out.'

He pulled a sack in either hand the length of the workroom, holding the pencil torch in his mouth. Then he went back, padlocked the storeroom and followed Gillis who was towing the third sack. With the three sacks by the door to the iron stairs, he locked the workroom. While Gillis waited, he opened the door to the stairs narrowly and surveyed the yard below. Two men walked across the street entrance of the yard and then there was no one. Gillis pulled the sacks on to the metal platform of the stairs, the wind still thudding at the brick walls but the rain almost gone.

Sandboy walked back into the building, slid the key

into the alarm and turned it full circle. Even if the mechanism overran in the morning, the first presumption would be a fault in the timer or the clockwork. He walked quickly on to the platform, closed the door and locked it.

'We'll get these down the bottom, Gilly, in case there's trouble with the alarm bell.'

By the time the device had set itself again, they were at the foot of the iron stairs. But there was no sound of trouble. Sandboy walked quickly to the car, started the quiet engine and reversed into the canalside yard with the headlamps off. He got out, opened a rear door and helped Gillis lift the three sacks inside.

As the car swung round, Gillis began to laugh. 'It was that easy,' he said, as if he had never doubted it. 'It was that easy after all.'

Sandboy drove back the way he had come, the display windows of the stores in darkness, the neon animation blank and dead, the blaze of the theatres extinguished. By Clapham Common he stopped, went to the phone box, fed three coins into it, called Pender's number and pressed the silver knob of Button A as McGouran answered, hearing the coins fall.

'It's done, Mac,' he said quietly, gazing across the wet space of grass to the black trees. 'Any trouble? Good. Pack up and be ready to go in about twenty minutes. We'll leave 'em in the kitchen with a bread knife. They'll cut each other loose by breakfast. Any case, Pender's not likely to be pleading for the law. His keys we'll just leave on the table. It's got to look right. Pender or his manager has to be able to open up the workroom tomorrow.'

He slid into the driving seat of the black and chrome Rover.

'What about the car?' Gillis asked.

27

'We leave it one street from where we took it. That way they'll perhaps wonder if it really went missing or if the owner got confused or drunk. Not that it matters now.'

They drove for a few minutes without speaking. Then Gillis laughed again. 'It was so bloody easy!' he said.

From the outside, the house seemed to be in darkness. There was no sign of McGouran waiting for them. Then Sandboy saw the flush of wall-lights faintly reflected in the pebbled glass by the front door. He tapped on it, saw a shaft of light open inside and heard McGouran turn the lock.

'Right,' McGouran said. 'That's it. All set.'

'Once we've fixed it for the Penders to get loose. We can't let them be found like this. It's our secret – and theirs.'

'I can do that.'

But Sandboy stepped past him, followed by Gillis.

'Go and get in the car, Mac. We need a lookout.'

The Penders still sat in their chairs, able to wriggle their hands behind them but not to free themselves. Pender was staring a little aside, as if the old man could not bear to meet his captors' eyes. Mrs Pender's chin was on her chest and she seemed to be talking to herself, or possibly murmuring to her husband. Gillis stared at her, looked more closely, then tugged Sandboy's sleeve and walked into the dining room. McGouran was still in the hall but out of earshot.

'What the hell's he done to them? To her? Her face is wet, for Christ's sake! Why? Her hair is wet! Soaked! That bloody thug McGouran! He couldn't keep his hands to himself! He's given her a ducking! What in hell for? For nothing! They'd told us all we needed.'

'She might have passed out,' Sandboy said hastily. 'He could have used water to bring her round.'

'Passed out! Good Christ! I warned you, Sandy! McGouran's got something missing in his head. He enjoys this! Not just with something young and tasty but even a couple like the Penders. Get rid of him before he stuffs the pair of us! Passed out? Look at her! Look at her clothes. She's been roughed up! She's had her face held under water. And Pender's gone and wet himself. We can't leave them for someone to find like this.'

Sandboy looked back quickly into the other room. He said, 'Cut Pender free but pull the phone out. Then we go.'

'No. Look at her, for Christ's sake. They have to call someone. I never bargained for having anyone on my hands in this state. Good Christ! We leave the phone but not so they can use it the minute we go. If someone comes and finds them like this in the morning, our plan is buggered anyway. Pender was never supposed to talk in case he shopped himself. If the law finds him or hears about him like this, he'll have to talk.'

'Look,' Sandboy said, 'we need at least fifteen minutes to get rid of the car and split up. At least that.'

'You would have McGouran!'

'All right. The phone's in the hall. We cut Pender loose but stop him going into the hall until we're clear. Then we move.'

'How the fuck can you stop him going in there?'

'I will,' Sandboy said more calmly than he felt. 'I know what to do.'

They walked back slowly into the sitting room. Pender still avoided their gaze. Mrs Pender still murmured, her chin on her chest.

Sandboy spoke to them. But now he felt like a servant explaining himself to his master. 'Right, Mr Pender. We got what we come for. So we'll be letting you loose in a minute. But it's not the end yet. There's something we need to drop off. So we'll be coming back in about half an hour. While we're away, our friend that kept you company is going to be sitting in the hall with his shooter. One sight of you out there and he'll plug you. With my compliments. Got it?'

The old man nodded. Then at last he began to weep. His wife made sounds of consolation, wordless, incoherent. Sandboy walked round behind Pender's chair and cut the cord from his wrists.

'Now you sit there for half an hour,' he said, like a father to a child. 'What's on the other side of that door is something you never want to see.'

With his eyes on Pender, he backed to the doorway. On the far side, with Gillis, he took a small gilt chair and wedged it under the round matt steel knob of the handle. If he was right, Pender would be occupied in untying and attending to his wife for longer than it took to return the Rover to the streets from which it had come.

Sandboy closed the front door without a sound. He sprinted after Gillis, slid into the driving seat of the long graceful chassis and started the engine. It was so quiet that Pender would probably not hear it. They edged out from the darkness of Rooks Lane on to the Croydon road. There was a thin stream of traffic before dawn, enough to conceal them until they turned off Streatham High Road. Sandboy relaxed and admitted to himself that, after all, he had planned this better than he knew. There had been difficulties but those were the test of command.

As the grey winter light touched the house fronts, he

parked in the street from which they had set off. Along Streatham High Road the steel grinding of tram wheels on rails was now more frequent. The wind had dropped and the night's rain was no more than an irregular finger tap of dripping pipes and gutters.

'You two go first and let me get rid of the car,' Sandboy said. 'One suitcase each. Thing with pussies is how small they fold up.' Once again he spoke as though furs had been his whole life. 'Tram stop,' he said. 'One at a time.'

Gillis began to sing softly, colouring his nervousness. Sandboy took a cigarette from a square silvered case. He tapped it twice on the smooth metal. 'Got a match?'

'Don't you ever . . .' Gillis stopped.

McGouran touched the outside of his pocket. 'No,' he said.

Gillis twisted in the passenger seat. 'Almighty Christ, McGouran!' He turned back to Sandboy. 'Of course he hasn't got a match! That fucking box is still on the table, by Pender's chair! And McGouran had his glove off, showing off the knuckles!'

Sandboy put the cigarette back in the case and slipped the case into his breast pocket. His heart was thudding but his mind was calm. Best to pacify the others. 'One thing sure,' he said quietly, 'we can't go back for it now.'

Gillis twisted round in his seat again. 'You really had to fuck the whole thing up with that performance about the knuckles and the gun and the matches,' he said for McGouran's benefit. 'You really had to . . .'

But McGouran laughed. 'You want to act your age, Gillis, and not your shoe size. Whatever we did, Pender can't go to the law without dropping himself in it. Any case, he can't tell anyone what we looked like, where we came from, where we went. All the things that matter.'

'He knows what you sound like,' Gillis said, staring the other way. 'A fucking thick-headed jock!'

'You can't tell someone's voice when they're talking through a scarf.'

'Shouting,' Gillis said, 'shouting through the scarf with a voice like Harry Lauder!'

'Be your bloody age, Gillis! You can't tell a voice from shouting. You have to listen to it quiet and careful. There's bugger-all Pender can do.'

Sandboy intervened. 'But you did have that glove off, Mac, when you put the matches on the table. It must have prints on. Remember? You were still showing him the knuckles.'

'Makes no odds,' McGouran said. 'They won't fit anything to me. I've been through all that before. Prints are no use to them until they find me. Which they won't.'

'And the bullet in the picture rail?' Gillis asked.

Sandboy shook his head. 'He's all right there, Gilly. That gun's never been in trouble. They can't even know it exists, let alone identify it. It's a target weapon, that's all. We always counted on that.'

'Almighty Christ,' Gillis said again, outnumbered by the other two, 'leaving a set of prints on Pender's table!'

'Come on,' Sandboy adjusted his hat in the mirror. 'Pender can't run to anyone. I want to be out of this car before it's properly light.'

'Right,' McGouran said. 'I'm going first.'

He opened the rear door and lugged out a cheap suitcase in which his three furs were now folded. He slammed the door shut, turned and moved off in a heavy walk against the street light.

'The first chance he gets,' Gillis said morosely, 'he'll

go for the money like a starving pigeon after a dropped sandwich.'

Sandboy said nothing but he shook his head slowly as if to acknowledge that he had heard and noted the comment. He began to whistle, improvising on a Cole Porter number.

'Almighty Christ!' Gillis said furiously. 'McGouran! Look at the sight of him! Even the way he walks! Will you just look at him!'

Chapter Four

Far out to sea, lightning slit the cloudbanks somewhere towards the French coast. Sonny Tarrant watched its jagged brilliance through lines of thin rain slanting across the unlit pier and the winter sands. The wet paving of the promenade, lit by strings of coloured bulbs between the lamp-posts, was deserted in the squall.

Bulky and a little dishevelled by this time of the evening, he stood in his dressing gown and watched the darkness beyond the black marble facing and chrome handles of the third-floor balcony. At an angle, other windows rose in another court.

In profile, at an uncurtained window, there was a woman in a blue dress, a cigarette in her mouth and a tall glass in her hand. Tarrant had watched her often before. She turned now, so that her back was to the window, and then turned again. She was smiling at someone and her lips began to move. Then she stepped back and there was nothing but the wall of the brightly lit room, a table with two chairs, like a stage when the curtain has risen but the actors have not come on.

'Tell you what, Ma,' he said without looking round, 'anyone that could lip-read could know every word that's said in some of these flats, the way they carry on with the curtains back. That'd tell a story.'

His eyes rested patiently on the same square of light, waiting for the woman in blue to come back. To watch men and women secretly – women most of all – gave Tarrant a pleasure he could not precisely define. But it was important to him that they should not know he was watching them. Nor had he any wish to meet them or to speak to them, which would somehow spoil the sense of being their secret captor or possessor.

It was quite different, of course, with the men and women who were paid to be watched in private. They satisfied his curiosity about love and passion yet there was no secrecy and no possession. But among all his playthings, with all other men and women, Sonny Tarrant worked quietly and with sure purpose.

A blue-white spear of brilliance split the sky above the steady tide, recalling his attention to the storm. After a long pause the distant thunder came again. Above the shrubs of the promenade gardens, in the hour before midnight, the Pavilion dancers were foxtrotting like over-wound clockwork toys within their tall brightly lit windows. The music of the band playing a foxtrot arrange-ment of 'Who Stole My Heart Away' filtered to him through the cold air.

Without turning round, he said, 'What we ought to do, Ma, is hire that Manders girl again. Yvonne. The one we used to 'ave. Her that come and give us a tune on the old Steinway. You liked that, didn't you? Bit of old Chopin and a top-notcher like Rachmaninov. Nice to have that on a winter evening. Ask one or two friends in to listen to her, perhaps.'

His slow voice sounded prematurely middle-aged with its hard-earned gentility, a manner of dropping a final 'g' in imitation of polite society, an old-fashioned

35

way of pronouncing 'roof' to rhyme with 'woof' and taking 'room' halfway to 'rum'. Even when he said 'ain't', he made it sound flashy and sporting.

Mrs Tarrant sat curled in her spaciously padded arm-chair with the coquettishness of a young girl. A mirrored sideboard behind her was littered with the glasses of their guests, the dregs of Sidecars, a Tom Collins, Egg Flips and Manhattans. The girl who came in daily would clear them next morning.

'Get our young lady in to play for us, Ma,' he repeated encouragingly, sensing that the old woman had already lost the thread of the conversation.

Mrs Tarrant pulled a face like a sulky child. 'It don't come cheap, Sonny,' she said reprovingly. 'Not as cheap as when you might go and listen to the piano in the Winter Garden for next to nothing.'

He turned at last and grinned at her. 'What's expensive to her is cheap as sunlight to us, Ma. We got no reason to go and sit with that mob in the Winter Gardens. Not when we can have it all here for ourselves. Nice to have a bit of music played to us. An' we can tell her the ones we want. Can't do that down the Winter Gardens.'

Without replying, she picked up the picture-paper at her side and began to study it with a frown of displeasure. Tarrant turned to the balcony window again. Thin rain blew in a scurry of drops, across the zigzag path and the lower promenade. The plate glass caught his reflection against the darkness outside, a tall man with a long intelli-gent face. His blond hair seemed to pile itself naturally on his head with the suggestion of a Pompadour wig.

Sonny Tarrant's speech and manner betrayed him as something baser but the look of equine intelligence was no illusion. At a glance, there was even the promise of amiability in the line of his lips. But the smile never came. It was only the natural set of his mouth which gave him this false look of joviality.

In the dark window, he looked through his reflection without interest. To hire the girl who played the piano would have pleased him. Despite the natural cruelties of his profession, he was equally moved by great music and great events. The cries of a man or the screams of a woman under some form of pain that he judged necessary to gain his ends were no more to him than the shrilling of cut metal or wood sliced in a circular saw. But those who dismissed him as a man without feelings were in error.

Like music, great events and their actors inspired him with his own sense of personal destiny: the two minutes' silence on Armistice Day for the dead of the Great War, the flags drooping in an autumn chill by the cenotaph, Whitehall lined by silent battalions, the solitary bugler; Horseguards Parade in the spring, the trooping of the colour before the Sovereign by the most famous regiments, bands playing the slow march, the young Prince of Wales, jaunty and debonair in the saddle, taking the salute on his old father's behalf. The hope of the future splendid in his full-dress uniform as Colonel-in-Chief of the Welsh Guards.

That evening Tarrant had felt the thrill of being present when history was made. A quiet, confidential voice had spoken to him from the woven speaker panel of the art nouveau radiogram in the corner of the room. The words came as if to a royal ambassador or a cabinet minister: 'The King's life is moving peacefully to its close.'

In his mind Sonny Tarrant rehearsed the sombre tone of the announcer.

At lunchtime the same voice had reported to him that, 'The King presided this morning over a meeting of the Privy Council, where Councillors of State were appointed for the duration of His Majesty's illness. The Prime Minister and members of the cabinet travelled from London to Sandringham early today.' The great events followed one another so swiftly that the listener became an actor in the drama. A man who had presided over the great powers of the state that morning was dying by nightfall.

On a mirror-glass table in the room behind him, the phone rang. Tarrant listened without moving until it had rung six times.

Mrs Tarrant sighed. 'Answer it, Sonny. Do.'

He walked slowly to the table, picked up the ivory-white receiver and listened.

'When's that?' he said at last. 'That so? When exactly? _Last_ night! Why didn't the silly old bugger say somethin' sooner? No. No. Of course, I'm sorry to hear about Vi, especially. Poor old lady. No, don't touch anythin', Foxy. And no police. At least not yet. They'll only ask why they wasn't invited before. We'll decide first who the suspects are and what needs doin' to them. Law can always have 'em if it suits us. Some'ow I think this might 'ave to be a bit more private.'

He listened for a moment, then said, 'No, Foxy. Put a stop to that. Especially we don't want no little gutter-snipes from the papers sniffin' round old Pelly Pender. I'll be up first thing tomorrow. And, soon as you can in the morning, send flowers and hothouse grapes to the hospital. Belgians, if you can get 'em. Where is she, by the way? All right. Best you can get. A big bunch, decent whack. Roses too. Times like this, flowers can make a few friends. No names to the hospital, of course. Not a word to a soul. More I think, more I'd say we'll handle this one private. Time I finish with the little bastard, whoever it is, he'll be runnin' cryin' to the hospital, carryin' a bag of his fingertips in his hat . . .'

He put the receiver down and walked to the two padded chairs, sitting down next to the old woman and taking her hand gently. 'We just got a bit of bad news, darlin'. That was Foxy. Poor old Mrs Pender been took to hospital. You know? Vi Pender. Old Pelly Pender's missus. Nice old lady. Been a bit of a ruck at the old couple's place last night. Seems she been took to hospital with a heart attack.'

'Has she?' Mrs Tarrant looked up anxiously into her son's eyes, troubled by her failure to remember who the Penders might be.

'Break-in, apparently. It so upset the poor old lady she been took bad.' Tarrant stood up again and looked at the window. He spoke in a level assured manner of authority, learnt from the voices on the radiogram. 'Let me find the little toe-rag that caused it, I'll give him a bloody heart attack all right! 'Fact, he'll wish it killed him long before it does!'

The old woman stared at the dark sky beyond the window, her gaze gentle but vacant. 'They can't say you don't remember your friends, son,' she said wistfully. 'It's nice you sent the flowers.'

He looked at her quickly and then away again with a movement of the eyes that betrayed an uncharacteristic moment of unease.

'See if there's any more late news on the wireless,

son,' she said hopefully. 'Hear again about the poor old king.'

He went to the tall HMV radiogram in the corner and turned it on. As the perspex panel was illuminated and the valves began to glow, there was a long humming while it warmed up and then a faint sound of bells. After a pause, they heard the abrupt pips of a news bulletin, an announcer's voice that was mellow and self-assured, reading an official statement: 'Death came peacefully to His Majesty the King at eleven fifty-five p.m. tonight, in the presence of Her Majesty the Queen, the Prince of Wales, the Duke of York, the Princess Royal, the Duke and Duchess of Kent...'

'Poor old man,' said Mrs Tarrant.

'... King Edward will fly to London from Sandringham tomorrow morning for the meeting of the accession council and the proclamation at St James's Palace...'

Tarrant sat down beside her again. He took her hand once more. 'Well, darlin', that's it then. There'll be changes now, Ma, with the new one. You'll see. He's not one of your old brigade. Seen a bit of life, same as we have. Been with ordinary people, like us. In the trenches even. More like the new sort they have in other countries. It's what's needful.'

'Is it, son?' Mrs Tarrant asked only to be reassured. He ignored the question.

'And, in a way, he's our sort, Ma. So far as any of 'em ever can be. 'Course, you can't help feeling sorry for the poor old fellow that's dead. But it ain't a bad change. Take it all in all.'

Mrs Tarrant gave a giggle of frivolity. 'And perhaps

you and the new one might both find yourselves a nice young lady each!'

He gave her hand a squeeze and winked down at her. 'You're still my girl, Ma. Ain't I always said? Not one of 'em could ever be what you are.'

He got up, then stooped to kiss her and went back to the balcony window, staring at the dark sea. The rain had stopped, only a breeze shivered the puddles among the shrubs and paths of the gardens. Tomorrow, like the young king, he would be in London. Two men of the new order. An unexpected chill touched his spine, like the excitement of fine music. Just for that moment, it seemed that he stood at the centre of great events in his own right.

February

Revuedeville

Chapter Five

'This girl of yours,' Gillis said, 'Yvonne or Lady Blue or whatever she is. She gets paid every time Dicky Dash or someone uses a song of hers? Paid every time?'

Sandboy pressed down the tip-up seat. He lowered himself into it and then folded his raincoat in his lap. The afternoon pause in the non-stop performance of *Revuedeville* was almost over, a flush of footlights touched the neutral-tinted curtains.

'Whoever uses it, they have to pay. It's her song. Property of Lady Blue.'

'God,' Gillis said, 'That must be worth something to her.'

'To Manders, more like. He looks after the money for her.'

'Lady Blue?' Gillis said.

'A joke,' Sandboy said. 'Just a joke. Something she was called once.'

The double-branched wall-lights began to dim. A man who played the piano and the drums, set up where a pair of classical pillars rose at the side of the oblong stage opening, had returned to his seat. The top of the conductor's head caught the footlights as he sidled back to his place below the stage. Two usherettes costumed like

45

Dutch dolls closed the curtained doors under the green electric 'Exit' signs.

'Don't forget McGouran when you see him,' Sandboy said. 'McGouran is to lay off until we square Samuelson with the first coat. I'm seeing Samuelson tonight, taking the ocelot. My other two stay here with you. That's safer. I checked the prices. You go outside here, Swan and Edgar in Piccadilly. An ocelot like this is ticketed for a couple of hundred at least. It's almost leopard skin. Even being sold on, that's got to be a hundred up. And that's the cheapest of them. Main thing is to get old Samuelson on the hook first.'

They were sitting under the curve of the side balcony as the house lights faded from the dark wooden dado and the bare angular space of the intimate revue. The orchestra broke into a single 'chord-on' to announce its presence and the murmurs of talk among the scattered afternoon audience died away.

'Why Samuelson?' Gillis asked quietly. 'Any special reason?'

'Just say he's been researched,' Sandboy said, 'Ask anyone in the trade, anyone down Praed Street for that matter. He was caught fencing once. Years ago. Thought to be honest since. That's a joke! Being caught just showed him how to be a bit more careful. He's like Pender, only cleverer than Pender was. Samuelson lives by stuff like this.'

There were ten fair-haired girls on the stage, dressed as Ruritanian hussars in shakos, tunics, skirts that ended at the tops of their thighs and white boots that buttoned to mid-calf. A tall brunette was the commander.

'Bang upon the big drum and clash upon the cymbals, sing as we go marching along . . .' The dancers changed formation into a single line, arm-linked, boot-heels and toes clicking and clacking on the polished wood. Behind them rose a two-dimensional fairy castle.

'I'm seeing him by appointment,' Sandboy said, 'so I'd say I got his attention when I phoned. Worst he can say is no. But why should he? Coat belonged to my fiancée that sent it back when she broke the engagement. I gave it to her in the first place. Has to be sold. Samuelson's got a story to tell if anyone asks him. Why should he care if it's true? I could just have took the coat and pawned it, come to that.'

'Seeing him by appointment,' Gillis said and grinned at the stage. The girls were now heel-and-toe clicking as if marching on the spot, powdered thighs quivering a little in the white glare of footlights.

'He knows he could slip a coat like that into stock and collect a couple of hundred for himself,' Sandboy said, 'and not declare the sale, most likely.'

The line of soldier-girls had left the stage. The lights dimmed, except for a steel-blue spot at the centre, picking out a naked dancer covering herself with two curved ostrich fans, long white plumes tipped with cherry red. She turned and moved with the precision of a sentry. One fan covered her nakedness the instant before she twisted into profile. The second replaced it in the moment that she turned full to the front. Her body, elegantly stretched, moved quietly and rhythmically to the beat of the music.

'Samuelson's like Pender,' Sandboy said. 'He's in no position to complain.'

Gillis paid him no attention. The ostrich fans stopped short at the dancer's knees, showing perfect calves and ankles bare. This and the trick of never looking at the

47

audience, as if in fear of her modesty, held the scattering of afternoon spectators silent and motionless. Sandboy gave her his attention more reluctantly. He had seen and done much that was unexplored territory to the likes of Gillis.

The tempo of the tango quickened. The dancer fled to the shadows and the spotlight pursued her like a lover. It held her captive as she twisted this way and that behind the fans. At last she sank to her knees and touched her forehead to the back of her hand. The lights went out, then came on again for the moment in which she was permitted to pose proudly naked with the fans held clear, kneeling motionless, shoulders and flanks powdered white, only her back and breasts moving slightly with the breathlessness of exertion.

There was a thin clatter of applause. The curtains closed and the footlights played on their folds as the orchestra burst into a beat-up arrangement of 'My Old Man's a Dustman . . .'

'This is him,' Sandboy said. 'Watch this. Banned on the BBC.'

Dicky Dash in his flower-pattern suit, his soft white hat, preposterously rounded eyes and pouting mouth, sprang on to the narrow strip of stage before the curtains and raised his arms to the balcony as if it had been Drury Lane. In one hand he held a silver-topped cane. His delivery came at the speed of a printing machine.

'Thank you very, very much, ladies and gentlemen. It's a pleasure to be here at the Windmill this afternoon. But you've no idea how exhausted I feel. I feel really poorly. Do I look poorly? Go on, say, "Ahhhhhhh," if you think I look poorly. Go on, lady, say, "Ahhhh . . ." '

'He's used three of her songs so far,' Sandboy said.

'I been running all the way to get here on time this afternoon, ladies and gentlemen. I have. Running all the way. I was held up in Regent Street. I was. There was a man on the kerb selling watches. And he kept asking me to buy a watch, first this and then that. And I said no . . . and no . . . and no . . . In the end, he said, "Do you want to see a nudist watch?" He did, he said it. So I said, "What's a nudist watch?" And he said, "Things you'd get arrested for". So I was hurrying along and I bumped into this lady and I said, "Sorry, ducky." And she said, "Don't call me ducky. Do I look like a duck?" So I said, "Well, only when you're walking away, dear." So she said, "I'll have you know my husband calls me Dimples." I said, "I don't see any dimples." And she said, "But you're not my husband." '

The band laughed uproariously to make up for the thin teatime audience.

'You met him?' Gillis asked. 'Why's he dress like a nance?'

'He's not a nance. He does it for the act. That's all.'

'Mind you,' said Dicky Dash, 'I don't always walk everywhere. Me? No, I don't. I was driving through town the other day. Turned a corner, went up the next road. Never saw it was a one-way street. That minute a policeman stops me and says, "Where you think you're going?" So I said, "Well I don't know. But it can't be much good, whatever it is, because they're all coming away from it." '

'You met him?' Gillis asked.

Sandboy shook his head. Dash was at the microphone again.

'This is it,' Sandboy said.

'Now what I'm going to do next, ladies and gentlemen,

because you've been such a good audience . . . You have
been a good audience . . . I'll tell you something. I was
almost booked for the Glasgow Empire this week. Certain
death. That's the place where if they like you, they let
you live. Anyway, you've been such a good audience, I'm
going to sing you a brand-new number. First time it's
been heard, here at the Windmill Theatre. A brand-new
song entitled, "I like a bit of real applause but I'd rather
not get clapped . . ." And while I sing it, I'm going to do
a bit of a dance. Yes, I am . . . Tell you what, though.
They've got a lovely band here. Haven't they? Lovely
conductor. Lovely man. You know what? He said to me
the other day, "Dicky," he said, "I'll have you know that
liquor has never passed my lips." Blimey! Makes you
wonder how he gets so much of the stuff into him . . .'

Sandboy lit a cigarette as Dicky Dash rolled his preposterous eyes, swung the silver-topped cane and broke
into his dance routine.

> 'Who do you think you are,
> All the swank and la-di-da,
> If you knew all that we know
> About your ma and pa,
> Who would you think you are . . .?'

'This is good,' Gillis said, surprised.

Dicky Dash watched his own shoes with marvelling
eyes, leaning back, feet twinkling as if he must fall, then
straightening up again. He threw the silver-topped cane
forward and caught it at the last moment.

> 'Who do you think you are,
> Astrakhan and big cigar,

If you knew what your missus says
About your la-di-da,
Who would you think you are . . .?'

Gillis chuckled with delight that Sandboy should have
a girl who wrote such songs for the stage.

'Who do you think you are,
Driving in your Rolls Royce car?
There's Piccadilly ladies
In the Trocadero Bar
Who know just who you are . . .'

'This Lady Blue of yours . . .' Gillis said.
'She wrote it. All right?'
'You want to keep your foot in the door there, Sandy.'
Sandboy tapped his cigarette on the metal ashtray
fastened to the back of the seat in front. 'Oh, don't you
worry,' he said quietly, 'I mean to. And it won't just be
the door either.'
'And not just your foot, either. What's the boss think
about all this?'
'I'd be surprised if Manny cares. If it wasn't me, he
must know it'd be someone else. He could be her father,
for God's sake. What he doesn't want any more, he can
hardly complain if she gives elsewhere.'
He turned in his seat. The illuminated clock under
the wall-light by the rear exit had just passed four. He
looked round. 'Stay if you want,' he said to Gillis. 'I'm
going soon, if I have to see Samuelson at five. This time
of day, in this weather, it could take a while to get to
Paddington.'
'I'll come,' Gillis said. 'As far as Piccadilly anyway.'

They watched Dicky Dash leave the stage in an uproar of applause, provided for the most part by the band, then made their way to the end of the row of seats. Beyond the velvet curtains of the exit doors, the steps went down to the street with a second flight to the side. Gilt script and an arrow on a dark signboard indicated the lounge bar and cloakroom. Sandboy gave his ticket to a girl at the cloakroom counter and took his suitcase.

In Shaftesbury Avenue the stores were still open and the first clerks were only just leaving the insurance offices in the yellow-tinted fog. Late editions showed photographs of policemen on point duty, dimly outlined by naphtha flares. The fog that had come that morning was still hanging over the city, masking the street lights, turning every breath into a small white cloud, making the traffic sounds dull and distant.

In Piccadilly Circus, two men in the display windows of Swan and Edgars were removing the black and purple swags of silk with which they had been draped for the royal funeral. The late king's portrait hung, stripped of its surroundings, the worn but trimly bearded face, the eyes wearied by sickness. At the corner of Regent Street, the newsboys' placards bore a younger image: 'OUR BACHELOR KING.'

'If the worst comes to the worst,' Gillis said humorously, 'you could always give her the mink. Might do you a power of good in that quarter.'

Sandboy grinned. Close by, a fog signal went off as if someone had blown up a paper bag and burst it. 'I'll take my chance with old Samuelson. I reckon we know the worst there is to know about him. With a bit of brass, you never quite know. She might be telling stories to Manny. She could be telling stories to me. And remember what

52

we agreed about the phone. Always the same message for either of us. Your bank wants to speak to you. No one's likely to argue about that.'

They stood by the iron palings which protected the flight of steps going down to the underground station and the public lavatories. The dark yellow fog seemed lower now, as if the clouds were no more than twenty feet above the traffic and the pavements. Then, for the first time in their friendship, Sandboy and Gillis shook hands as they parted.

Chapter Six

The tram swung wide round the corner by the Cumberland Hotel and the wet, mist-hung outline of Marble Arch. It whined and rocked down the Edgware Road past the turnings of pillared terraces behind frozen shrubberies. Sandboy looked down from the upper deck on the crawling beetle-trail of cars in the splashed colour reflections of the lamplight. The tram rode through them, swaying and clanging.

He stood up and braced himself against the grinding of the brakes and the slowing rhythm as he walked down the length of the deck towards the stairs at the rear. The next stop would be his. Below him, the conductor shouted, 'Sussex Gardens!' A bell clanged, and the driver pushed his shining brass lever. The tram took off again, its wheels screaming on the rails as it followed a slight curve to the centre of the road.

Just before the corner of Praed Street, Sandboy touched the bell and began to descend the stairs awkwardly, his suitcase in one hand. He stepped to the pavement. The sick white-green of the gaslights flickered in the puddles as the tram jerked forward, whining into the northern distance of Kilburn and Maida Vale.

The fog lay down the length of Praed Street's rooftops, like a low cloud of poison gas, past the dark ugly front of the hospital to the glass vault of the railway terminus. Windless lamplight scoured Sandboy's face with its chill. Moisture gathered silently and dripped along the fronts of little shops selling sweets and groceries and newspapers. Down sparsely lit side streets and passages, children in overcoats played in the winter murk. A group of little girls waited their turn for the skipping rope. In the asphalt courtyards behind the tenements of tall houses with broken windows, lines of underclothes hung like white dismembered ghosts.

Sandboy passed the office suppliers with its window of second-hand typewriters and metal cabinets. He turned into Mr Samuelson's doorway. The long gas-lit shop was divided by a wooden counter, beyond which the customer was allowed only at Mr Samuelson's invitation. The rear of the space had been furnished like a sitting room with dining chairs at a table and a black marble clock on the mantelpiece of what had once been a back parlour. A circular metal fitting, set with four hissing lamps, was suspended by three chains from the centre of the ceiling. Mr Samuelson's stock hung in dimly lit cupboards to either side.

Samuelson himself came to his counter as the bell on the shop door jangled. He was tall, thin and a little stooped. A white halo-fringe of hair round a bald head, combined with the oatmeal tweed of his suit and waistcoat, gave him the look of an itinerant preacher or corn curer. Two bloodstone seals hung on his watch-chain.

Sandboy put his suitcase down. He was about to hold his hand out but thought better of it.

'Mr Samuelson? We made an appointment, Mr Samuelson. Mr Hammond. We spoke on the phone.'

'Did we?' Mr Samuelson widened his eyes a little. 'Did

we? I don't recall speaking but if you say so, Mr – Hammond? – I'm sure we did.'

'About the sale of a coat?' Sandboy said. 'Full-length ocelot?'

'Well,' said Mr Samuelson helpfully, 'I certainly sell coats. Whether I could find you a full-length ocelot at the moment, I'm not sure. I think perhaps not. People who want that sort of thing nowadays prefer leopard.'

'I'm the one with a coat to sell.' Sandboy said pleasantly. 'I explained on the phone. It's a return. From a lady I'm not marrying any longer.'

He lifted the case on to the counter and snapped open the lock. Drawing back the tissue paper in which it was wrapped, he let Mr Samuelson see the leopard pattern of the ocelot.

Mr Samuelson lifted a fold of the coat and felt it. 'Send the doings back with it, did she? This young lady?'

'Doings?'

'A receipt or bill of sale, for instance.' Mr Samuelson lifted his head and looked into Sandboy's eyes for an uncomfortably long moment. 'Questions apt to be asked as to the provenance of articles like this. You must have thought of that, I'm sure.'

'Provenance?'

'In other words, where it came from, Mr – Hammond? Where you got it from.'

Sandboy laughed. 'All I want is to have it off my hands, Mr Samuelson. She had the receipt. She had it with the coat. But I'm not likely to get it back now, am I?'

Mr Samuelson sighed and looked down at the coat. 'So what – what exactly – did you have in mind, sir? As to price, exactly? In the case of a garment like this with no – provenance?'

He ran his finger and thumb over the fold of the coat. Sandboy could have sworn to himself that the old fraud had taken the bait.

'Hundred and twenty, Mr Samuelson. They're ticketed two hundred, two fifty even, down Swan and Edgars.'

It was about right. Samuelson would know that Sandboy could be talked down to a hundred or a little less. But Samuelson said, without looking up.

'Still, this isn't Swan and Edgar. Let me tell you something, Mr – Hammond? Coats of this sort aren't ticketed at so much as a hundred in Praed Street. And this isn't a usual sale. Is it? More of a fire sale, I'd say.' He lifted his eyes again. 'Fifty,' he said, 'if it's what it ought to be.'

'It's kosher,' Sandboy said and once again Samuelson held his gaze.

'If I was you, Mr – Hammond? – I wouldn't use words I didn't understand.' He indicated the coat again. 'Do you mind?'

'Have a good look at it,' Sandboy said encouragingly.

Gently, as if it had been thin silk, Mr Samuelson unfolded the coat from the suitcase and carried it to the table in the rear of the shop. He took a magnifying glass from his pocket.

'It's ocelot,' Sandboy said reassuringly. 'No one's saying it's leopard.'

'What it was when alive doesn't concern me. Now it's dead, that's another matter.'

He lifted the coat above his head and held it against the gaslight. Then he shook his head and laid the ocelot on the table again. The angle of the magnifying glass followed the hem and seams.

In the street a horse-drawn cart rattled and bumped, its dark sacks of house coal stacked in tight rows. A delivery boy stood between the shafts of an Aerated Bread Company Cart and watched it go by.

Presently Mr Samuelson straightened up. 'You met Mr Pender, have you?'

Sandboy felt as if the shop with its fungus smell of rotten timber had gone dark all round him. He stared at Samuelson, then said, 'I don't think I know a Mr Pender. Why?'

'He made this coat,' Samuelson said, walking back to the counter.

Sandboy felt that he should laugh but shrugged instead. 'All I did was buy the coat, Mr Samuelson. I wouldn't know who made it.'

'Short engagement to the young lady, was it?' Samuelson looked at him and the laughter went cold in Sandboy's heart.

'Month or two. Why? What's that to anyone?'

'You gave the young lady this coat to celebrate your engagement. As I understand it. Now she's broken off and you want to sell the garment. Right?'

'Yes,' Sandboy said, 'but the price'd have to be right.'

'Never mind the price,' Samuelson said.

The shop bell jangled again as a child came in and threw the evening paper on the counter. 'WOMAN LEAPS ON BANDIT CAR'. The bell rattled and cold air caught Sandboy's legs as the child went out again.

'Listen . . .' Sandboy said but Mr Samuelson was folding the coat back into the tissue paper.

'No, you listen, my young friend. Short engagement to your young lady, was it? Only, sometimes, when a coat like this is made, it has little pinholes that spell letters and numbers. Even the customer never knows. No one does that doesn't know where to look after years in the trade. But what those little marks say is who made it, when, and what its serial number is. I ask if it was a short engagement. This coat was made about a month ago. Let's say it goes through wholesaler, retailer, ticketing in the store, you couldn't have had it more than a week or ten days ago. That's what I'd call a short engagement.'

Mr Samuelson turned up the hem of the coat. 'Just there,' he said, 'written in pinpricks that show up with a light behind them. If you know where to look and what to look for.'

'Ask the man I got it from,' Sandboy said. 'About three weeks ago.'

A passing bus rattled the window of the shop.

'All right,' Sandboy said, 'fifty, then. What you said to begin with.'

Mr Samuelson pointed at the window, the crowds pressing homewards, the lamps hazed by moisture. 'Look,' he said contemptuously, 'it's been a foggy day. I done no business. I took no money. I'm not buying. That's all.'

'Fifty,' Sandboy said again, 'you'd double that and more inside the week.'

Mr Samuelson looked at him as if he hardly knew how to explain a simple truth to one so foolish. 'You been used as a mug,' Samuelson said. 'Bought it off some spiv, hoping you might put it into circulation at twice the price. So you might Mr – Hammond? But not through me. First I thought you might be plain-clothes. I been stung once that way. Years ago. Never again. But you're something else. And I don't want to know what.'

Sandboy began to close and fasten the suitcase. 'You don't happen to know . . .'

'No, I don't happen to know anyone else.'

'Fair enough.' Sandboy picked up the suitcase. 'You had your chance.'

'You ought to meet Harry Bidolph,' Mr Samuelson said reminiscently. 'He had his chance too.'

Sandboy stopped. 'Who's Harry Bidolph?'

Mr Samuelson's eyes narrowed a little in recollection. 'About your age. Ten years back. Thought he was smarter then the big boys. Thought he could be a bit of a young buccaneer. They could have topped him but they decided he'd be better as a living advertisement that the entire village could see. He'd shafted some very important people. One or two in prison and he thinks to move into their shoes. Others thought not. So they reckon Harry Bidolph went under a tram. Easier to do than on a railway, the wheels going down into a groove. When they caught him, they reckon they gave him a simple choice: left arm at the elbow or left leg below the knee. Half an hour to make his mind up while someone found a tram left overnight at a stop.'

Mr Samuelson gave a short painful cough. He removed the cigarette from his mouth, studied it, then looked back at Sandboy. 'I know what's what, my young friend. If that coat come from where I think, I wouldn't give you two bob for it.'

Sandboy turned to the door. An elderly woman in only a black dress and a straw hat rimmed with artificial flowers paused to stare through the window into the shadow light of the interior.

Sandboy shrugged and straightened his trilby. 'All right, you had your chance.'

'Get rid of it,' Mr Samuelson said.

Sandboy walked towards the railway terminus, through the crowds coming up from the underground railway, the tap of women's heels, the evening papers in every hand, the charcoal-grey overcoats, the gas flaring through the yellow-grey fog. The fog was everywhere now, even in the station, where the towering smoke and steam from the locomotives gathered under the glass curve of the roof.

He pushed past the news cinema, Wymans bookstall, the coffee stall. In the foyer of the Great Western Hotel there was a row of wooden telephone kiosks. He went into the first, put down his case, slid two coins into the box and called a number. He slammed his palm against the silver button as Gillis answered.

'Gilly? It's gone wrong. Gone wrong with Samuelson, anyway. He twigged Pender. We might try the other way. Just pawning and never reclaiming. But not yet. Someone knows something. Get hold of McGouran. Stop him doing anything till it's all clear. He could be off on his own, otherwise, trying his luck.'

He listened for a moment. Then he said quietly, 'Never mind what you have to do. He can't be that big a fool. Just get hold of him and stop him.'

He put down the phone and followed the passageway connecting the electric-lit foyer of the hotel with the underground station. For half an hour, until the carriage emptied, he sat with his suitcase on the Circle Line train. Then he took the folded softness of the ocelot from the suitcase and placed it on the opposite seat. It could have come from anywhere on the line. It might be swallowed up in the Lost Property Office for months. But in the moment before the doors began to open at the next station, he saw a hundred obscure ways in which an abandoned coat might be traced to the man who had left it. The plots of the yellow-back Edgar Wallace novels that lay among the cushions of the Manders' drawing room assured him of it.

He scooped up the soft length of the coat and got off with it at the next station.

Chapter Seven

Mr Samuelson unhooked the old-fashioned earpiece from the upright telephone set. He hesitated until a brewer's lorry had passed, rattling the glass of the shop window. He hesitated for a moment after that. Then he called WHI for Whitehall, paused and added 1212.

'Mr Samuelson for Inspector Rutter, if you'd be so good,' he said quietly.

There was a pause and then he heard the voice of a man who sounded as if he might have his feet up on the desk or was relaxing under a sunray lamp.

'Hello, Sammy, my boy. What've you got for me then?'

'Something to do with skins, Mr Rutter.'

Rutter shook his head, as if at the hopelessness of Mr Samuelson's case. Behind him, the lower half of the office wall was covered by the varnished wood of a Victorian dado. There was a mantelpiece and a hatstand, an unused picture rail two feet below the high ceiling. Despite the size and darkness of the room, only the desk-light was on. The angle of its shade threw the beam diagonally across the surface of the blotter and a stack of several files, magnifying them to grotesque shadows on the far wall.

'Skins.' Rutter removed the cigarette from his mouth

and pressed it out in a brown bakelite ashtray below the lamp. 'I suppose it would be skins, Sammy, that being your trade. What skins are these?'

Samuelson stared at the passers-by as he spoke, the typists and clerks separating from Praed Street to their boarding-houses and bed-sitting rooms in the long Paddington terraces and squares.

'There's something going on, Mr Rutter. I had a young chancer in here just now with an ocelot to sell. Don't know him from Adam. Usual story of it being not wanted or not liked by the lady.'

'Had a smell about it, Sammy?'

'More than that, Mr Rutter. He might have got away with his story but that coat was never second-hand, I'd swear it.'

'How's that, then?'

'He never knew about the pinpricks, Mr Rutter. Before they leave the furriers, they have pinpricks in the lining where no one thinks to look. Like a code. It numbers them. You can even tell who made them and when, if you know where to look.'

'You ever see this face before, Sammy?'

'Never, Mr Rutter. But what I don't believe is him buying this ocelot new in the last few weeks and coming to sell it to me at half its price already. Anyway, he didn't look as if he had that much money about him.'

'Before we start talking money, Sam, you wouldn't have any idea where this coat began its life?'

'Oh yes, Mr Rutter,' Samuelson sounded offended by the suggestion that he might not know. 'You know Pelly Pender?'

'I've heard of him, Sam. In several incarnations.'

'I'd swear this coat was still in his workroom as late

as three weeks ago. Not more. You tell me how it could get to wholesaler, retailer, showroom, customer, not be wanted by some young lady it was given to, not taken back by seller, and offered to me – all in that time.'

'And there's been no whispers?'

'No whispers, Mr Rutter. But if this coat was pinched, it was never pinched on its own. No one who got into a shop or a storeroom would take one ocelot and leave the rest. They don't work like that.'

'I know how they work, Sammy. You don't have to tell me.'

'Suppose I'm right,' Samuelson insisted, 'minks and ocelots and sables from the same job could start turning up all over the place in the next few weeks. Hasn't happened yet or I'd have heard something. I'm just telling you to watch out, Mr Rutter. You jump on top of this one, you could have a result to remember.'

'Yes,' Rutter said non-committally, 'and so I could.'

'That all then?' There was no mistaking the sudden tone of displeasure in Samuelson's voice.

Rutter became relaxed to the point of drowsiness. 'You'd never make a policeman, Sam. What I can see as rewardable is you asking this face to come back for a further discussion, with Mr Brodie or I listening. But, then, you never did that. Did you?'

'You should have heard him, Mr Rutter. He might be green but he wouldn't fall for that. It was a deal to be done now or never. He was anxious. Too anxious. And it's not just him I don't fancy. I don't want dealings with the sort of people who might come looking for him and whatever stolen goods he might have. If they hear I asked him back for another chat, I could need stitches in a hurry. And if I tell them I only asked him back to please you, I'd be carved up as well. It's all very well, Mr Rutter, to talk brave where you're sitting.'

Rutter pushed three cigarette stubs round the bakelite ashtray. 'Never mind, Sammy. We'll have a drink on it soon. Real money, though, depends on the insurers. No one's gone crying for insurance, so far as I know. Not Pender, not wholesalers, not showrooms. Unless you can tell me different. We don't even know for sure who's supposed to have lost this pussy. It could be Pender. Could be anyone. Could be no one. Still, if there's more to come, you'll be the first to hear. That's a promise.'

'Manufacturer has to be favourite, Mr Rutter. Perhaps wholesaler, but there's hardly been time for anything else. Since Christmas, that coat was made.'

'Leave it with me, Sammy. I'll enquire here and there.'

The line went dead. Samuelson hung the black bakelite earpiece on its stand. 'Bastard,' he said softly.

Rutter got up and turned on the central light. He crossed to the latticed window, which was far too small for the size of his office, and closed it. Two buses and a car passed down the Victoria Embankment under the skeletons of its winter trees. Across the river, County Hall stood bleak and massive, as if awaiting the staff of a soviet commissar. He turned and went out into the panelled corridor. Immediately outside his room was the door to an old Victorian lavatory. On the opposite wall hung a four-foot Bartholomew's map of England and Wales with the counties in individual colours.

At this level, Scotland Yard was a mosaic of Victorian byzantine gothic. As Rutter never tired of explaining to his visitors, the most famous law-enforcement building in the world had started life as a rejected design for an opera house. His own office was somewhere within the ecclesiastical red-brick summit of the scenery tower.

He turned to the far end of the corridor with its large square room looking towards the toy meccano set of Charing Cross bridge, the constant rumble and rattle of trains passing to Waterloo. There were half a dozen desks for sergeants, only three of them occupied at present. With its chalk-dusted blackboard and easel at one side, it might have been a schoolroom. Just outside, in the corridor, three black telephone receivers stood on individual shelves, supervised by a grey-suited civilian operator. The man got up, walked into the sergeants' room ahead of Rutter, and called out, 'Line two for Sergeant Maybury!'

Rutter beckoned the eldest of the officers. 'Frank! Have we still got a report that came in about a Mrs Pender? Violet Pender? Recently? Hospital report?'

Sergeant Brodie went back to his desk, opened a drawer and took out a slim brown file.

'Bring it through,' Rutter said.

Frank Brodie, clean-shaven, cleft-chinned and ginger-haired, followed him. Unlike the others, he had been a sergeant with Rutter, had been left behind by promotion, and still retained a private familiarity with his commander.

Rutter sat down in his swivel chair. 'Samuelson just phoned. Furrier in Praed Street. He was offered a full-length ocelot coat this evening by a face that no one recognizes. An amateur. Didn't even know that furs have an identity code pricked out in them. Samuelson reckons this one was made by Pelly Pender not more than a month ago. The face was supposed to have owned it longer than that. Therefore, he can't have come by it legitimately. What's the story on Mrs Pender?'

Brodie stood under the centre globe, the lights of Lambeth and the river glinting in the little panes of the window behind him. He opened the cardboard folder on his hand and sifted through the pages. Then he stopped and turned the last page back. 'Mrs Violet Pender. St Thomas's Hospital. Brought in early on Monday morning before last. Heart attack.'

'There was more to it,' Rutter said.

Brodie ran his finger down. 'There was, but not officially. She'd had a history of heart trouble. But when they examined her, the old girl also had marks on her wrists. As if she might have been held or tied. The house surgeon asked her about this on the second day. Mrs Pender said she'd been winding string.'

'Winding string? What's she bloody well mean? Winding string?'

'It's what she said.' Brodie began to read out the report in the flat unimpressed tone of its composition. 'Garden twine or string that was used in the garden. Like winding wool, I suppose.'

'God Almighty! What's the house surgeon say?'

'Looks more like cord or thin rope to him. But Mrs Pender was quite definite and made no complaint against anyone.'

'And during the two days she was in hospital before this chat with the house surgeon, she no doubt had a visit or two from Pelly Pender himself?'

Brodie took a page from the file and handed it to Rutter. 'See for yourself, Jack. Old man Pender came in with her when she was admitted. He was there every day afterwards. If they needed to make up a story, they had time enough to get it straight.'

Rutter stared at the pinpricks of city lighting in the

darkness of the casement window. He took his rolled-silver cigarette case from his breast pocket, opened it, and offered it to Brodie.

'No thanks, Jack.'

Rutter took a cigarette and lit it. 'So, if her wrists were tied, Pender's hiding what?'

Brodie closed the folder. 'Pender was always close to the wind, according to intelligence. Never quite been in trouble, though. Not quite. Problem is, he also moves in very private circles. Those he does favours for do favours in return. He's the kiddy that could take stolen furs, unpick them, cut and stitch until their own mother wouldn't know them.'

'Any proof?'

'Nope,' Brodie said. 'But he'd be well looked after. He's not a man that would be likely to get robbed by a professional.'

Rutter shook his head and Brodie went back to the sergeants' room. It was fifteen minutes later when he returned, still carrying the cardboard folder.

'Mrs Violet Pender,' he said in a tone that Rutter knew too well.

'What's gone wrong?'

'I had a word with St Thomas's, Jack. The house surgeon himself. Mrs Violet Pender died. She had another attack last Thursday and that was that.'

'Why in hell didn't they tell us?'

'No reason they should, Jack. I asked 'em that. Someone sent us that report on suspicion. We said no more. They thought we had no further interest. Her death was caused by heart failure, pure and simple. No question. She'd been under the doc for years. Could have happened any time. Nothing to do with her wrists and not much left to see on them anyway. They saw no need for an inquest, her having been under constant medical supervision. No post-mortem even. You can see their side of it, Jack. Funeral yesterday afternoon. Croydon Cemetery. No one's going to let you dig her up on the strength of that.'

'Sod it!' Rutter said helplessly. 'One thing, though, Frank. Samuelson clears the way a bit. We give the grieving widower a decent interval. Then we go down to Purley and test old man Pender's size in thumbscrews. I don't like what I hear about this anonymous face in Praed Street. A new generation that fancies itself, taking on the old bulls. And it'd be us sweeping up fingers from the tramlines first thing every morning.'

March

Picturedrome

Chapter Eight

A flood tide rattled and hissed on the shingle, under iron girders and wooden decking. Sonny Tarrant's glance fell like a shadow across the white-painted kiosks of the pier approach and the fish-scale silver of the roofs. Out of the wind, the morning sun was warm as early summer. The electric script of the neon signs was dead but the stalls that sold camera films, sweets, cigarettes and Sunday newspapers were open.

With ungloved hands stuffed into overcoat pockets, he walked past the seats that were sheltered in the lee of the glass-panelled windbreak. The headlines of the *News of the World*, *People* and *Sunday Pictorial* ran like messages tapped out from a doomed liner: 'GIRL CHEATS WHITE SLAVE GANG . . .', 'GERMAN ARMY ENTERS RHINELAND . . .', 'FRENCH TROOPS MAN 300 DEATH TURRETS . . .', 'ADMIRAL ARRESTED IN WOMAN'S DRESS . . .'

The cold morning air made his thoughts clear and hard as diamonds. Bland and unremarkable to the world, he clenched his fists in the deep pockets. His mind reflected the sword-edged purpose of a Roman emperor or a Renaissance prince. Muffled against the wind in his russet-brown, military-tailored coat, Sonny Tarrant paced the decking of the pier, a self-made commander of a new age.

The dead past lay honoured and buried at Windsor on a cold January afternoon. A new debonair voice from his radiogram struck him with a fine thrill of expectation. Simple and vital, it offered power to new men, speaking to Sonny Tarrant as a friend might speak: 'I am better known to you as the Prince of Wales . . . Although now I speak to you as King, I am still that same man . . .'

The cold tide glittered like ice in the early sun. Soon the bars and arcades at the end of the pier would be open on such a day as this. Other men and women judged the return of spring by blossoms or migrant birds. In Tarrant's calendar, the coming of new life was signalled by the whoop of the Ghost Train, the electric splutter of dodgem cars, the strident chords of a steam organ.

He stood by the blue promenade rails, the clipped green of privet behind him, and shaped his purpose with a locksmith's precision. What he intended for Manders must wait until Pender had been put right. He had scarcely known Vi Pender, but his help had been asked. For that, he needed a slightly dishonest favour from a generally honest man. It might be refused, but he was practised in shaping demands so that there was no room for refusal.

The trick was justice for Pelly Pender without recourse to the law. Tarrant knew to the last inflection of his voice how that trick was to be done. He lifted the corner of his lip, allowing himself a smile at the startled headlines in the papers. The Nazi sleight of hand in the Rhineland, well judged on its larger scale, was a second-rater compared to his own.

Impatient to put himself to the test, he lengthened his stride through the broad, empty shopping streets towards the upper end of the promenade. He supposed that ex-sergeant Charley Archer had never taken a bribe, either in his police career or since. But what he wanted from Archer was so small that it would seem scarcely dishonest, at first. He walked between the tall fronts of department stores that rose dark as the rock face of a canyon in the Sunday morning quiet. The sales concourses behind the display windows were unlit, only the winter sky above the roofs a pale soaring blue. A seagull circled in the fierce cold overhead with the patience of a vulture.

Beyond the bend of the hill, he turned into the curving driveway of the Garden Royal Hotel, a Second Empire front with mansard roofs overlooking the sea below. Its white-rendered portico lay behind a shrubbery of laurel, ivy, bay tree and monkey-puzzle. From its warm lounges and private suites, the winter sea between the evergreens was as blue to the hotel's guests as Rapallo or Cap Ferrat.

A uniformed doorman touched his gloved fingers to his cap and held open the glass door.

'Morning, Mr Tarrant, sir.'

The man was new. He had not yet learnt that Tarrant disliked employees speaking uninvited to himself or his guests. In this case, he forgave inexperience.

'Speak when spoken to, Nobby,' he said gently. 'That's what our visitors pay for.'

He walked into the vestibule and then remembered the words, 'speak when spoken to'. It was what one of the three little guttersnipes had said to poor old Vi and Pelly Pender. Tarrant felt a controlled rage at the thought that his own rules of conduct for subordinates should have been soiled in this way. His arms at his sides, he clenched his fists hard again and then relaxed them. It was a trick of curbing temper that his mother had taught him, years ago. Because he believed in it, it often worked.

The lobby of the Garden Royal was a wide concourse of caramel and white marble paving with a central dome of coloured glass, its vestibule a cross between a conservatory and a shopping arcade. Behind the dwarf palms in brass urns edging its semicircle, there was a barber's shop, a jeweller's display window, a florist and tobacconist. It was a place of cigars and orchids, perfumed pomade and diamond clusters set in gold.

The sleekness of the marble underfoot gave him a feeling of walking on ice or air. A pianist in the lounge bar was evoking ripples and cadences from a Chopin waltz, so that the casual elegance of the music hung like perfume in the tall rooms. In the lounge there was an amber twilight of expensive linen blinds drawn against the brilliance of sun on the glittering tide.

Tarrant crossed to the wide mahogany sweep of the reception desk, knowing that Charley Archer would have noticed him long before he got there. It was Archer's job to clock new arrivals without being seen himself.

A door at one end of the counter opened and a half-bald, dark-haired man looked out. He was a muscular fifty-year-old. His suit of grey flannel had the smooth and expensive nap of well-groomed billiard cloth. His hair showed the close razor-trimmed neatness of a toy soldier. He opened the door at one end of the counter and let Tarrant through.

'Morning Charley Artful.' Tarrant watched to catch any resentment in Archer at the threadbare joke. There was none.

They went into the security officer's room, which contained only Archer's chair, desk, filing cabinet and a second chair occupied at various times by hotel thieves, guests unable to pay their bills, prostitutes removed from the bars or lounges, victims of robbery or of violence by those who shared their beds.

Tarrant sat down and looked amiably around. 'We must try and do somethin' better than this for you, Charley. I said as much to Manny months ago.'

'It's all right, Mr Tarrant,' Archer said. 'It does me.'

Tarrant looked at him steadily, letting Archer feel that a silence was developing between them. Then he said abruptly, 'I'm wonderin', Charley, if you might help me over somethin' very personal.'

Archer seemed relieved it was no worse. 'I'd try, sir, naturally.'

'On'y, I mustn't put you in an invidious position. So you got to say straight out, if you feel I'm doin' that. And no hard feelin's. Right?'

'I can't see how you would, Mr Tarrant.'

Tarrant lay back a little in his chair, the bulge of the tightly suited stomach visible between the open flaps of the overcoat. 'I come to you, Charley, because I got a high opinion of you as an able man. Always been well-impressed by the way you done a difficult job. Firm but sensitive. Still, you know that, I'm sure. I always thought you'd go all the way. Whether it's here or elsewhere. And I'd like to see it happen here. But what I don't like is makin' promises I can't keep.'

'That's fair enough,' Archer said.

Tarrant's lip rose in its half-smile. 'All the same, Charley, and I say this because I know it won't go further, you might have caught a rumour that Mr Manders and I ain't been idle over the business of the Luxor Hotel. It's near enough an hotel that might have the cinema as part of it. Now, this plan bein' a joint enterprise, it's not entirely in my gift to make promises. But, say it should go through. There'll be a hotel manager needed down there. If that made a vacancy in this little office, there'd be a need here. Somethin' to suit the sort of man you might know of. A chap that's well on his police career, say, and lookin' to move into somethin' more long term. Police havin' to retire so early and not much of a screw meantime. I say all this just to show I don't come empty-handed.'

'You never come empty-handed to me, Mr Tarrant,' Archer said quickly, the impassive face reddening a little. 'You don't go empty-handed to anyone. You wouldn't know how.'

Tarrant's smile softened at the compliment. 'Help me or not in my little difficulty, Charles, you're the best man for this job. The two things don't depend on one another. That got to be understood.'

'What d'you want done, Mr Tarrant?'

There was no change in Archer's face, except a slight movement in the dark eyes. Tarrant shook his head. 'Mrs Tarrant, Charley. Between you and me, I had a little trouble with the poor old lady. Poor old soul. It's not her fault.'

'Sorry to hear it, sir.'

'Thing is, Charley, she woke several nights ago when I was up in town. She thought she heard someone movin' about in the flat. And she could be right. I don't say not.'

'He'd have to get past the porter on the desk and the locks,' Archer said sceptically.

'Well, I don't think he could, Charley. 'Course not. That's just it. But suppose some Celluloid Alf could get past the porter or climb a drainpipe to a corridor window.

Then he might ease back the bolt of a Yale lock with a strip of perspex. Not likely, but possible.'

'He might,' Archer said grudgingly.

'Before comin' to you, Charley, let alone the law, I been right through the flat and come up with nothin'. I thought the old lady had a bad dream. Anyhow, then I saw a box of matches on a table in the business room, where no one generally goes but us two, not even the girl that cleans, as a rule. Now, we got no cause to use matches and wouldn't leave them in there anyhow. Can't be accounted for.'

'What's a burglar want with matches?'

'What do they want with anythin', Charley? Look, what I've done is bring them to you. I haven't touched them, 'cept to tweezer them into a bag.'

Tarrant laid the cellophane bag on the desk. The yellow box of Swan Vestas showed a sandpaper edge scraped red by match heads.

'I don't like to ask, Charley, except you're the only one I know with contacts on the force. Of course, I could go to Superintendent Landis and he'd be very good. He'd start a first-rate investigation, I know that. I'd welcome him, if it was just me. But it's not. And if the poor old lady's mind's playin' up, which I think perhaps it is, then havin' a set-to of that kind might make it all the worse. Other hand, if it is somethin' like a break-in, then I can't be away in town and have a moment's peace with her there on her own. See?'

The square face with the clipped moustache looked back at him. Archer was not going to be easy.

Tarrant's mouth moved in its half-smile. 'Someone's used that matchbox, Charley. Struck matches on it. Fingered it. A thousand to one, they're ordinary prints of an ordinary person. Came there innocently. I don't want to bother Ray Landis and your friends down CID over somethin' like that. Nor poor old Mrs Tarrant. But there's one chance in a thousand, it's been left by some villain that got into the flat. In that case I'm in a bit of bother.'

Archer seemed relieved again that it was no worse. 'You want the matchbox looked at, Mr Tarrant? Dusted?'

'Just that, Charley. Then, if there's a print on it that fits someone with form, I suppose it had better go all the way. If not, we can just let it go. Must be the girl who cleaned went in there, perhaps, without askin'.'

Archer was still grateful to have saved himself so easily. 'I can ask someone, Mr Tarrant. What I can't do is promise, of course. But I think I know who could check that for us. As a matter of routine, more than anything. After all, if there was a break-in inquiry and they found prints, you'd get to hear anyway. Or you could have had prints as such lifted by a private inquiry agent. I can't promise, sir, but I can't see a problem.'

'I don't need promises, Charley. I know you'd do it for me if you could. I wouldn't ask you but for worry about the old lady.'

'See what we can do, Mr Tarrant.'

'And I shan't forget you, Charley. You shan't be the loser, nor your friend down the division, you know that.'

As Tarrant walked away across the lobby he hoped that the box had been fingered by the little guttersnipe who ordered the terrified old couple to 'speak when spoken to'.

Chapter Nine

The Luxor Picturedrome stood on a quiet tree-lined street at the corner end of a row of expensive little shops. There was a florist, a high-class fruiterer, a wine merchant, a dress shop and a small tea-room, closed in the Sunday afternoon stillness. The shops were identical in style and, like the cinema, had been built into the rear of the Luxor Hotel block, whose front opened on to the promenade. Shops and cinema served the grand hotel and its suburb of white houses behind hedges of laurel or yew, an enclave that seemed exempt from sickness or crime or death.

On its quiet corner, the Luxor Picturedrome shone with a modernism of black glass and white tiles. The square ventilation tower was neatly and discreetly stitched with its name in red neon script, rising in the cold blue of the winter day.

The Luxor was a second-run cinema, picking up new releases a month or six weeks after the chains of Odeons and Gaumont-British theatres had finished with them. Tarrant went up the wide steps, past the chromium-edged display cases. The monochrome stills offered George Formby in *No Limit*, showing on Monday to Wednesday, followed by *It's Love Again* with the soubrette dancing of

Jessie Matthews from Thursday to Saturday. A sign above the doors boasted Western Electric Wide-Range Sound.

He took out a key and let himself in at the black metal door by the glass-fronted pay box. The flush of the wall-lights behind engraved and frosted glass had been turned on in the foyer but the chandelier was dead. Someone had unhooked the velvet cord across the shallow steps of the poppy-scented foyer with its amber carpet soft as snow. Ignoring the heavy portholed doors to the stalls, Tarrant put his hand on the sleek chrome rail and went up quickly to the circle landing.

On weekdays, the Circle Café served teas and hot snacks, its balcony looking down on the foyer below and across the street outside to the trees and bandstand of Victoria Park. Today the tables were bare and unlit, the counter empty, the kitchen door locked. Over all lay a sweetish smell of disinfectant.

Sonny Tarrant walked past the colour photo-portraits of Hollywood stars and the doors that sealed the circle auditorium like the portico of a pharaoh's tomb. He went up narrower stairs to the private offices. From close at hand came the chatter of a projector gate. But there was no sound of voices. Someone was projecting a silent film in an empty cinema. His lip lifted a little with the amusement of what he might find.

At the top of the private stairs stood a metal fire door with a poster on it. An angled modernistic machine directed a beam like a searchlight against a sky-blue background: 'Gaumont Kalee 18: A Complete Soundfilm System.' He pushed open the door and walked into the harsh acetone smell of celluloid adhesive fluid, the scents of hot metal and dust.

Two Gaumont Kalee Universal projectors stood silent

and unlit, attenuated prehistoric shapes, angled at the porthole shutters. The sleek bronze steel of their housing was pierced by tiny windows showing sets of cogs and angled mirrors, metal guides for the film and valves in the soundbox. Their two steel cases for the full and empty reels would be unused until Monday afternoon, the lens and shutter gate dark.

Two young men stepped out from behind the nearer machine. One was tall and slim with ginger hair that would never look tidy. Tarrant knew the other.

'Hello, Sandboy. Who's this stranger, then?'

'He's a mate, Mr Tarrant. Gilly. I'm just showing him round while the others watch the flicks. Mr Tarrant, Gilly.'

Tarrant nodded but otherwise ignored the introduction. 'Where's our friend Manny?'

'They're all in the circle, Mr Tarrant. They got the little screen and the Bell and Howell. Mr Manders is running it.'

On a bench at one side of the projection box was a pile of round cardboard containers for reels of 16mm film, blue boxes with their Pathescope Safety Film triangle in orange. Tarrant picked them up and glanced at the titles on the white strip round each box's circumference. *Suzanne Learns the Ropes*, *French Follies*, *The Blonde Bandit Takes Her Medicine*, *Lolotte et Ses Deux Amies*.

He put the boxes down and walked across to the projection shutter in the front wall. The two young men pretended to go back to their conversation. In the auditorium below him, a six-foot silvered screen with black edging was propped against the parapet at the front of the circle. Tarrant caught a smudged unsteady image of a man in a gown and mortarboard, a woman of thirty or so in a school uniform with her skirt removed. The beam of the film flickered uncertainly from the box shape of the Bell and Howell at the rear of the aisle, the image overlapping the black frame of the screen.

Faked celluloid dramas had not the least interest for him. He had seen too many, knew their tricks, even looked on while they were made. Several times, he had watched the camera at work when the ecstasy or distress was not acted at all. Now he gave his attention to the outline of the five people who sat together in the back row of the circle, just below the shutter: Yvonne, Nina, Manders and a couple who were strangers to him.

His eyes were soon used to the flickering darkness, making out the green walls, the domed ceiling in green and gold, emerald velvet curtains at the exit doors. He watched Yvonne and Manders' stepdaughter Nina with special care. In distinct ways, Tarrant despised them both. Yvonne Manders had the pretensions of a failed actress. Nina Manders, 'Little Madam', as they called her at seventeen, thought herself mysterious and high-strung. Underneath the fair Greta Garbo hair and green Slav eyes, she was merely, as Mrs Tarrant told her son, 'a bit common, a bit brass'.

He grinned at their backs. Nothing on the screen could equal the amusement, sometimes the excitement, of seeing how two such women betrayed themselves as they stared at the grainy and erratic image of Suzanne learning the ropes. Tarrant, the unseen onlooker, smiled almost good-naturedly as his subjects unwittingly surrendered their secret expressions to him.

Without speaking, he turned at last and went back to the door of the projection box, about to go down and join the others. Then he stopped and looked at Sandboy. 'Listen, son. You waitin' to drive them back after this?'

84

'Yes,' Sandboy said.

Tarrant gave a sideways wave of his hand, wiping out the idea. 'Forget it. They can come with me in the Chrysler. You show your young friend around.' He paused, as if trying to make up for his earlier indifference. 'What's more, if you two boys got time, go up the Garden Royal. Lounge Bar. You have a drink up there, and tell 'em from me that you don't pay nothin' for it. See? Tell Mr Archer on the door, he'll see you right. And have some grub while you're at it. Pair of you look as if you could do with a good tightner. You two lads have anythin' you like. On the house.'

The door closed. Gillis said, 'That's Sonny Tarrant? That's all?'

Sandboy stood at the rear of one of the Gaumont Kalees. He turned a knob, starting the motor with a sputter and a whine. Then he turned it off again. 'That's him.'

Gillis walked over to the projection porthole, where Tarrant had been standing, and looked down. 'He doesn't know a bloody thing, Sandy. He can't. You heard him. Go up the Garden Royal. 'ave a drink. You 'ave anythin' you want. He talks like a prat! Chrissake, you're his blue-eyed boy. I thought he was supposed to be some thug with hair grease, strawberry nose and brass knuckles. What I've seen of him, even McGouran could take him. In fact, McGouran worries me a fucking sight more than Tarrant.'

'McGouran's nothing,' Sandboy said. 'But the less Tarrant knows, the better. You think he's nothing? This place is his, even if it's got old Manny's name on it. So's Brandons Garages. He's got Manders like a rotten plum at the end of a twig. Ready to drop in his hands the minute he wants. There's agreements drawn up so Tarrant can collar this lot any time he chooses. Only thing is, it suits him to have Manders on the notepaper for the moment. Just so long as Sonny doesn't have to account for where all his money came from.'

'What if Manders won't move over when asked?'

Sandboy grinned. 'I 'spect he'd have to take a long walk out to sea on a very short plank.'

Gillis picked up the cardboard film boxes and looked at the titles as Tarrant had done. 'McGouran's stuck his three pussies in a pawnshop near Euston. Stuffed 'em for all he could get, as quick as he could get it. He thinks the shop owner's safe because he's used him before. No one's that safe! And McGouran's never going to have the money to get the furs back. Almighty Christ, that old woman's dead, thanks to him. If it ever gets out, McGouran good as killed her. Where's that leave us?'

'No one killed her,' Sandboy said stubbornly. 'You heard what happened. She died a fortnight later. It could have happened to her anyway. All you and I did was talk to her. That never killed her. We might have frightened her. But not killed her. Come on!'

Gillis sat down on the stool. 'Listen. Those three coats McGouran pawned can't be left there. Not now that old woman had to go and bloody well die. They're like a bomb waiting to go off under us, the moment McGouran's time is up for redeeming them. You know anything about pawnshops, Sandy? If McGouran doesn't redeem them, which he won't have the money to do, they go to auction. Less than two months from now. They'll even be advertised. You think Samuelson was quick? They'll be identified and traced a lot faster than old Samuelson could do it. What then?'

Sandboy turned the projector fan on and off.

'I warned you about McGouran,' Gillis said. 'I told you the bastard wouldn't wait. Whatever we all agreed. He must have his money. Spouts the lot for a tenth of what he might have got.'

'What's his rush?'

'McGouran's a thick jock. And he's got a hop-head tart with a real habit to feed. Of all the girls lying around, bloody McGouran would pick one that uses dope! So, no sooner he gets his hands on those coats than he runs like a rabbit to a bent dolly shop in Dalgetty Street! He thinks it's safe because he's used it before! Almighty Christ,' Gillis said, 'that's why he shouldn't use it now. If this goes really wrong, it could tie him to killing the old woman! And his coats could tie us.'

'All right,' Sandboy said quietly, 'we'll do what's needful.'

Gillis turned back to the projection shutter, as if Sandboy's concession had satisfied him for the time being.

'Stop worrying and give your eyes a treat,' Sandboy said.

Gillis squinted into the dark. 'Which of them is yours?'

'Chestnut, between Manny and the blonde.'

'She looks all right,' Gillis said generously. 'What's Manny think? You still reckon there's nothing between her and him?'

Sandboy joined him at the shutter. 'He's an old man. He's got no more use.'

'You're not sharing her with Tarrant as well?'

''Course not,' Sandboy said irritably. 'She just goes up to see Tarrant. Old Mrs Tarrant's there as a rule. Lady Blue plays their piano to them. Fucking great grand piano! Anyway, I'm told Tarrant's like Manny. He doesn't do it with anyone. Just likes to be seen around with a nice bit of brass. Watches sometimes. Pays some girl and her boy to do it for him or perhaps three at a time. Only not with Yvonne. She's class, another league. Strictly for show. Any case, with Manny, she doesn't need to earn money.'

Gillis shook his head. 'You got anyone in this town that plays straight up and down the wicket?'

'Only me,' Sandboy said.

'Who's the blonde?'

'Nina. Little Madam. They reckon she's Manny's step-daughter. First time round, he was married to a woman that died but already had Nina. I don't think Manny ever did anything with the daughter. He picked up Yvonne about ten years ago when she was on the stage. Any case, he's no danger to a girl now. More like a father to Yvonne, even.'

'You had a go with the blonde?'

'Funny thing,' Sandboy said, 'I never really thought of her, me having got Yvonne. And I couldn't very well have both in the same house. I honestly never thought. Then one night I had a dream of being at a Christmas party at Manny's. When we all left we kissed goodbye. Just on the cheek. I went to kiss Nina and she was all Russian blonde and green eyes. I went to kiss her and somehow it was her mouth, French kissing in the dream, and she opened her mouth and it was her tongue round mine. I never thought of her like that before. I suppose I must have wanted her without knowing. And then I couldn't stop thinking about it. Even though it was Yvonne every day, I had dream after dream about Nina. Just kissing and lying about together. So when Manny really had his Christmas party, I tried it under the mistletoe, on her mouth.'

'And then?'

Sandboy laughed. 'She didn't run but she turned her face sharp. I just about kissed her earhole. But those dreams. I used to wake up really fancying her. I used to wonder if she was having them too. Couldn't get her out of my mind.'

'Until you kissed her ear,' Gillis said derisively. 'This keeps up, my son, we'll be taking you down the vet's.'

'I'd like to do her, though, if I got the chance,' Sandboy said wistfully. 'I really would.'

Gillis turned back to the sleek dinosaur shapes of the two big projectors. 'How do you manage it so that there's never a gap between reels in a film?'

'Easy.' Sandboy touched the panel at the rear. 'There's a motor switch at the back here to get the second machine ready. You turn the knob to "Start". All that does is just get the motor humming without running the film. When the reel on the other machine gets close to the end, there's a blip in the top corner of the picture on the screen. When that comes on, you turn the knob on this machine to "Run". There's a ten-second countdown. Then the other machine goes off and this one takes over. They don't run together. Almost automatic.'

'Just like that,' Gillis said admiringly.

'Worst thing is, if the film breaks and you're not watching the light box. The soundtrack isn't synchronized with the picture on the strip of film. The picture gets projected from the light box. But the sound comes out the soundbox, down here, when the film goes through it ten seconds later. So if it breaks in the gate of the light box, which is usually where it does, you hear the film going on but there isn't any picture.'

Gillis nodded, his interest at an end. He put the cardboard film containers back on the workbench. He said, 'Those bloody coats. That bugger McGouran. If the old man in Praed Street could tell straight away that yours came from Pender, they'll know these the minute they see them in an auction. They'll go back to the dolly shop, Lawsons, and they'll have McGouran's name. They'll find where McGouran lives, same house as me in Harringay. That's two of us found.'

Sandboy sat down on a wooden stool by the nearer Gaumont projector.

'I tell you,' Gillis said, 'if they're wise to that ocelot you took Samuelson, these other three are sitting there like a time bomb and we're too close. It's not just stealing pussies any more, Sandy. We're talking about an old woman that's died. Someone could have to jump off for that, in theory at least. This can't be left.'

Sandboy bit the edge of a thumbnail. 'What's done, is done.'

Gillis shook his head. 'No, Sandy. We could put it right but we'd have to do it soon.'

'How's that?'

'We go and get 'em,' Gillis said. 'We go and get the three pussies from the dolly shop, same as we got 'em in the first place. That way, we can wash our hands of McGouran. Take the coats abroad somewhere. Do what we want with them. Just get clear.'

Sandboy bit the edge of his nail again. 'Fuck that for a game of soldiers,' he said.

'Fuck sitting here and waiting for the whole thing to blow up under us. If we leave them there, we're handing out a visiting card. How long before someone puts them together with the one you took to Samuelson? How long then before the law brings Samuelson here to have a look at you?'

'Samuelson's nothing. He couldn't have known who I was. No one would. That's why it might have worked.'

Gillis sat down on the other stool. 'I had a word last week with a man that has reason to know. Samuelson's a nark.'

Sandboy coughed, laughed and coughed again. 'Samuelson's a fucking crook.'

'So what?' Gillis paced to the projection shutter and back. 'Let's say he's crooked and a nark. That makes it worse. I want those coats back. It's easier than last time. For God's sake, we're not going to anyone's house to hold them hostage. Just a smelly little dolly shop off the Hampstead Road. We just come and go. A quick break-in and a quick break-out.'

'Supposing it's that easy,' Sandboy said doubtfully. 'Once we're in, though, how do we know which coats? There could be dozens hanging there. It's only some secret pinpricks Pender leaves in his.'

'Forget the pinpricks,' Gillis said. 'McGouran was so pleased with himself, he started flashing the pawn tickets. I got one of the numbers, a green one, 4938. He probably took the coats there in one go, the bloody fool. In that case they're in sequence. Anyway, there can't be many of that sort hanging there. Not in a dump like Dalgetty Street! And we do it when the place is empty.'

'With one sight of the gun if it's not.'

Gillis shook his head. 'Sod the gun.'

'We take it,' Sandboy said. 'Of course we don't use it. It wouldn't have been used last time, but for McGouran. Just show it, if we have to. It stops arguments and saves fights. We don't even load it, if that worries you.'

DONALD THOMAS

Gillis said nothing. From the circle seats below the projection box, the chatter of the Bell and Howell projector had stopped.

'Put it this way,' Sandboy said, 'It'd be better to have it and not need it, than need it and not have it.'

There was movement below them. One of the women in the circle seats said something and another laughed. Sandboy closed the square shutter. In the acetone smell of the darkened projection box the sunshine of the March day belonged to another world.

April

Little White Lies

Chapter Ten

Beyond the black and gilt Victorian tavern-front of the Rising Sun, the Wolseley turned left from Derby Gate into Whitehall. Rutter sat in the back seat next to Brodie. The driver turned left again at the traffic lights, past the fairy-tale spires of parliament and the underground station. Downstream from Westminster Bridge, the waves of the river chopped and slapped against the masonry of the Embankment. A cold breeze crossed the incoming tide, the sun a hard gleam on jumping water.

'I don't much care about Pender lying as such,' Rutter said at last. 'But after a couple of months of this, I do care about why he goes on lying and who makes him do it.'

'He needs a nasty shock,' Brodie said helpfully. 'Local bobbies a bit too sympathetic. A bit too apt to be impressed.'

Rutter lit a cigarette, and shook out the city final of the evening paper, which like all final editions had been on the streets since lunchtime. Ignoring 'NIGHT OF TERROR IN SPANISH RIOTS', he opened the centre photo guide to the *Queen Mary*'s maiden voyage.

The gates between the high brick walls of Pender's driveway had been left open. To either side, close-textured hedges screened the white flat-roofed houses with their curved corner windows, lawns and covered pools.

Rutter and Brodie entered a long room with two leather chesterfields, a cocktail cabinet, a baby grand piano and tables that were arranged with photographs in silver frames. Through the far window a gardener in a cap, his jacket removed to show shirtsleeves and waistcoat, mowed the lawn in long even strips.

Pender sat hunched and hostile in a chair beyond the tall Minster fireplace with its copper screen. He stood up as they came in but made no movement towards them. He was short but bulky in a light brown suit of plus fours. The eyes were still large and solemn behind his glasses. The jowls had a doggy sadness.

'Mr Pender.' With his hat in his hand, Rutter spoke in a crisp gravelly voice that proclaimed sympathy without showing it in the least. 'Inspector Rutter. Sergeant Brodie. Sorry to bother you again, after your interviews with our colleagues in the division.'

'Pity you couldn't be sorry enough to let the whole thing drop.' Pender sat down in his chair again like a sulky child.

'Perhaps I can save you trouble by talking now,' Rutter said evenly. 'I can understand the shock that your wife's death must have been to you.'

Pender said nothing. Rutter took the armchair opposite the old man. 'We need information, Mr Pender, on routine matters.'

'I wouldn't call it a shock,' Pender said quietly.

Rutter closed the folder he had begun to open.

'In her state,' Pender went on, 'she could go any time. Bound to go some time. Sooner or later. Lucky she held on so long.' He looked up and stared into Rutter's face, daring him to think otherwise.

'But then,' Rutter said smoothly, 'the circumstances of Mrs Pender's death have been discussed with you. Your answers, made in the presence of your solicitor, are on record.'

A glance of annoyance troubled the old man's solemn eyes. 'I hope I shan't need the solicitor back this afternoon.'

Rutter opened the folder again. 'I wouldn't think so, Mr Pender. We need to ask you about your stocktaking, as a matter of routine. That's all. Have you missed any items in the past two months? Probably less than two months, but let's say as long as that.'

Pender's eyes and mouth rounded, his face fuller in astonishment. 'No! No, I have not.'

'And you would know, of course, Mr Pender? You would know if anything was missing? There would have been checks in the past two months?'

'There've been checks in the past two weeks, let alone months,' Pender said sharply, 'for what it matters to you. Supposing how I run my business is any of your concern.'

The irritation passed and the face fell into its lines of gloom.

'My concern, Mr Pender,' said Rutter smoothly, 'is that an ocelot coat made in your workshop in early January was being offered for resale a little more than two weeks later. There seems no way in which a coat could have been made by you, passed to the wholesaler, then to retailer and showroom, could be bought and resold in the usual way within so short a time. If your stock control records do not account for this transaction, perhaps you might like to speculate on how it came about.'

'You seen this coat, have you?'

'What matters is . . .'

But Pender had snatched the initiative. 'You come back when you got the coat, not just a story.'

Rutter sat firm. 'For all I know, Mr Pender, you may have other outlets. Apart from your wholesale trade. That's all. But, if goods from your premises are passing through the wrong hands, that concerns many other people. Not least your professional association. If it does not concern you too, I shall be interested to know why.'

Pender got up. 'I'll make it nice and easy. I keep books. I keep them to the last detail. The income tax and the Excise would have me if I didn't. Stock control down to the last item. Right? Now, I been through those books, as if I needed to, because of the things been said about me by people like you. Have I been robbed? Have I been attacked? Have I been fiddling? All the rest of it. Every garment that come from me can be accounted for. Furs coming in, coats going out. Not one gone missing.' He sat down again.

Rutter glanced at his folder. 'So all we have to decide, Mr Pender, is how a garment valued at more than two hundred pounds, dated as being made by you in early to mid-January was apparently offered for sale, allegedly after retail purchase, before the month was out. If I was asked, I'd have to say it's a classic sign of a fur being sold on by someone who had no business to have it. I could be mistaken. But, in this case, the furrier who was offered it refused to buy for just that reason. That's why I'm here.'

Pender's face was growing red, like a child about to burst into tears. But he did not burst into tears. 'And this ocelot you can't produce was known to be mine? How?'

'The codes pricked out in it.' But Rutter knew before

he answered that the interview with Pender was about to go wrong.

'Oh, dear.' Pender's shoulders gave a single heave of dry laughter. The anger changed to mockery. 'Is that all? They really shouldn't let you out on your own, Mr Rutter.'

'I don't understand.'

'I'll say you don't! Haven't you ever heard that one of the tricks of the game is getting a coat without a marking and putting one in? A bit of rabbit knocked up in Shadwell or Hackney and all of a sudden it's a Swears and Wells from Regent Street or some West End outfit? It never come from my workshops. That's why this garment you're talking about seemed to go through the trade like grease through a goose. Suppose it ever existed.'

Rutter fixed his eyes on the wall beyond Pender, as if he had no answer. Pender came back at him. 'In the trade, Mr Rutter, a Pender's fur is something with a reputation and a bit of class. I even have to keep the labels under lock and key, so some cutter with a grudge don't take them and sew them into coats that are rubbish. See?'

Rutter nodded and let the old man run on.

'You could have said all this on the phone and saved yourself a journey. Nothing got past my stock control. What you heard about and never saw wasn't stolen. But it might well have been a fake. Take the trade as a whole, I'd be in the top dozen they'd try to rip off by faking.'

'If that's what happened,' Rutter said helpfully.

'It happened,' Pender was enjoying himself now, 'if what you heard was true. Either way, I'd say it's down the bottom of the class for you. What you can do, though, is find out who's faking and put a stop to it. I'll be on to you about that from time to time. It's what you're paid your wages to stop!'

He stood up. Rutter and Brodie followed him.

'Anything else, was there?' Pender asked.

Rutter shook his head. 'Not really, Mr Pender. The other officers and your own solicitor will have told you the rest.'

'What rest?'

'Perhaps it hardly applies.'

'What hardly applies?'

'Well,' Rutter said, 'if there had been theft, if there had been violence used, if Mrs Pender had suffered injury, there is a point where you would make yourself an accessory by concealing such a train of events.'

The scales of mockery and anger came down on the side of bitter fury as Pender glared at him. 'You sail that close to the wind again, my friend, you'll bloody wish you'd stayed on dry land. You leave my property now. And you don't come back. My wife dies after a fortnight in hospital with a heart attack and you come round here asking me if I killed her? Who the hell d'you think you are? You leave here now. Anything else you got to say, you talk to my lawyer.'

Sergeant Brodie watched the outburst from a little distance. There was always the chance that in such a tantrum Pender might say more than he had intended. In such a state, the agitation of anger in the eyes was almost indistinguishable from fright. But anger might also mask the fright.

The two men walked back to the car. On the common, a hockey team scurried and hacked at a ball. A whistle blew across the trodden grass. The teams broke up and went back to their positions. Rutter put his hat on and turned up his raincoat collar.

'Fakes! No one fakes Pender's coats. They're not worth it.'

The whistle split the cold afternoon air again.

'Next time,' Brodie said, 'he'll have his lawyer all right. I'd say that was your last chance of getting Pender on his own.'

At six o'clock, as the rush-hour traffic rumbled on the Embankment below his window, Rutter washed his hands in the grey-veined porcelain basin next to the Victorian lavatory. In the tarnished mirror his face that evening looked to him as bad as Pender's. The jowls were set harder, however. Like frozen butter. There were lines down them. Deep, straight and thin. Aslant his face, they might have been taken for razor scars.

Time, the universal razor-boy, had marked him like the loser in a street fight. But still, Time was carving its mark even-handedly on Mr Samuelson, Pelly Pender, Sonny Boy Tarrant and a host of those who thought themselves immortal. He dried his hands, combed his hair and felt a little more cheerful.

Chapter Eleven

Sandboy studied the pale green frosted bowl of the centre light. He folded his hands on the pillow behind his head. Afternoon sun glanced high from the ornamental lily pond and played in ripples of light on the bedroom ceiling. With the chignon of her chestnut hair brushed and ribboned, Yvonne sat naked on the pink basketwork dressing-table stool with its padded silk top. The straightness and narrowness of her back, the hard slenderness of her pale legs marked her as a dancer.

Among the rose-tinted hangings and Chinese carpets, the kidney shape of the dressing table with its bleached wood and green leather inlay was ranged with her half-empty jars of white or pink cream. From where he lay, Sandboy tried to count the combs and the scattered instruments of a manicure set, as he waited for her to be ready. At the centre was the white-gold ring which she had taken off, a flame-opal set with a small diamond either side. Manny's Christmas tribute a dozen years ago.

He watched her take the stopper from an engraved Lalique perfume bottle, sniff at a tawny droplet of Guerlain's Shalimar and put the stopper back again. Then she stood up.

Sandboy chuckled. 'There's pink marks all over your arse from the creases in the silk.'

She turned, the hair drawn neatly back, the large soubrette eyes shining with laughter. 'You are a disgusting little tyke, Sandboy. What are you?'

He grinned back at her, knowing that from the first time they met she had been as excited as a little girl by such intimate vulgarities. It pleased him that she left her delicacy, with her morals, outside the bedroom door. Lady Blue behaved with him more like a kitchen-maid with the master of the house, than the mistress of the house with a minion.

Sandboy grinned at her again. Lady Blue was well drilled and sharp mannered but randy as a sparrow underneath it. A little lubrication by vulgarity and flattery worked wonders on her. Manny had given up flattery, with everything else, years ago. She turned back to the tilted oval of the mirror.

'I never told you, I heard Dicky Dash sing your song. Did I?' Sandboy asked. '*Revuedeville* at the Windmill.'

Yvonne seemed not to hear him. He noticed that the elastic of the crêpe de chine underwear had also left a pink imprint round the pallor of her narrow waist and another round the curve of each dancer's thigh. His eyes followed the flat belly and the slight backward jut of the hips. She was the only woman he had ever known who thought nothing of taking off every stitch of clothing. Girls of his own class would have hesitated far longer.

'Did I? Tell you about Dicky Dash and your song.'

She heard him now, as she drew one of the hairpins from between her teeth, slid it into the chestnut sleekness of her crown and said, 'No. Why?'

'I went to the Windmill with a mate of mine. I told him about you dancing with Jack Buchanan. Dicky Dash sang your song. The la-di-da one.'

Without turning round, she said quietly, 'Some differ-
ence between a gentleman like Jack and Dicky Dash.'

'You sticking up for Jack Buchanan because you were
in a show with him?'

She turned, the chestnut hair tidied in its chignon,
the fringe and her wide-eyed amusement making her
seem younger than she was. Sandboy caught sight of
them both in the glass and thought she looked no older
than he with her light dancer's body.

'Only in a show on tour, darling,' she said emphatically, 'as Manny never tires of telling everyone. We
opened in a heatwave and closed in a heatwave. Unfortu-
nately, it was the same heatwave. That was Ivor's play.'

'Ivor Novello?'

'So you do know about something other than the girls
at the Windmill!'

'You were in a show with Ivor Novello?'

'Not with him, dear, by him,' she sighed. 'When it
went on tour. When I think of them – Jack and Ivor – I
wonder what they're doing now. And what I'm doing
here . . .'

'What Manny says, that other one's a nance.'

She twisted round. 'That's a filthy idea.'

'Well, was he?'

Lady Blue unclipped an earring. 'Manny thinks
anyone who falls short of Oswald Mosley and his black-
shirts is a nance. All right? That's the extent of his
interest.'

There was a sound from the room below and Sandboy
sat up.

Yvonne giggled. 'He won't be here for hours yet. And
anyway it doesn't matter.' She turned back to the mirror
and said softly, as though to herself. 'If it mattered, you'd

have been out of your job a long time ago. After all, dear, we're not exactly the quietest people at night, are we? If he doesn't mind it then, almost in the next room to where he's sleeping, he can hardly complain about it on your afternoon off!'

'He's never tried it with Nina?'

Yvonne turned round again and brushed a fleck of cotton from the front of her thigh. 'Little Madam is his stepdaughter, for goodness sake!'

'So what? It's been known. He's not blood related.'

She sighed and took a final look at herself in the glass, committed now to bed. 'No one – no one at all – tries anything with Nina. There's nothing there to try.'

Upright as a statue, she knelt astride him on the wide bed, sank down and said softly, 'Now, Mr Sandboy, let's see if you can do that voodoo that you do so well.'

She was so light on him that he felt he could have lifted her on the palms of his hands. As he turned her the afternoon sun from the lily pool dappled the ceiling above them again. Behind her closed eyes, Yvonne gasped and clutched in a world of her own. For a long hour afterwards, he watched her sleep.

'Lady Blue,' he said at last, 'Lady Blue.'

She opened her eyes and smiled. Slowly the strength of the sun in the curtains, from the tide and the line of the cliffs, mellowed and dwindled. When she moved towards him again, Sandboy said, 'Manny's a lot older than you are.'

'I'm a lot older than you are.'

'I mean, he's likely to die long before you. What happens then?'

Yvonne laughed. 'I don't become Mrs Sandboy, if that's what you mean.' Her finger drew patterns down his face. 'When you were a horny young man of thirty-five, I'd be fifty and past caring. When you were just getting into your stride at forty-five, I'd be sixty. So much for that.'

He turned over on top of her, as if holding her down. 'What about the hotel and the picture-house?'

'If Manny dies, Sonny Tarrant runs them. Likewise the other way round. There's an agreement. Little Madam and I get Manny's share of the profits from Sonny. An income. It's what anyone would want that's not interested in business.'

'That why you're screwing old Tarrant now?'

She began to struggle, partly in fun but with growing energy. 'I am not screwing Tarrant! Get off me, you pig!'

Sandboy let her sit up. 'But you're going up to his place now.'

'To use his piano, you cretin! And his mother's probably there. They bought a Model B Steinway. Have you any idea what that is? A Model A is the biggest, the sort of thing you only get in a big concert hall. Just playing the chord of C major makes you feel like God. Even a Model B is more than you could have in a house this size. I like to play the sort of music he likes to listen to.'

Sandboy tried to seem puzzled. 'Then who is he screwing?'

She lay down on her elbow again and turned to him. 'I shouldn't think he's screwing anyone. Why should he be? He doesn't have to be. Manny's not screwing anyone . . .'

'So far as you know. Tarrant's a lot younger than Manny.'

'So far as I care. Manny gets by. Perhaps Sonny gets by as well. Who knows?'

Sandboy stroked her face. 'You think Tarrant might be a nance?'

Yvonne giggled. 'Ask him and see.'

'What time you got to be up there?'

'An hour or two,' she said. 'What I want to know from all this gutter talk is why you aren't screwing Lady Blue . . . In the meantime, which gets meaner all the time, as the song says . . . Whatever happens later, there's the meantime on our hands . . .'

Through the early dusk of the spring day, Sandboy turned the midnight-blue Chrysler Airflow past the Odeon and the Metropole Hotel, the theatre bills in red and blue promising Billy Cotton's Stage Band at the Hippodrome. Beyond the brightly lit display windows of Brights and Bobbys, the road skirted the formal gardens stretching to the sea, then climbed between Edwardian villas where the wooded cliff stretched to the beach. The evening sky had faded to a dull pearl with spots of rain in the air. A freighter lay low in the water, waiting to move up the Channel on the next tide, lights blazing like a showboat at the heads of its derricks.

It was not to be Mrs Tarrant's flat this time but dinner and music at Tarrant's own house, the gates open but a chain across the driveway, the green tiling of the roof just visible above a massive rhododendron hedge, like a fortress wall. The first mauve flowers of the year seemed luminous against the wreath-green of the dark leaves.

Yvonne stopped him before he could turn into the drive. 'Just here,' she said. 'Far enough.'

Sandboy opened the door for her. 'So much for Lady Blue.'

She looked at him without smiling this time. 'Lady Blue goes back in the box with the toys, until next time,' she said, turning away, 'Don't wait. Someone will bring me home.'

'Just a minute!' Sandboy called her back.

He reached into the car and took from the back seat the box of chocolates and the bunch of roses that Manny had chosen for Mrs Tarrant. He handed them to Yvonne, a dark ghost between the hedges of rhododendron.

Chapter Twelve

In a sparkle of morning sunshine, Tarrant entered the rear of the Garden Royal from the street that ran behind the sea front. There was no porter at the drab swing door of the 'town' entrance. It was used for the most part by guests slipping out to the theatres after an early dinner. The shallow rise of wide carpeted steps led up to an access corridor at the back of the main hall. The passageway was windowless but with a pointed skylight of patterned glass. The chocolate and cream pattern of the marble floor was lit by a long row of display cases on either side, fashioned in Venetian arches of dark oak. Tarrant glanced at an arrangement of gold and sapphire on black velvet, a silk shirt, a white leather evening bag, a bottle of perfume.

The outer door of Archer's office was to one side of the rear hall with its brass standard lamps and soft shades, its Egyptian settees and floral carpets. Tarrant strode past the signs for the Lifts, the Gentlemen's Toilets, and the Telephones, indicated by panels of black glass with illuminated lime-green lettering. An old man in shirt sleeves rode up and down in the lift, polishing its button panel. Tarrant knocked lightly on a heavy door of polished mahogany between two electric-lit Regency display cabinets holding artificial flowers. He opened the door without waiting for a response.

'Hello, Charley. I gather you got somethin' for me, after all. I hear you might've struck gold.'

Archer got up from his desk, the impassive military neatness of his face showing neither pleasure nor annoyance at Tarrant's intrusion. 'Whether or not it's what you hoped, Mr Tarrant, is another matter.'

He sat down again, drew open the top drawer of his desk and took out the cellophane bag with its yellow matchbox inside. Tarrant glanced at it over the man's shoulder and smiled at Archer's back. Archer stood up and handed the bag to him.

'It's a wrong 'un, Mr Tarrant. At least, the finger on this belonged to someone that's on file.'

Tarrant's face registered the quiet dismay of a victim. He sat down on the second chair and looked at Archer for a moment without speaking. 'I was afraid it might be, Charley. I tried to think not. In fact, I've even had one or two other ideas that could explain everything.'

'Sorry, Mr Tarrant,' Archer said. 'That's how it seems.'

Tarrant looked up again. 'Don't you be sorry, Charley! You did something for me that a lot of people wouldn't. I shan't forget that, nor your friend that helped. You can tell him so. Next time round, the favours are on me.'

'There's no need, sir,' Archer said.

Tarrant slipped the cellophane bag into his pocket. 'These other ideas I had, Charlie. There's one I got to get off my chest. This finger on the box. It never belonged to anyone heavy? Not someone big scale?'

Archer shook his head. 'Small-time, Mr Tarrant.'

The creases of anxiety fell from Tarrant's face. 'Then I think I might have solved the mystery, Charles. Something I never thought of before. A little while back, we had workmen in the flat. Contractors' men. They could come from almost anywhere.'

Archer stared at him.

'What I mean, Charley, I don't want the law to roust some young chap that once put a foot wrong and now got honest work of a kind. Some lad who might have smoked a fag in his tea break, while he was working up the flat, and left the matches behind. See?'

Archer nodded slowly, as though he preferred not to understand. Tarrant grinned at him. 'I don't want people that work for me thinkin' I'm a monster, do I now?'

Archer shook his head and sat down. He drew up one knee of his grey flannel suit to preserve the sharp trouser crease. Tarrant smoothed the palms of his hands together.

'I got a list of the ones that worked there, in the flat, Charley. Now I don't want to pry where I shouldn't. You know that. I wouldn't want to hear names or addresses, let alone how anyone went off the rails. Just the last name. Just the surname, Charley. I can check that in two minutes.'

'I don't . . .'

Tarrant chuckled. 'You don't tell me, Charley, that your friend told you about the file and never mentioned a surname! Someone you worked with all that time?'

He smiled softly as Archer uncrossed his legs. Charley Archer was going to walk the plank and was beginning to realize it.

'He wouldn't be taken on as a contractors' man if he'd shot the Pope, would he, Charles? If he's one of them workmen, we can drop the whole thing. But if I have to call in your friends, Mrs Tarrant having heard noises in the night, some poor devil might get rousted, even though he paid his price long ago.'

'It's just a matter of the rules, Mr Tarrant.'

Tarrant beamed at the rich humour of the objection. 'What you and your friend done – and what I'm not goin' to forget you for – was just a matter of the rules, likewise.'

Archer sat in the little office like a predator outwitted by a trap.

'Wasn't it?' Tarrant asked amiably. 'Look, I don't want you to identify anyone, Charley! All I ask is a surname or anything that can cross him off the list.'

It was the end of the plank. Archer said, 'McGouran. That's all I know.'

Tarrant looked blank for a moment. Then he smiled and stood up. Archer stood as well.

''Course there was,' Tarrant said effusively. ''Course there was him. I remember. They called him Mac.'

'Then that's all right?' Archer's voice feared it might not be.

Tarrant looked down at his polished shoes and shook his head. 'It's more than all right, Charley,' he looked up again. 'The poor old lady had a bad dream, perhaps, or heard things that weren't what she thought. Just bein' a bit upset over all the work goin' on in the flat. Simple as that. And I could have had all your friends turnin' the place over for nothin'. This got to be the answer. The workmen left them matches. That may be the end of it – but what you saved Mrs Tarrant, as well as me, I shan't forget.'

There was no mistaking the man's relief, Tarrant thought. As so often on these occasions, it was almost as if the favour had been the other way round.

'I'm glad it's no worse, sir.'

Tarrant looked at him. 'You and Mrs Archer be at home Sunday morning?'

Archer looked puzzled. 'Yes.'

'Your good lady like a drop of fizz, I dare say? Glass of the boy?'

'Yes, sir, but . . .'

Tarrant waved gratitude aside. 'Then don't you go out Sunday until the delivery van's been.'

Archer stared at him. Now that the trap had served its purpose he showed the first little signs of anger. 'There's no need, Mr Tarrant. There really isn't.'

Tarrant shook his head once, as if in admiration of such loyalty from a servant. 'There's every need, Charley. You got no notion how worried I been, over poor old Mrs Tarrant. And what you done, you acted like a friend. And I don't often say that to those that work for me. 'fact, I don't think I ever said it quite like that to anyone before. Not in all these years.'

Charley Archer lowered his eyes. Like so many of Tarrant's victims, he had summoned up anger or resistance only when it was too late.

May

Silver Steel

Chapter Thirteen

Sandboy was with Little Madam in the games room of the house that Manders had built behind the cliffs after his marriage to Yvonne. As he came into the room, Nina was wedged behind a table, trying to open a side window in the cramped space allowed her. The sunlight across the garden and the lily pond caught her slim figure, the length of her pale blond hair, the enigmatic glance of the green eyes. Almost everything about her made sense to Sandboy, though, as he crossed the room to help her, it seemed to him that Manny's stepdaughter was taller and slimmer than he had remembered.

Behind the table, among the piles of boxes and abandoned toys, the two of them were squeezed together so closely in their efforts that he could not help touching the smooth green wool of her cardigan and the soft weave of her long fawn skirt.

He heard himself explaining that the catch on the window had always been stiff. But now she seemed indifferent to the problem. Moving nearer, to get past her, he felt her arms close round him. Before he could speak, she kissed the side of his face. Sandboy held her and, at the same time, fell back into an armchair by the window, pulling Nina on top of him. As they lay in a loose embrace, he thanked her for some kindness that he could not quite identify. Nina asked why she deserved thanks and he explained lamely that it was the trouble she had taken. With his arms round her, his fingers traced the outlines of her ribs and backbone.

To one side, he noticed that the door of the games room was still open, revealing them to anyone who came past. Nina now lay motionless in his embrace, as if contented but indicating that she had gone as far as she was prepared to go or perhaps passively that he might do as he pleased. Her voice was quiet and encouraging, though the words passed from his memory as soon as she spoke them. This time she had taken a cold decision to be seductive. It was something that even Little Madam could do when she put her mind to it.

As he moved a little, Nina asked if he was coming to her party. Freeing one arm, she took his hand and began to examine it. Sandboy, who had been changing the engine oil in the Chrysler, felt uneasy at the grimy state of his nails. For a moment he and Nina exchanged kisses on the cheeks. Then he turned her head firmly and kissed her on the mouth. Somewhere outside the dream, a man's voice said sharply, 'Christ! Is he no' finished yet?'

Sandboy opened his eyes, remembering at once that he was no longer in his own room or even in his own town. By his watch, it was almost eight o'clock in the morning. So far as he could calculate, his dreams of Nina were always in the minutes before waking. Beyond the foot of the couch, the north London sky through the shabby net curtains of an attic window was warm and cloudless. From the landing below, next to the room in which Gillis lived, the same voice said, 'I have no' got all bloody day, Gillis!'

A door opened and Gillis said amiably, 'What's your rush, Spurgeon? Get yourself dressed first, for God's sake!'

Sandboy moved on the makeshift bed, lifted the blanket and pulled himself up. Sometimes, as on this occasion, the girl in the dream was recognizably Nina. On other occasions, she was an indistinct figure, known to him intuitively. Manders' villa had no games room. That, like almost every location in his dreams, was fantasy. But this was the first time that he and Nina had been lying down with their arms about one another.

He stood up, the floor creaking and yielding underfoot as he crossed to the little window. It looked out across rows of identical roofs further down the hill, sooty little gardens and a builders' yard just this side of the railway embankment. Sometimes, like this morning, the dreams of Nina were so vivid that he could not believe she did not share them. In the moment after waking, he thought it inconceivable that he did not enter her thoughts as she entered his. But she showed no sign of it.

He tipped water from the metal jug into the china basin and began to wash his face. He was half dressed when Gillis came up the stairs.

There was nothing for breakfast. Like McGouran and like Sandboy, Gillis would eat wherever he happened to be. At Holborn Coffee Stall, they stopped at the counter for cheesecake and two cups of sweet Camp Blend, poured from a bottle and diluted in hot water.

The junction of Euston Road and Hampstead Road was London as Sandboy always imagined it, the rhythmic trams taking the curve at Mornington Crescent for Camden Town, the fresh green of plane trees towards Great Portland Street and Regent's Park, the squawk of car horns, grinding of brakes on steel, the clang of the bell at tram stops, flickers of colour, the brisk tap of women's heels, the flutter of curtains at open windows along the soot-grained brick of terraced houses.

As they waited to cross the heavy commercial traffic of the Hampstead Road, a motor-bus with its banner-advertisement along the upper deck obscured the shops opposite: Bravington's Wetwrista Watches – King's Cross and Branches . . .

'Off the main road,' Gillis said, 'over there. Dalgetty Street. It couldn't be better for us.'

As they threaded the traffic to the far side, a gust of warm summer wind filled the width of the road, blowing from beyond the white modern fortress of the Carreras Cigarette Factory.

'Stand here,' Gillis said. 'You can see the front of Lawsons down the other pavement.'

From open windows above the corner of Dalgetty Street, the insect whine of a dentist's drill competed with the muted sounds of a dance orchestra drifting down from an attic radio. A clatter of glasses and a barrel-house piano rang from the open doors of the corner saloon bar, where a barman busied himself drying newly washed glasses.

There were several shops in the terraced grime of the side street. 'Lawsons Second Hand Jewels and Silver' stood opposite a little café with patched cloths on rickety little tables, a fly-spotted net curtain across the lower half of the window, the New Argyll Restaurant. Lawsons was a single-storey structure where a house had been demolished at the centre of the row. It consisted of a solid brick front with black-painted doors and a grilled display window between them. The signboard hanging out above the street proclaimed the shop as another 'cash jewellers'.

The notices over the two doors distinguished them as 'Sales Entrance' and 'Pledge Entrance'.

'That,' Gillis said, 'is where McGouran spouted his coats. Soon as he heard a whisper about your trouble with Samuelson. Hocked them with a man he knows called Rayner that runs Lawsons and then he vanished. If Samuelson knew there was something queer about that one coat of Pender's, you can bet the news is round the dealers. Even sniffed by the law. So when there's three coats put up for auction and Rayner has to register McGouran's name . . .'

'McGouran's gone for good.'

Gillis scuffed dirt off the edge of his shoe. He looked round, then spoke with quiet energy. 'The way McGouran carries on, they could track him down in a week if they wanted to. His woman needing hop, for instance. And they'll go asking Pender. The police will. The police, Sandy. They like catching people and hanging them. It's what they're for. And that blasted old woman is dead, which is all it takes, if we did it or not!'

Sandboy said nothing. They turned slowly into Dalgetty Street, talking together. Gillis said, 'You imagine McGouran being grilled by the law. You really think he wouldn't try to save his own neck by offering them our names? 'Course he bloody well would. First thing he'd do!'

'We weren't even there when McGouran half-drowned that old woman, or whatever he did to her . . .'

'You think it matters?' Gillis said quietly. 'I asked about that. If you're all in something together, it doesn't matter if you didn't actually do her yourself or weren't there when it happened. Malice is what they call it. If they play it clever, they can hang you for it. You think they wouldn't? I'd hate you to be wrong.'

In the warm spring morning, Sandboy felt cold and sick at the threat. The sights and sounds of the sunny street seemed far away for a moment, as if through a haze of winter flu or too much drink.

'Suppose we end up doing Lawsons for nothing? McGouran could have got the coats out by now – somehow.'

But Gillis shook his head. 'I kept that ticket number of Mac's. Yesterday I phoned them, pretending to be a punter that didn't understand the rules. I made sure it was the girl answering, not Rayner, and I didn't tell her what the goods were. I asked how much longer there was to run before that number went on sale. Four weeks. They're still there all right.'

'I'm scared we'll get in deeper,' Sandboy said. It was the first time he had ever spoken to Gillis of being scared. But he was. If the coats could be had without trouble . . . But if not . . .

Gillis said, 'You can go further down Dalgetty Street and come out the other end. There's a little yard at the rear of the shop and an access lane to the back of the whole street. At least have a look at it. I tell you, it's not difficult.'

He glanced aside at the shabby café with its long net curtain, as if to check whether they were being watched, and said, 'So long as we pick the right time.'

'What's the right time?'

'A Saturday. Saturday morning.'

'How in hell can I do it on a Saturday, Gilly – of all days? I'm in a projection box a hundred miles away.'

'That's right,' Gillis said. 'You're going to have an alibi, or something close enough. Lawsons close on Saturday at twelve. I sat in that dump of a café the last two weeks and watched them. I'll watch from the corner pub this week to check.'

He looked round, as if to make sure there was no one walking behind them. 'Half an hour before they close, not later, they collect up the cash and the jewellery – what's portable – and take it down the National Provincial Bank in the Euston Road. They're away a good twenty minutes. There's two of them. The governor, Rayner, in a grey hat, white scarf and blue suit. The other's there for muscle. He could be carrying a truncheon or a gun for all I know.'

Gillis glanced across the road at the sign that advertised 'Cash Jewellers'. 'If it works, and it will, it puts us in the clear. Even if they registered the coats to McGouran, they can't know where the coats came from if they haven't got the coats. And that clears us. Better still, we can sell 'em.'

'After Samuelson? How?'

'I thought about that,' Gillis said calmly. 'Samuelson was a mistake. London could be a mistake. First find out where these markings in the coats are, and cut them out. Do whatever we have to and get rid of them. Then we take the coats abroad, somewhere that's got no problem about speaking English. Dublin. You can walk across that border, if you have to. We sell them there. No police looking and it's a place where Pender's friends wouldn't operate. I thought about this a lot, Sandy. I'm not saying we necessarily have to do it but it could be the bonus. And whatever else we could grab while we were in Lawsons would be a bonus too. If this worked right we could get rid of everything we got from Pender and a bit more. Six top-class furs. We can still come out ahead.'

'I'd rather find McGouran. Get some money somehow. Send him back to get the furs from Lawsons. We can still do Dublin after that. But it'd be safer.'

'All right,' Gillis said reasonably, 'you find the money in the next week or so and we'll do that. Except that McGouran's got the bloody pawn tickets and no one knows where he is. So you'll have to find him as well. I don't know where to start looking. And you won't be in London anyway.'

They walked in silence by the last of the dingy little shops.

'It's so easy,' Gillis said desperately, 'it's so neat. Furs aren't Lawsons' thing. These are hardly under lock and key.'

A group of children were chalking out hopscotch on the pavement at the far end of the street. The claws of dread clung tight in Sandboy's guts. At the same time he felt an irrational surge of anger against the old woman who had died. Without her they might have been free. Now he was being forced into the robbery as surely as if she had given an order.

'All right,' he said to Gillis, 'Show me. I'll go that far.'

They crossed the street, away from the children's game. Gillis looked round and spoke again. 'Saturday morning, they walk down to the Euston Road but there's a car parked somewhere near. So for all I know they take the furs and everything else home for the weekend. But that won't happen till they get back from the bank. And they won't just leave them in a car meanwhile. There's a grill on that display window in the street but you can see through into the shop. There's a counter inside, then the shop behind it, then a door into a back room that opens on the yard at the rear. Right? The stuff is kept in the rear room, metal door, bars on windows.'

Sandboy shivered in the warmth. 'You reckon the place is empty for twenty minutes?'

'At least. After all, the good stuff has gone to the bank. They don't seem to lock up properly, not as if they weren't coming back. Even if there was anyone there, it couldn't be more than an assistant. Say, a shopboy or the girl that answered the phone. That's the worst. And only in the front shop. When I watched, I reckon it was empty. They lock the street doors while they're away. They wouldn't do that if they were still open for business. And we're not going into the front shop. There'll be a locked door between us and anyone who's left in there.'

'Show me,' Sandboy said again. Numb and cold, he walked with Gillis along the lane that ran between the little rear yards of Dalgetty Street and its neighbours.

'Just there, the back of the building,' Gillis said. 'Look. They drive the car up here to load. Over the wall, there's an outside toilet joined on to the building at the back, same as all the other houses. Only, instead of having an outside door to it, they've padlocked that, barred the windows, and it must have got a door directly into the rear room of the shop. That's our way. They'll hardly lock up the toilet while they go to the bank with the valuables, having a locked door between the shop and the back room anyway. Even if they do, we can make a bit more noise once we're in. Just walk on tiptoe a minute and look over the wall. You can see across.'

The rear yard, like most of those in the street, had once been a small garden, now paved over. The brick outbuilding was at one corner, about ten feet long by five feet wide. Sandboy could see that its small window was barred, the original door bolted and padlocked.

'And there'll be a bloody great bolt or lock on the inside as well,' he said.

They walked on. Gillis shook his head.

'We go in on the hinge side of the outside door. That dumb bugger Spurgeon owes me a favour. He's got a cane I can borrow. Two and a half feet long. You can just slip it up the coat sleeve with the end in your hand. Silver steel. You can slide a two foot steel tube over the end as well. Gives you ten tons leverage – and silver steel won't snap. You could bust open any set of hinges in this street. Have the front door off a house in half a minute. And Spurgeon can drive.'

'Where to?'

'Just in case he's needed,' Gillis said. 'Once we get through into the building, we'll be in the room where all the goods are kept. Anyone looking in from the street at the front shop won't know we're there. Even if there's an assistant left in the front, we'll be in the back room behind that locked door. Anyone hears anything, they'll think it's the governor come back and locking up the rear of the building for the weekend. See? And we got a way out at the back. Honest, Sandy, we've hardly ever had one as easy as this! In and out in two minutes. Spurgeon waiting with a motor in case we need a bit of speed to help us get to where we're going. That's a promise.'

'And then?'

Gillis chuckled as they came back into Dalgetty Street. The ragged children were shouting and jumping one-legged.

'Cardboard suitcase each. Sort that you can fold up. We go in at about eleven thirty. Once we got what we want, we come out the back. Can't be more than eleven forty, if that. We walk down to the street, cross Hampstead Road. Two hundred yards from Euston Station. There'll be thousands of people carrying suitcases on a Saturday morning. No one's going to remember us. We're at Euston by eleven fifty, probably before. We separate for home. I wait for Spurgeon. He's to pick me up in the car at Euston at twelve. You go down the tube. Northern Line to Waterloo. Seven stations, fifteen minutes. Call it twenty. You're on Waterloo platform twelve ten. I checked the times. There's a twelve thirty express. Gets you in two thirty-five. Fifteen minutes walk to the Luxor picture-house. Say two fifty. What time's the first film?'

'Three,' Sandboy said. 'Doors open two fifty. So that's not an alibi.'

'It is if you play it right. You get there usually half an hour or so before the first film. Right? Load the projectors and so on? You could rewind the films and thread the projectors the night before. Yes?'

'Could do. Not supposed to. It puts a bend in the film, being held like that for so long. Makes it more likely to tear.'

'But no one would know?'

'Probably not. The reels are cased in, so they'd have to open up the projector to look close at the gate or the soundbox. No reason to.'

'Listen,' Gillis said, as they came out again into the traffic of the Hampstead Road. 'You thread the projectors up, get everything as ready as you can the night before. Leave the escape door from the projection box to the outside stairs unbolted on the inside. When you get back on Saturday afternoon, you go up that outside fire escape to the box. It's round the back. No one's going to see. About five to three, you come down and talk to various people. Tell them there's no soap in the washroom, anything. Make sure they see you and think you must have been up in the projection box all the time getting the films ready. After all, they never saw you come in. When you walk down the stairs they'll think you must have been up the projection box before they arrived. How else could you be there? Say two thirty?'

'About that.'

'And that door to the outside escape stairs is always bolted at night?'

'Has to be.'

'You go in that way, they'll think you must have been there before anyone else. Two thirty? Impossible you could have been in Dalgetty Street at eleven thirty in the morning, if you were in the projection box at half past two. But it won't come to that. That's just the worst.'

'If it was to go wrong . . .'

As they crossed through the traffic, Gillis gave a low whistle of admiration at an Armstrong-Siddeley Typhoon Coupé, its hood down, the engine purring, the long sweep of the green body sparkling in the sun. Beyond Euston Arch lay the station approach.

'Any trouble here, we've got Spurgeon with a car in the next street. Agreed? Without that we don't do it. All right?'

'The alibi. Someone sees that the projection box escape door is unbolted on the inside and bolts it. I can't get in.'

Gillis shrugged. 'Slip in with the queue when the doors open at two fifty. No one's going to stop you. Odds are, they won't even see you. Anyone asks, you went next door to buy a packet of Woodbines or something. They don't sell those in picture-houses. Seeing the projectors will be ready by then, they'll believe you must have been around before, threading them.'

'It could still go wrong. Depends too much on railways and underground trains. Suppose I don't get back in time?'

'Wherever you are, you phone whoever's at the Luxor or Manders in his office. Talk as if you were at home. You feel lousy. Bad attack of the runs. But you fixed the film up that morning, all it needs is a rewind boy to press the buttons for the first house and someone to run it again after that. Then, soon as you get off the train, go to the first chemist and get a bottle of kaolin and opium. As if you'd just come from home. Make sure they remember you.'

'If the law thinks . . .'

'The law doesn't think,' Gillis said firmly. 'It just knows that it's wasting its time taking a story like they'd have to court. Anyway, it won't happen. Five minutes in Lawsons, we can save our necks and make a bonus. Bit of real money. Put right everything that stupid bugger McGouran got wrong. Even the old woman being dead. We got to do it, Sandy.'

They passed the taxis, the waiting porters with their barrows and entered the echoing uproar of the station concourse. Gillis punched him lightly on the shoulder and grinned. 'Stop worrying, boy. I told you. It's a piece of piss.'

Chapter Fourteen

Manders, Yvonne and their guests occupied two rows of armchairs set out across the lounge. Sandboy watched them in the shadowlight as the reels of the Bell and Howell projector turned. The narrower gauge of the 16mm film sputtered as the motor fed it through the metal gate of the light box. When the sides of the reels caught the reflected light, the tightly wound celluloid had a prismatic reflection, like finely spun black silk.

The screen had been erected at the far end of the room with a single box-like speaker positioned just below it. The Bell and Howell was raised on a stand in the hall, so that its beam projected far enough to fill the black-edged silver with its monochrome images. A wavering reproduction of sound filled the curtained room. Its gliding and soaring waltz evoked Viennese operetta, powdered wigs, tinsel, hot chocolate and silk dresses.

Sandboy checked the focus of the carefully styled titles as the film settled down, the white copperplate script on the censor's black certificate. Then the famous names shimmered in white against a dark velvet sky lit by pulsating galaxies . . . Ivor Novello . . . Mary Ellis . . . a plaintive music of dreams before the burst of melody and the elegant italic aslant the screen . . . *Glamorous Night* . . . *From the Drury Lane Play* . . . Sandboy felt curiosity at a film by a man whom Yvonne had known so well. Ivor, as she called him, was one to whom she must once have spoken every day.

The over-costumed figures played a heroic young king, a gipsy singer who loved him, a Nazi prime minister and his gang. There was talk of forced abdication, a police state, and the firing squad. But the music made Sandboy think of Manders' London, grand hotels and tea-rooms, velvet-seated theatres and parties in evening dress.

As the film unwound steadily, he could see the day-light outside, late-afternoon sun lying full across the garden. The drawn curtains of the French windows could not quite keep it out. Along the cliff, the red glow had not yet dropped below the line of the ridge. It caught the slopes and the chines, the miniature monkey-puzzle shape of the gorse with its deep yellow flowers, bluebells, feathery pink grass, purple heads of clover, the rising branches of pine beyond the cliff edge. There was something furtive, perverse, in closing out such a view to enjoy the pleasures of the dark.

In the half-light, he watched Manders and his guests. Yvonne and Nina were next to one another, adjacent arms on the arms of their chairs, Yvonne's hand lying on the girl's as if in the excitement of the film or family affection. Tarrant was watching the screen with an expression that might have been a tolerant smile. Manny sat a little apart at the end of one row, as if the performance had nothing to do with him. His large, dark-haired, intelligent head was matched by a face that showed a slack and weary sadness. Mrs Tarrant looked at the screen as if it had been blank. The only other guest whom Sandboy recognized was the crony they called 'Alfred' or 'Freddie', a baggy-trousered landlord who owned properties in the shabby

131

length of commercial streets beyond the railway station. With Manny and Yvonne, he was a bumbling, subservient guest at West End restaurants or Christmases spent in the Strand Palace Hotel.

The performance of *Glamorous Night*, the play within the film, swept past in a shimmer of muslin curtains, the little dancers in Swan Lake tutus, laced feet fluttering like birds. There was a pause while Sandboy changed the film to its second reel.

'How about that German fellow for prime minister, Manny,' said Freddie pleasantly. 'All the black uniforms and leather belts? Stand no nonsense from His Majesty either.'

Manders turned on his elbow and looked solemnly at Freddie in the seat behind. 'Yes, Fred. But we all know who's behind rubbish like this that they put on the films. Don't we? And there's people half-daft enough to be took in! But I hope we got a majesty now that's not half-daft and won't be took in.'

Freddie chortled self-consciously.

'Only a film, Manny. That's all it is. Bit of fun. That's all.'

'Who's your choice then, Freddie?' Manders leant on his elbow, keeping his back turned in displeasure. 'Another performance by Ramsay-bloody-MacDonald, the Loon of Lossiemouth? Mr Stanley Baldwin the champion pig breeder? Got a phiz like a bloomin' porker himself. Old Lloyd George? Liberal animal in a Tory skin! Old Winston and his followers? I tell you one thing, my friend, the only followers old Winston's got are his unpaid tradesmen. You ask some of 'em what they think of him!'

'Sir Oswald?' Freddie asked helpfully, turning to wink at a woman beside him. 'Got the answer, has he?'

Manders looked away, his face tight with indignation. 'Sod Mosley! All he wants to be is another Musso-the-Wop-with-the-bristly-chin! Things moved on a bit from that in the last year or two, Fred. There's others and better in the game now. When it all happens here, if it does, it won't be Musso. You can bet on it. Gone too far for that.'

'Old Moustache-Face?'

Manders shrugged, softened after his outburst. 'Ah, who knows, Fred? What it won't be is any more of the old gang, we hope. No more posters of bloody Baldwin with "Safety First" and "Trust Me" underneath his fat face. Him and all that lot are for the rubbish dump, first off. They had their chance, years ago.'

'Manny could be right, Fred,' said Tarrant amiably. ''Ave to see if we can't squeeze you into some of them riding breeches and leather boots. Do you up a treat.'

'And this king wouldn't stick his neck out to save the old gang neither,' Manders said. He gestured at the screen. 'He knows better than this poncing nancy-boy knock-about.'

Sandboy switched off the lights and turned on the motor for the second reel. They watched the rest of the film in silence. At the end, Sandboy began to rewind the two reels. The curtains were opened and early evening sun filled the softly carpeted and silk-draped lounge. Manders and his guests stood or sat with plates and glasses in their hands.

Sandboy began to dismantle the projector, its screen and speaker, and pack them away. In the corner of the leather sofa he noticed the hard orange shape of a Hodder and Stoughton 'Three-and Sixpenny Title', a green parallelogram stamped in its corner. Edgar Wallace, *The Square*

Emerald. Manders saw him looking and picked the book up.

'Here you are, son, 'f you 'aven't had it already.'

Sandboy thanked him. Behind him Yvonne was talking loudly to the men gathered round her. 'Freddie,' she called suddenly, 'that girl Ozanne in the front row of Ivor's dancers. The tall and dark-haired one with the rather pointed nose. Were you there at the party when Jack B said that they reckon she's a slapperat? It's how she gets into these shows?'

'Oh?' Freddie, standing by the window in his large-waisted trousers, shook his head, either not under-standing or not caring. 'No. Did he say that? He may have done. I don't recall. Is she?'

Thanks to Freddie, Yvonne's piece of scandal fell flat, but not before Mrs Tarrant, standing closer than Yvonne had realized, asked, 'What's that, dear?'

'What's what?' Yvonne turned, her face showing more annoyance than embarrassment at being overheard by the old woman.

'A slapperat, I think you said. I never heard of that one in my day. What is it?'

Tarrant had got up from his chair, the lip lifting from one side of the strong upper teeth. He walked towards them and stopped.

'Not something you need worry over Mrs T,' Freddie said hastily, glancing at Tarrant. 'Fast and loose, that's all it is. No better than she should be, I dare say.'

'But what is it specially, if this girl that dances is one?'

Yvonne waved an explanation at her. 'A glutton for punishment, if you know what that means,' she said indifferently.

'Oh,' Mrs Tarrant kept the same vague and foolish

smile. 'That's it, then?' There was no doubt that she seemed disappointed.

Irritated by the interruption of her story, Yvonne walked out into the hall. Tarrant followed her. Sandboy, from where he stood, heard Tarrant's muttered anger but saw only Yvonne.

'You don't bloody do that again, my girl! Not in front of Mrs Tarrant! And then walk off from her like the fucking Queen of Sheba.'

Yvonne stood with her face lowered in front of him, biting her lip like a disobedient but defiant child. 'I thought I pulled it off rather well,' she said quietly.

'Listen,' Tarrant said, 'behave yourself or you'll get somethin' you won't enjoy. And you might find a bit more trouble gettin' them little packets of fun for you and your so-called friends. Got it?'

Yvonne shrugged. Tarrant's voice was still quiet but he was furious. 'What you and your theatre friends talk about is your business. But I won't have nothin' mucky bein' said in front of Mrs Tarrant. You got that, 'ave you? Bloody look at me, when I talk to you!'

She raised her eyes. Tarrant's hand moved fast. Sandboy saw it for a fraction of a second as it slapped the further side of her face. He did not hit her hard, scarcely more than a vigorous pat on the cheek. The fright in her eyes was shock rather than hurt. Sandboy watched them with a sudden intense excitement, which took him by surprise. He did not feel the least resentment at what Tarrant had done. Yvonne, chastened in this manner, became instantly and inexplicably more desirable.

'You want grief,' Tarrant said, suddenly soft and reasonable, 'you can have as much as you like. There ain't no shortage.'

Now that he had released his anger he seemed irrationally calm, talking like a man who would never have raised his hand to her. 'Get the boy to take you for a drive round,' he said indulgently. ''Ave a look at the fairy lights on the prom. Get some air an' think about what you got to do later on.'

Twenty minutes afterwards, Sandboy turned the leather-cushioned Chrysler Airflow away from the cliff drive. Yvonne sat in the back, her eyes still wide with astonishment, a sparkle of tears still visible in the fading light. He drew the car off a quiet road above the town where the chines sloped to the sea. It was dusk, the lights of the promenade lamp-standards across the bay like a double row of pearls on mauve silk.

'How about here?'

The little drama in the hallway had sharpened excitement in both of them. After the initial fumbling with clothes there was too little room in the back of the car to lie full length. In the clumsiness of their appetite, curled up together like puppies, Yvonne began to giggle.

'Did you see her face? Old Ma Tarrant's face! She got more than she bargained for this time!'

'Shut up about her,' Sandboy said, drawing down a handful of elastic and crêpe de chine. 'Tarrant must have Manny on a short string, if he can smack your face like that at home without being minded.'

'None of your business,' she said with a breathless and impatient laugh. The laughter suggested that there were deeper secrets than he would ever be allowed to know.

Later, he asked her, 'You and that Nina, holding hands in the dark, while the film was on. What's that all about?'

Yvonne was tidying her hair with the aid of the

driving mirror, sitting in the front seat beside him now. The faint interior light of the car was switched on. 'It's not about anything.' She looked at him in the mirror. 'What did you think it might be about?'

'I don't know. You can't fancy her. I shouldn't think. You wouldn't have any need for that sort of thing.'

She snapped a powder compact shut. 'That's right, I can't and I wouldn't.'

'Still, she is fanciable. Anyone could see that. I dreamt about her once or twice.'

He waited, testing the ground. She put the powder compact in her bag and snapped that shut as well.

'Nice for you,' she said, 'but don't tell me. I don't want to hear about it.'

Glancing aside at her in the near darkness, it seemed to Sandboy that he was studying her for the first time, seeing the profile of a stranger. But it was only a trick of silhouette.

Alone in the projection box on the following afternoon, he thought again about Yvonne and Nina. By contrast, the talk of prime ministers between Manders and Freddie was dead lead. He could scarcely have told one name from another. But Sandboy understood something of what he saw on the screen at the Luxor, as the Movietone News blazed its headlines in a square frame against shifting images: 'TURMOIL IN TURBULENT SPAIN . . . THREAT OF FASCIST REVOLT IN UNHAPPY COUNTRY.' The camera was trained on the monumental front of a public building, and a stationary tram surrounded by a crowd. In the background an improvised armoured car went past, built on the chassis of a van with gun slits at the front and a turret on its top.

As he watched, the camera moved to a body lying in

the street by a burnt-out building. A casualty was being carried into a doorway on a stretcher. Two policemen dragged a prisoner from a street skirmish, a man in an overcoat and silk scarf. A third policeman stood by with a rifle. Away from the film, Sandboy counted an audience of thirty scattered through the cinema on the sunny afternoon. The agony of Spain dissolved in a jolly march tune and GIMCRACK'S 8–1 NAP AT LINCOLN RACES.

He waited for the newsreel to end, started the motor on the first projector for the main film, rewound the newsreel and loaded the second Gaumont Kalee with the main feature. In the warmth of the afternoon, he opened the iron door to the fire escape to let in some air. There was nothing to be done for half an hour until the first changeover. Sandboy stood on the iron platform, took a packet of Capstan cigarettes from his pocket and lit one.

At this height, there was a view of the cottonwool wash of cloud above blue water at the street's end, the pale summer colours of downland green, a grey-blue tide running slack and a hazed sky in the cool wind. The flower beds of the promenade gardens were neat as embroidery in pink, red and mauve. Holiday couples wandered among them, lost and without purpose. Further out, a white-funnelled steamer churned backwards in its broad paddle-wash from the timbers of the landing stage and then swung forward on its afternoon excursion.

He leant his elbows on the rail and thought of Nina, the green Slav eyes and pale blond Greta Garbo hair. There was a drift of teatime music from the pier pavilion orchestra, a jaunty voice and a tinkling accompaniment: 'Rosie, You Are My Posy.' In the cooler air on the iron platform, Sandboy smoked and listened with half his mind to the soundtrack of Ronald Colman in *The Man*

Who Broke the Bank at Monte Carlo, timing the end of the first reel.

As he watched the gulls on the ledges of the opposite roofs, he knew that it would have excited him to tell Yvonne about his dreams of Nina. Perhaps if Nina knew of them, from Yvonne ... But to tell Yvonne would be stupid, perhaps dangerous. He must first know what went on between Yvonne and Little Madam ... between Manny and Nina, come to that ... between Tarrant and Yvonne ... What went on in their world of musical comedies at London theatres, ribboned chocolates, red roses, Christmas at the Strand Palace, parties where Jack Buchanan or Ivor Novello talked to them as old friends ... scandal and slapperats ...

There was still a flush of salmon-coloured sunset in the night sky when he left the projection box at the end of the last performance. The fairy lights were strung out between lamp-posts in boiled-sweet colours the length of the garden walks. Across the town, the evening air was stagnant, warm with the hot-nougat smell of candyfloss, the quietness of a coming storm.

Sandboy lit a cigarette and cut across the gardens between the glass moons of lamps among dark evergreens. He walked up the hill and past the railway station, way from the hotels and dance bands towards the commercial length of Queen's Road. There were little pubs with fake Regency bow windows, blackboards in the doorways with the price of drinks competitively chalked.

Beside the little printer's shop that offered wedding stationery and cartes-de-visite, he slid his key into the latch of the door that led to his rented rooms above. The printer's shop had once been the ground floor of a house and the narrow hallway at the foot of the stairs still had its old mahogany hatstand with an oval mirror at the centre. Sandboy took his hat off and noticed in the half-light of the gas an envelope that must have come by the afternoon post.

The envelope was propped at the base of the oval mirror. It had been addressed to him in capitals and bore a 'Brighton and Hove' postmark. He frowned and picked it up. It was light enough to be empty. As he stood on the bare threads of the stair carpet, he folded the envelope and felt no sheet of writing paper inside. Alone in his room, he put a match to the gas mantel, let the glare of white light settle down and tore open the message. There was nothing inside but a newspaper cutting, a single three-inch column under a foggy picture of a sham-medieval lodge above the signal gantries and dark mouth of a railway tunnel. With a sudden feeling of sickness he read the cutting.

MAN'S BODY FOUND IN PATCHAM TUNNEL

The body of a man was found early on Tuesday morning at the northern entrance to Patcham Tunnel. He was identified yesterday afternoon as James McGouran, aged 22, who had lately taken lodgings in Stanhope Place, Kemp Town. The deceased had a ticket from Crawley to Brighton in his pocket. A carriage door-handle was logged as unfastened upon the arrival of the 9.43 at Preston Park.

Police were unable to speculate yesterday as to how the deceased met his death. Mr McGouran had sustained severe injuries to both head and body. Multiple fractures were found, consistent with falling from the train. At either end of the tunnel, local trains are restricted in speed to 15 mph over a distance of a mile. Moreover, the 9.43 was held at the signals both before and after the tunnel on Monday night.

A broken cardboard 'periscope' bought from a novelty shop was found in the grass several yards from the body. There have been complaints for several months of groups of youths travelling on the local trains, where there are no corridors and the compartments are isolated from each other. This is done to spy upon those 'courting couples' who think themselves alone. Evidence was recently given of youths adopting the foolish expedient of standing on the outside running board of a carriage during low speed or delays, while having one arm round the coachwork of door or window, in order to spy into the next compartment.

No reason can be given for the present accident. It is conjectured that the deceased may have attempted something of this kind, perhaps at the instigation of others, and may have been hit from the back by the tunnel wall, unaware of it as the train approached the northern entrance. An inquest will open at Brighton Town Hall on Monday.

Sandboy read through the cutting again, searching for something that might explain McGouran's death to him. There was surely a word or phrase that he had missed, a hint that might make the second reading less fearful. But there was nothing. He read it a third time and, as he did so, the claws of fear tightened again in his entrails, as if claiming him. At last he put the scrap of paper down and stared across the room. It was too late to go out now, to do anything that night. In any case, he did not know what there was to do. The fear that became his companion was without end. As he faced the night alone, he felt as he supposed a man must feel when first told of his final sickness.

Chapter Fifteen

'We come away with nothing, we can't be any worse off than we are now!'

From the public telephone, among the camellias and rhododendrons of the promenade gardens, Gillis came to him like the tinny counterfeit of a human voice.

'Listen,' Gillis said, 'we got even more reason now. What we decided to do. It can't be left. It's ticking under us now, faster than before. Under you more than me. We got to get the coats, if we can. Better we never had them in the first place. But we did. An' if we do this deal right, we come out ahead. I can't speak plainer. Not on a phone.'

'There's three minutes on this thing before they cut us off,' Sandboy said. 'I paid for three minutes so they'd leave us alone. After that someone could start listening in anyway. Let's get it straight about Mac. He could have been a peeping Tom, like the paper said.' He clutched the call-box phone whose black bakelite earpiece was dank from his own summer perspiration and that of countless others. 'He was that stupid.'

'And if he wasn't,' Gillis said, 'then someone did him proud and left him there. And suppose he was able to talk while they was doing it. Suppose they made him. These are experts. When they'd finished, they might do him in on the train, then chuck him out. Might do it outside, then let it hit him in the tunnel. Either way, the state he'd be in, who could tell what happened?'

'But how come they haven't got the coats back? If he told them?'

'They can't have found the counterfoils. What's it matter? You got to think of what they might have asked before they finished with him. And what he might have said!'

'No word from official quarters?'

'There wouldn't be,' Gillis said. 'If we hear from them, it'll be about the old girl. Almighty Christ! What a mess! We got to do what we agreed.'

'One thing,' Sandboy said, 'Sonny's been all right. Getting me to take the Manders woman about, all that.'

'Listen,' Gillis said again, 'your friend in Praed Street can't have said much yet to Sonny or his mates, if anything. We'd have heard of something. But the minute those things go for sale, Praed Street will know, most likely he'll be at the sale himself. And then he'll remember the visit he had. The face he saw. The voice he heard. I'm the one that might stay clear.'

'We don't know Sonny . . .'

'Fuck's sake,' Gillis said. 'What's it matter? You're too close for them not to notice you. All it takes is them to find that ocelot with you and you're on the same train as Mac. Get rid of it. Any others we do it fifty-fifty. And this time we're not lumbered with Mac.'

Sandboy wrestled round in the box and watched the trippers filing on to the pier in the midday sunshine. He made a last stand. 'If they don't know you, Gilly, why're you so keen on Lawsons?'

He heard Gillis sigh. 'Listen. If it's you, then it's me anyway. Say they talked to you, like they did to Mac.

How long before you introduced them to me? See? These are professionals. You'd give 'em your own mother. As for official sources, we can't even show them that Mac was the one with the old woman. That's us now.'

'It was down to him!'

'Try telling them and see how hard they laugh,' Gillis said. 'You reckon you'd do your one-way walk and not name names? They got their ways, my son. Lips sealed and you walk. Name the others and you might not. There isn't a man alive who'd take that walk alone if he didn't have to. Human nature.'

One of the strollers in the gardens, an elderly man in shirtsleeves, detached himself from the others and stood by the phone box, patiently. Sandboy clenched his left fist at his side.

'When do we do it?'

'Week Saturday. You got enough back-up to cover you several times over.'

'I got to think about it.'

'All right,' Gillis said. 'Think about it. Today. And while you're thinking have another read of that bit I sent you from the paper. Shave off that gigolo moustache too. It's a give-away.'

'The one I took to Praed Street – ' Sandboy looked at the man outside the box and hesitated ' – we take it with the others?'

'You joking? Burn the bloody thing before it burns you,' Gillis said and the line went dead.

Sandboy pushed open the door of the kiosk and stepped out from the heat into the light breeze drifting with the tide. The square clock above the pier approach stood at five past two. Gillis was right about the ocelot.

Even Dublin would be too close if Samuelson started to talk.

He turned away from the gardens and strode towards Queen's Road, a tall, dark-haired figure in shirtsleeves and grey flannels, his upper lip shadowed by the doomed moustache. The little shops and business premises beyond the railway station seemed dustier and dirtier in the fresh sunlight. So far, it was the gun not the ocelot that he had taken care to hide. But Gillis was right. In the fright and confusion of the last twenty-four hours, Gillis was the only voice of reason.

He went straight up the stairs, drew the coat in its tissue paper from under the wardrobe and laid it out. The tawny pelt with its dark irregular blotches, once the smartest possession of his life, lay ugly and dead across a chair. Sandboy felt an irrational fury as he stared at it.

Impossible to burn it at the size it was. From a table drawer he took a six-inch sheath knife in a leather slip. There was no time to do it here. Wrapping the knife with the coat in its tissue paper, he folded the parcel into a large paper shopping bag from Beales department store. Locking his door, he went down to the communal bath-room, soap and razor rolled in his towel. Five minutes later, he had shaved off the David Niven moustache.

Twenty past two. He would have to move like hell before they missed him at the Luxor for three o'clock. With the light bulk of the shopping bag in one hand, he walked and ran along the busy pavement of the long commercial road, down the hill. He went in at the little door by the glass-fronted pay box of the cinema.

'You're late,' Mrs Hallam said indifferently, glancing up from the ticket rolls that she was feeding into the automatic machine.

146

'Shopping,' Sandboy said, thinking how perfectly that fitted the Beales bag. Then he remembered an item in the evening paper. 'You been in Beales this week, Mrs Hallam?'

'I been here this week,' she said without looking up.

'They got the *Queen Mary*. Model of it. For the maiden voyage and the Blue Riband. Eighteen feet long in a tank that ripples like the sea. All the portholes and windows lit up from inside and reflecting on the water. It's good.'

She ignored this but no one would question his story now. He went up the stairs into the projection box and turned on the lights. There was time to load the two Gaumont Kalees and the small Bell and Howell that showed the advertisements. At three o'clock he dimmed the lights over the scattered audience, moved the switch that drew back the neutral-tinted curtains from the screen and turned on the first motor.

While the advertisements ran, he took out the coat and tried to cut its seams with his sheath knife. The ocelot skin seemed tough as elephant hide. Concealed behind the metal bulk of a Gaumont projector, Sandboy struggled to rip through the coat as the soundtrack of the advertisements and general interest features played from the speakers.

'Skidding ends where concrete begins. Concrete roads wear so long that no one yet knows their limit of durability. They are all-British, made of local materials. Eighty-five per cent of their cost goes into wages . . .'

He swore quietly with the exertion, the sweat beginning to gather at his hairline. But the knife was through, rending the coat as he drew it down. Surely he could burn it in eight pieces. He cut the two halves into quarters. Then, as he cut these again, the knife caught the back of his left thumb. Sandboy looked round, saw the regulation First Aid box on the wall and fixed a plaster over the cut. At last the ocelot was in eight sections, the silk lining torn free. He stuffed the pieces back into the bag and stood by the nearest Gaumont Kalee. The first reel of the Crazy Gang's Flanagan and Allen in *A Fire Has Been Arranged* would run for almost forty-five minutes.

He knew what to do, had thought of it over and over as he hurried down the dusty length of Queen's Road. With the film running, he had only to get down the stairs, past the offices, and unfasten the yard door which gave access to the basement boiler room. Then he could come back to the projection box up the outside stairs of the iron fire escape, take the bag back down that way where no one would see him, burn the fragments, lock the door to the yard and come empty-handed up the inside stairs. No one need see him carrying the bag.

Twenty minutes would be enough. It was a chance in a thousand that the film would tear or jam. He would know if it did, the soundtrack being audible over most of the building. So long as no one saw him with the bag, that was the main thing.

Before starting, he unbolted the fire-escape door. Going quietly down the inside stairs to the circle balcony, he saw no one. The usherette, Maureen, was inside the auditorium and the Circle Café was still empty. From here, he went through a door marked 'Private', turned away from the little corridor of offices and hurried down bare stone stairs to the yard door. He pushed the inside bar up, went out into the dazzle of sunlight and closed the door after him. Three minutes. Back up the fire escape to collect the bag with its fragments of the ocelot. The yard had blank walls on every side, except for the frosted glass of the toilets. No one was in sight as he went back down again with the shopping bag, in by the yard door which he fastened after him, and down a further flight of white-painted stone steps to the basement boiler.

Around him, the pipes were lagged with asbestos, like so many limbs in white plaster. Though the heating was turned off, the boiler was still running to provide hot water to the kitchen and the handbasins. Eight minutes gone. He lifted the latch of the square iron door on the boiler and saw the miniature mountain ranges of red-hot coal. The heat dried his eyes as he took the lining torn from the coat and threw it in. It burnt up like gossamer. Then the first irregular oblong of the pelt flared more slowly.

Listening for footsteps on the stone stairs behind him, he threw a second piece of the coat on to the last embers of the first one. He still heard no one on the stairs. In summer, the watchman would have banked up the fire just before the performance and would have no need to come back for an hour or two. A third fragment of the coat went in. Fifteen minutes. It was longer than he had hoped but he heard above him the reassuring rumble of the soundtrack. A fourth oblong of the pelt burnt. And then a fifth.

It was twenty-seven minutes before he had burnt all the pieces and the paper-bag. He hurried back up the steps. As he came out of the door marked 'Private' on to the circle balcony, the usherette was standing by the wide stairs, holding her torch.

'Hello, Maureen.'

But a man and woman with their tickets held out came to the top of the circle stairs and she turned towards them. All the same, seeing him come out of the offices like that, she must have thought that he had been called there to see Manders. Sandboy went back up to the projection box. There would still be ten minutes of the first reel to run and he could swear that no one had been there while he was away. In any case, he had his explanation ready. He could hear himself saying, 'Sorry, just had to nip to the lav.'

And that would fit the back-up story for Saturday week, the pretence of being unwell. For the first time since reading of McGouran's death, he thought Gillis was right. They might still come out ahead.

He started the motor of the second Gaumont Kalee and waited until the circle appeared in the top right-hand corner of the film on the screen. Then he pressed the 'Run' button, let the ten seconds pass, and turned off the first machine. As he began to rewind its reel, the door of the projection box opened.

'Hello, bonfire! What you been doin', then? Burnin' down the buildin'?'

Sonny Tarrant's bulk almost filled the doorway, his lip slanting in a half-humorous grin.

'Mr Tarrant?'

Tarrant walked in and closed the door.

'You been burnin' something up here? Smells like it.'

'Earlier on, Mr Tarrant. Clear up at the digs.'

'I should say you had!' Tarrant peered through the shutter at the auditorium, 'Stuck to your clothes. You smell like a stoker. What I wanted was Manny. Seen him, 'ave you?'

'Not this afternoon.' Sandboy switched off the rewind.

'Ah,' Tarrant seemed satisfied. 'What you done to your hand?'

'I just caught it on the metal gate threading the advertisements,' Sandboy said, smiling at his own clumsiness.

'Oh? State of that plaster, looks more like it been in a bonfire to me. But that was this morning, you said. Unless you had another one since. Never mind, son. I'd get a clean plaster on that, if I was you.'

June

Smash and Grab

Chapter Sixteen

'Raining like this,' Gillis said, 'it won't look odd wearing mackintoshes. You worry too much, Sandy. Stands to reason, Tarrant couldn't have seen you burn that coat. How could he? Any case, doing it in bits like that, you could have been burning anything. What's it matter? How's he to know?'

Sandboy shrugged. They sat at an individual marble-topped table in the small and busy Lyons Tea Room on the Hampstead Road, the electric lights turned on in the darkness of a summer storm. From here they would see Rayner and his escort as the two men walked from Lawsons to the National Provincial Bank. Above the city, on that late Saturday morning, lay a deepening blackness, like a descending fog. Here and there, where the lights of the shops or the street had been turned on, they seemed to touch the vapour with a purple flush.

'And you look better without that moustache,' Gillis said cheerfully. 'You won't tickle her thighs so much.'

Sandboy stared past the grumbling trams and sodden litter to the Snooker Club, 'New Members Welcome', on the nearer corner of Dalgetty Street. Gillis glanced aside, towards the counter. Its two silver urns were steaming with coffee and tea, beyond cheesecakes and sandwiches under vaulted glass. There was still no one close enough to overhear him.

'Stop worrying,' he said quietly. 'He couldn't know about that skin. Anyone been through your place would have done something about the gun first. That been moved?'

Sandboy shook his head. 'Under a bit of loose floorboard by the gas, taped under the board itself.'

'If he never bothered to look for that, he hasn't been there,' Gillis said. 'After all, the gun's one thing even Pender wouldn't forget to mention.'

Rain clouds had not quite masked the summer day. Through a gap to the west, the dark sky filtered a yellow light across the brickwork of Dalgetty Street, but the electric shop signs and the brightly lit interiors brought a sense of nightfall at lunch time.

'You didn't bring it?' Gillis asked. 'The Walden?'

Sandboy patted the pocket of his raincoat. 'Only for show. You rather have a boxing match on your hands? They don't argue with this. They seen too many films.'

'Like McGouran!' Gillis said sourly. 'He only had it for show! Not loaded?'

'It might as well be.'

Gillis shook his head, feigning disbelief. From where they sat, in the window of the shop, they could just see the front of Lawsons. The pavements and tiles of the street shone after the summer downpour. On their Euston Road hoarding, the bill postings for Iron Jelloids, Bovril, and Ovaltine, were wrinkled by the morning's storm.

'Watch it!' Gillis said suddenly. 'This is them.'

He stood up, pushing aside the smeared plate that had held poached egg on toast. Sandboy turned casually and saw the blue-suited man with his grey hat and an umbrella held open. His companion was younger and larger.

Gillis glanced at the wall clock. 'Quarter past eleven. That's prime. We could be out and down Euston Station by half-past.'

They pushed out into the noise of the street as Rayner and his assistant walked away towards the Euston Road.

'Spurgeon . . .' Sandboy said.

'He's there if needed for a quick move. That's all.' Gillis threaded through the traffic. Like Sandboy, he was pulling on his gloves. 'But far the best way home for you is the underground and the station for me. Get clear in the crowd, not be remembered getting in a numbered car round the corner.'

They came to the opening of Dalgetty Street between the Snooker Club and the open doors of the public bar. The pianola that was fed with pennies by the customers was playing the 'Jealousy' tango.

'Once we're over the wall,' Gillis said quietly, 'we wear the scarves. Not in the street. But, anyone sees us in the yard at the back, it's best to be covered. All you got to remember, Sandy, is that even if the coats aren't there, we're no worse off for trying. At least we'll know where we are. We got nothing to lose.'

'Where's the steel cane?'

'Spurgeon'll pass it to us with the cardboard cases as we go into the lane. They're flat, don't even look like suitcases till you open 'em out. No weight to speak of.'

They walked quickly past the street doors of the uneven pavement. Children sat on the stone steps in the shelter of the lintels, keeping dry. Gillis swung right into the first turning, making for the lane that ran behind Lawsons. Spurgeon had parked the car close to its entrance. As Gillis approached, Spurgeon stopped him, as if asking for a light for his cigarette. When they separated, the silver steel cane and tube was in Gillis's sleeve, the flat cardboard in his other hand.

The high-walled access lane behind Lawsons was deserted. Heavy rain had driven off the children who might have been playing there. Gillis put down the cardboard and pulled the triangular mask of a woollen scarf across his nostrils, mouth and chin. Sandboy copied him. This time Gillis had slipped easily into command. Pender's furs had been Sandboy's plan, this was not.

The stone wall was easy. Gillis went first, swivelling over, waiting for Sandboy to hand him the steel cane and the cardboard. They jumped down on the paved surface. Sandboy unbolted the yard door from inside to leave an open retreat.

The wooden door of the outbuilding was still padlocked and bolted. Gillis screwed the steel tube over the final length of the cane, extending it to almost three feet.

'All that trouble over bolts,' he said breathlessly, 'and they still left the door to open outwards. Hinges still on the outside!'

There were two exterior hinge plates screwed across the wooden door, one at the height of his shoulders, another just above his ankles. Gillis slid the tapering steel into the narrow crack between the door and its frame, just below the upper hinge. He took the end of the extension tube in his gloved hands, giving maximum leverage on the three-foot length.

'Get on the bar, Sandy. As far back as you can. This'll crack in no time.'

Sandboy added his energy. For a moment they strained to no effect. Then there was a snap and an abrupt rending of wood. The flat plate of the rusted hinge jerked, warped and then sprang clear. Gillis put his foot up and kicked the door. They had opened a gap on the hinge side, high up. He tried the silver steel cane again, just above the lower hinge. Kneeling side by side, they put their weight on the hardened steel until the lower hinge burst open. The door on that side sagged inwards. Gillis lifted his foot and kicked again, the sole of his shoe hitting it almost at waist level. Though the broken door was still held on one side, there was a gap where the hinges had been. It could be widened far enough by the weight of each body pressing its way in.

Inside the door was a floor of stained red tiles, the walls roughcast and whitewashed. There was a handbasin and a small mirror on a nail above it. At one side stood an internal door to the rear room of the shop. Gillis touched the handle and spoke quietly. 'It's open, Sandy! They haven't alarmed the place nor nothing!'

He turned the handle and pushed the door without a sound. Lawsons back room was lit by daylight through barred windows in the main rear wall. There were shelves with ticketed silver-plated tea-sets and ivory ornaments, oriental vases and ornate lamps, the domestic pledges of Euston and Camden Town. On the opposite wall was a row of individual wardrobes in dark-varnished mahogany, each of them about six feet tall by three feet across. One had a key in its lock.

The main door to the front shop was closed, presumably bolted on the far side and locked by Rayner before he left for the bank.

'Three minutes,' Gillis said softly, 'That's all it takes. He unlocked the first of the wardrobes with its key, found it empty and shrugged. He tried the key on the next wardrobe, only to find that the locks were not uniform. Removing the tube from the cane for convenience, he used the tapered silver steel to wrench open the second wardrobe door. It was filled with shelves of clocks and watches. The next contained brooches and bracelets, old silver set with large but semi-precious stones. The gold had gone to the bank.

Gillis wrenched open the fourth and the fifth of the wardrobes with no better result.

'They must have them somewhere,' Sandboy said. 'You sure no one came to claim them?'

'Certain,' Gillis said. 'I got Spurgeon to ask a question or two.'

'They could have them in the front room ready to go. They could have loaded them in their car already . . .'

'Fuck that!' Gillis said. He turned to the remaining two wardrobes, the tapering steel in the crevice of the first. He wrenched it and saw the broken door swing open on a row of cheap furs that had never come from Pelly Pender.

'What d'you think you're doing?'

She had been so quiet that neither of them had heard her. Gillis swung round and saw a girl who might almost have been a child, with fair fluffy hair and a plain blue dress, standing in the now open doorway between the front shop and rear storeroom.

Sandboy held the small silver grip of the Walden Safety Revolver.

'For God's sake . . .' Gillis said. But Sandboy was calmer.

'You don't move,' he said quietly to the girl. 'If you don't act stupid, you got nothing to worry about. Walk in here. Clear of that door.'

She hesitated.

'Do it now!' Sandboy said, his calm broken by sudden anger at the risk she had put them to.

'Don't fire the bloody thing!' Gillis shouted.

Sandboy had the girl in the corner of his eye when he glanced aside for a split second, as if to see what Gillis thought he might fire at. In that moment, Rayner's shop assistant stepped back behind the angle of the communicating door, slammed it and shot the bolt. Before either Sandboy or Gillis could speak, the clapper of a bell began to hammer out its alarm.

'Get out!' Gillis said. 'Now.'

'Do the last wardrobe!'

'They catch us here, they can tie us to old Pender's woman.'

'Do the last one! After all this! Give me the steel!'

He snatched the cane from Gillis, thrust the tip of it in the aperture and tore the wardrobe door from its fastenings. The furs that hung there were stoles and fox wraps, not a single coat.

'Move, for fuck's sake!' Gillis yelled. 'They're not here! They could be in the front shop! Keep that scarf on till we're clear of the back.' He was forcing his way out through the broken door to the yard with Sandboy at his back. Gillis carried the steel cane in his sleeve and Sandboy the flat cardboard of the unused cases. Gillis threw open the yard door and stepped into the rear access lane.

'Now pull the scarf down!'

They stood in the empty lane in the minute or so between the start of the alarm and the first response to it. With Sandboy after him, Gillis began to run the way they had come. At the end, Gillis slowed, looked out and turned.

'Spurgeon's gone! The car's gone! I'll swear there's plain-clothes police out there!'

Sandboy looked and saw, at the corner of a further street, two men in fawn trench coats and soft hats. They were looking uncertainly about them, trying to identify by its sound the location of the alarm. He ran back down the lane again with Gillis after him.

Gillis coughed and called after him, 'They could head off both ends! Get out of here before they cross behind and see us! Any trouble, we'll have to go through a house!'

But they came to the end of the lane without being seen and turned north, away from Dalgetty Street towards Mornington Crescent.

'Now we walk, not run,' Gillis said.

Two streets further up, on the far side, a black lorry was parked, its side lettered in white, 'Witham and Son, Coal Merchant: Delivery and Retail'. The driver was carrying sacks of anthracite on his back into the yards of the little houses.

Sandboy crossed the road and tossed the flattened suitcase cardboard into the back of the lorry, behind the bagged coal. 'Give us the steel!'

'What about Spurgeon?'

'Fuck Spurgeon! Let's have it!'

Gillis gave it to him. Sandboy lobbed it, hearing it fall deep among the sacks. 'Time they find that, it could have come from anywhere round half of London.'

Gillis turned a corner into a street that led back towards Euston, walking faster. 'Soon as we can, we split up. They're looking for two. And we get rid of the raincoats. Lose 'em where they won't be noticed, such as with a lot of others.'

'Where's Spurgeon?'

Gillis shook his head. In trilby hats and still rain-coated, they walked quickly down the long street of dusty yellow-brick houses towards the noise and movement of the Hampstead Road that crossed its end. Several streets away, Lawsons clockwork device was still hammering out its alarm.

They had covered a quarter of the street's length towards the safety of the Saturday crowds. Then the two men in plain clothes, who had been standing where Spurgeon parked the car, turned the corner towards them at the far end.

'Go back!' Gillis said sharply.

'Then they'll know it's us. They got nothing on us yet.'

'You got a fucking shooter in your pocket!' Gillis said. 'There's no way I'm walking past them. I'm not being tied to what McGouran did to old Pender's woman. And he fired a bullet into the picture rail. They could match it with that gun! Those two won't run fast enough to catch us, so long as we do it now. I know a way we can go.'

Less than half the street's length separated them from the two oncomers. With every step forward the chance of escape narrowed. Sandboy heard Gillis behind him turn and run. There was nothing for it then but follow, one hand clutching the soft trilby to his head. He glanced back once, but the two men were still there, walking at the same speed.

'They're not coming after us!' he shouted at Gillis. But Gillis turned right at the street's end, north again and down the parallel side street. There were local shops here, a fruiterer's with its trays lining the pavement, a newsagent and the revolving stripes of a barber's pole sheathed in glass.

The houses on the far side had been demolished a few years earlier to make room for square blocks of offices in London brick. It was still early enough on Saturday for some of the premises to be open.

'The reason they never came after us is they could cut us off both ends of these side streets,' Gillis said breathlessly. 'So there's one way out.'

"Case you forgot, there's a train to catch!"

'You got time,' Gillis said, reading 'Arcos and Co. Timber Importers' on a plate by the steps that led up to swing doors. He walked up to the door, passed through, and said to the boy inside, 'Arcos. Overseas invoice by hand. Urgent.'

The boy watched them go up the cement stairs to the next floor. At the first-floor window, Gillis paused and opened the narrow metal casement, looking up and down the street. 'No sign. Once they seen we're not in any of these side streets, they'll move on. Give 'em five minutes more and we're clear. You'll be all right.'

They went up to the second floor. The reception door of Arcos stood on one side of the landing, Hillas Rents on the other. From a door between the two sets of offices came a splash of water and a hiss of pipes.

'In here,' Gillis said.

Two interior doors were marked for men and women. Gillis opened one of them a little, glanced at the tiled and porcelain interior and then let the door close. The small lobby between the landing and the toilets had an open closet with a line of unused coathangers. Gillis stripped off his raincoat and hung it there.

'They must get dozens in here. Two coats left behind by foreign dealers. They'll never twig it.'

Sandboy took off his mackintosh and hung it next to Gillis's. He drew the silver weight of the Walden Safety Revolver from the pocket and slipped it into his jacket.

'See?' Gillis said. 'You still got time to be at Euston by twelve. You worry too much, Sandy. That's your trouble.'

Despite the loss of McGouran's three coats, the disappearance of immediate danger seemed like an escape.

'They never caught us,' Gillis said. 'Suppose the worst comes to the worst, we just cut and run – and run. Dublin. Timbuctoo. Anywhere, till it all blows over. They'll give up in the end. There'll be other cases to keep them busy . . .'

He led the way back down and into the street, busy with shoppers in the late morning.

'Keep in the crowd,' he said, 'and carry your hat. You don't look more like the chap that was in Lawsons than hundreds of men round here.'

They came out into the thundering traffic of the Hampstead Road, Sandboy now leading the way towards Euston Station. There was a gap in the vehicles, time enough to cross the road at a trot. Sandboy, still ahead of Gillis, heard rather than saw what happened. Afterwards he thought that, from the corner of his eye, he had seen a dark saloon car that had been parked by the kerb as it started up and pulled out at speed. Behind him he heard a thump like a heavyweight fist smacking into a punchbag.

Swinging round as he ran, he saw Gillis rolling absurdly up the bonnet of the heavy car, sliding past the windscreen, rising a little as if he had been trying to kneel or stand up and cartwheeling to the tarmac on the far side. The Hampstead Road came suddenly to silence and immobility. A tall tram ground to a stop. Two cars and a lorry pulled up sharp. People began to move towards the huddle of clothes and dead or dying flesh that lay in an arena of wet asphalt. Only the car which had hit Gillis disappeared, its speed undiminished, towards Euston Road and the city.

Chapter Seventeen

No one saw him as he stumbled down Drummond Street, across Gower Street, on towards the station forecourt and the Euston Arch. With his hat in his hand, Sandboy dodged the pedestrians. He ran past the narrow fronts of boarding houses and cheap hotels that were two minutes' walk from the train, their signboards painted with the names of Scottish towns and the English lakes.

Under the roof of the great station, the din of engines and the harangue of loudspeakers echoed among steel, tiles and iron-framed glass. Soot drifted down on plum-coloured carriages behind the steady upward funnelling of smoke and steam from stationary locomotives. The hands on the big clock pointed to five minutes past twelve.

Sandboy skirted a partition placarded with holiday scenes. Oban – Gateway to the Highlands . . . Killarney is Fairyland . . . He took out his ticket for Waterloo and ran for the wooden slats of the moving staircase, under an electric sign for the 'Hampstead, City and South London Tube'. He had made a note that morning of where the platform would be. If Gillis had been right, he could still be at Waterloo with five or six minutes to spare.

With his hat in his hand, Sandboy flew down the moving stairs, past the small wooden-framed advertisements for Pearl Assurance . . . Lavella the Suncream that Tans without Torture . . . A Clean Bill of Health with Wrights Coal Tar Soap . . . Fullers of Regent Street for Light Luncheons and Afternoon Teas . . . 3,500 Rooms at Imperial Hotels, Russell Square . . .

He was one of half a dozen passengers racing down the stairway. No one would remember him for that. He dived into the odours of dust and stale electric air. From somewhere at the bottom came the traction whine of a train. He turned into the platform entrance and saw the brightly lit caterpillar of carriages coming to a halt in the southbound Hampstead Tube.

Only as he sat down in the corner seat of the coach did he allow himself to think that Gillis must surely be dead, hit squarely by a heavy car at such a speed. Safer for him that Gillis should be dead rather than dying. But, in that case, there was no one in the world to whom he could any longer speak about Pender or Tarrant or the coats at Lawsons or the other coats that were somewhere in Gillis's possession. Spurgeon might do something about Gillis's coats, he supposed, if Spurgeon knew of them.

The electric carriages rattled and swayed, then with a descending howl pulled into the next platform. Sandboy stared at the station name and felt a chill cloud his brain. King's Cross. Almighty Christ! Gillis's words infected him. In his panic, he had taken the right direction but somehow reached the wrong station. Sandboy felt a cold certainty of being utterly lost in a mechanized labyrinth.

While the doors were still open, he saw a small map displayed at the end of the carriage. The Hampstead Tube line divided at Euston. He had known that it divided but was sure that he had chosen the right platform. His mind flew along the trail of possibilities. This branch line went round in a semicircle to the Elephant and Castle in south London. A change there and two stops northwards to Waterloo. If he went back, he must wait for a train here and then another at Euston. It was impossible.

Sandboy counted the stations on the map as the train pulled out again for the Angel, travelling further east. Nine stops and one change if he went on, nine and two changes if he went back. He must go on. Say two minutes for each station. Gillis had told him that. Sixteen minutes. Or was it only two minutes on the other line and longer on this one? Christ! It was ten past twelve now. How long to wait at the Elephant and Castle? Trapped in the blind tunnels, he knew for the first time that there was nothing he could do but hope.

As the stations passed, he tried to count the seconds between each, seeing the names of a city unknown to him as they slid past. Old Street, Moorgate, Bank, London Bridge, south of the river now, somewhere under Bermondsey and the docks where Gillis had been a child ... Gillis ... Suppose they had not been plain-clothes men in the side street ... Suppose the black car had been theirs ... Suppose that Spurgeon ...

At the Elephant and Castle, he was ready to spring from the train and run whichever way he was directed by the electric signs. There was only one way, down a passage with a curved roof and white tiling like a public convenience, up a flight of cement stairs, down another passage and on to a platform. The train was there. Empty and silent. A man in a dark uniform was waiting on the platform, further down the train.

'Where's this train go?'

'Only one way,' the man called back.' This is the terminus.'

'When's it go?'

'Two minutes.'

'Not before? I got to be at Waterloo.'

'It can't go till the line's clear. Not till the next one comes in.'

Sandboy flung himself down in a seat, the blood beating in his temples. Twelve twenty-five. In his desperation, he invoked Gillis's Almighty Christ. At last the motor began to vibrate and the doors hushed together. Sandboy stood ready to jump again at the next stop but one. He ran from the train, down the subterranean platform at Waterloo with the hands of the clock above the moving staircase pointing to twelve thirty-two. He was too late.

In a rage of frustration he ran back up the wooden staircase to the daylight, the same advertisements for hotels, and soap and afternoon teas flying past him. Southern Railway – South for Sunshine. On the station concourse the large square roman clock above the bookstall pointed to twelve thirty-four. There were other trains, trains he might change from to catch another somewhere. Sandboy sprinted for the platforms with their carriages in summer-green livery, the modern windswept lines of the new locomotives.

The platform gates were open but there were no passengers to be seen, only the ticket-inspector in his cap and tunic. Sandboy ran towards him. Surely the man would know if there was another train that might get him back by changing somewhere . . . by getting close enough to hire a taxi . . .

'Hurry up,' the inspector said.

Only then did Sandboy grasp that the train at the platform was the twelve thirty express which had been delayed. He ran for the first door of the nearest carriage, as a guard at the far end of the train raised a green flag and put a whistle to his lips. He found himself in a first-class restaurant car, neat tables down either side, spread with linen cloths, railway silver and pink-shaded lamps. He walked down, past the steward at the far end, and into the narrower corridors. There was a blast from the whistle and the long express slid forward with a shunting thump of steam.

Even on a Saturday in summer, there were not so many passengers at this time of day. Sandboy found an empty compartment almost next to the engine. There was a good chance that no one else would walk down this far. The pulse which had been beating at his temples since he left Euston began to slow at last. He stared at the sepia photographs between the tops of the opposite seats and the luggage rack above. Salisbury Cathedral, Cowes Royal Regatta, Plymouth Hoe, spray breaking on the rocky coast of Tintagel . . .

Through the narrow central window of the carriage, he watched without noticing as the congested roofs and streets of Clapham gave way to suburban roads, green spaces and plantations of pine trees through Wimbledon and Surbiton.

Gillis! Gillis had been right, of course. As he stared at the view, he knew that if the worst came to the worst, he must run and never stop. The weight of the small Walden Safety Revolver sat absurdly in his pocket now, but that must go with him. There were a few other possessions to collect from his room, about twenty pounds in cash. Gillis was right about Dublin too. Far enough away but no problem with the language. Anywhere that had cinemas and projectors would offer a job. A frontier that could be walked over. He remembered the holiday poster at Euston. Killarney is Fairyland – It could be done.

At last the express pulled in to Basingstoke. Sandboy watched the porters with their trolleys wheeling piles of brown holiday suitcases and cabin trunks labelled as Passenger Luggage in Advance. The sun was out again now, seeming all the hotter after the morning's rainstorms. There was a long pause, the station almost silent in the dust and smoke of the summer afternoon.

He heard a man's voice from a loudspeaker referring to the train as the one twenty-five express from Basingstoke. Sandboy glanced at his watch. It was one thirty-seven The train being late enough for him to catch it at Waterloo might make it too late on arrival for him to be in the projection box by three. There was no chance now of getting off the train and phoning them to say that he was ill, unless he abandoned the journey. Better to hope that he could still pull it off.

He began to calculate. Twelve minutes late – two forty-seven on arrival. If it lost no more time, perhaps he could almost get to the Luxor in thirteen minutes and be up the iron stairs of the fire escape by three o'clock. But just outside Basingstoke, where the line divided for Southampton or Exeter, the engine slowed and came to another halt, steam whispering from its valves in the quiet countryside. Because it was running late, it must now wait for an oncoming express to pass.

Sandboy watched another five minutes slip from him. Then, with an inward shudder of the windows, the Exeter to Waterloo train went by, the summer-green coaches streaming and sparkling into the distance of the fields and downland. The stationary carriages jolted and then began to move forward again. At Winchester, he almost convinced himself that he must get out and make his telephone call, pretending sickness. But there might be just time to do that at Southampton.

At Southampton it was two twenty. Rather than abandon the train for a telephone call, suppose it arrived fifteen minutes late, as seemed likely. He could be in the projection box by five past three. If someone else was in the box, he need only complain of having felt sick and insist that he had gone out on to the iron platform of the fire escape for fresh air. If they had found the escape door unbolted, it would fit his story. The alibi was flawed but perhaps the flaw need not be mortal.

In any case, the telephone call was no longer good enough. Only the alibi would do. When Gillis had made his plan, he had not allowed for such accidents as being seen by two men in plain clothes half a street away. It was far enough to cast doubt on identity, perhaps. But not unless Sandboy could be seen by Manders or the others as early as possible. It would be too late by the time he could go into a chemist's shop. There was even a chance the chemist might not remember him.

He closed his eyes against the pale afternoon sun. As if in a slow sequence of film, he saw Gillis, rolling on the bonnet of the dark car which had accelerated from the kerb. He heard the impact, saw the body rising, cartwheeling and felt the thud on the tarmac. 'He went straight at him.' Until now the words had not occurred to him. But as he stared at the platforms and the iron railway bridge of the station, he began to think that he had heard someone say them as he turned and ran.

The train pulled clear of the docks and the city into the stretches of forest. It moved more slowly, as if abandoning all attempt to keep to time. Sandboy knew that he was now committed to pleading illness at the cinema. That or running and running. As the express pulled in, it was five past three.

The alibi. He must insist that he had threaded the projectors soon after two thirty. Just before three o'clock, he had been violently sick, in the toilets, vomiting from time to time for fifteen or twenty minutes.

It was the best of a bad job, Sandboy thought, as he ran rather than walked. On a Saturday afternoon, it was easy to be lost in the summer crowds. At the familiar sight of the gardens and the pier, the slack wash of ebb tide, it seemed as if he must have dreamt the events of the morning. Sitting with Gillis in the darkness of a storm over the Hampstead Road . . . Watching Gillis killed in the aftermath of a failed robbery . . . On its corner by the length of the Luxor Hotel and the little shops, the white-tiled and black-glass cinema stood quiet in the strengthening sunlight. The pavement outside it was empty.

Keeping out of direct view from the pay box and the steps, he made for the yard at the back. He left his hat on a window ledge by the foot of the escape and went up the iron stairs. Raincoat or hat would have spoilt the story he had chosen.

As he came to the top, he touched the iron door and heard the unmistakable chatter of film passing through the metal gate of a projector. There was nothing for it now but to adopt an excuse of having gone out fifteen minutes earlier for air and having been sick. He pushed open the door.

The film was running smoothly through the nearer of the Gaumont projectors, the patterns of the light beam changing with the movements of the image. The warm enclosed air with its sharp chemical smell of acetone was thick and oppressive. Sandboy looked round and saw no one. He turned to the Bell and Howell. The advertisements had been run but not rewound. The film on the Gaumont Kalee had only started about ten minutes earlier.

Several people knew enough to start the two projectors. However this had happened, it fitted his story of having threaded the films and then been taken ill. But his instinct was to say nothing of how the machines had been started unless he was challenged. Let the others think that he had been there all the time.

He walked carefully down the projection-box stairs to the circle balcony, perfecting his inspiration as he went. The usherette was standing with her pencil torch by the heavy porthole doors of the circle auditorium in her aproned dress. She smiled as he went by, like Little Madam in his dreams.

In the foyer, Manders was talking to Mrs Hallam at the pay box. They glanced at Sandboy but neither of them spoke to him.

'I just got to hear the sound amplification from the level of the stalls,' Sandboy said. 'It sounds a bit boxy from up above.'

When he came out a few minutes later, Mrs Hallam was alone. He chanced a question that need not compromise the alibi. 'You wouldn't know, Mrs Hallam, if anyone threaded that second Gaumont Kalee today? Only it is threaded and if it's not been done today it'll still need a rewind.'

'You're the only one up there,' she said, looking up from a small ledger. 'You should know.'

'Yes,' Sandboy said, conceding the argument, 'only I

had to pop to the gents for a minute and someone could have seen it wasn't done and done it for me.'

She looked at him without sympathy. 'If you made sure of all the rewinding last thing at night, you wouldn't need to come asking,' she said. 'That's what you're paid to do. Not leave it in the projector to be wound next day. Mr Manders isn't a rewind boy. And I'm sure Maureen nor I aren't.'

'I'll see to it,' he said contritely.

As he walked back across the soft depth of the foyer carpet under the inset spotlights of the ceiling, he tried to reconcile the pattern of events. But Mrs Hallam and Manders acted as if they thought he must have been in the projection box at least ten or fifteen minutes before the delayed express reached the railway station. If they believed that, it was impossible he could have been in Dalgetty Street at eleven thirty.

He went back up the narrow stairs from the circle. Gillis was forgotten for the moment. The claws in Sandboy's entrails released their grip. He felt like a man condemned to die whose life had been suddenly restored to him, whole and complete. But in the projection box he faced the unforgiving logic of its machines. It was necessary to rewind the advertisements and general interest on the Bell and Howell. The feature film on the Gaumont Kalee was ten minutes in advance of the time when he could have started it. He timed the end of the reel and knew that it had been started at three ten. He timed the length of the Bell and Howell and knew that it had begun promptly at three.

Not three five or three two, not even three one, but three precisely. They were often a minute or two late in starting, but not today. The motor had been started on the first projector, and the film switched on, by someone who surely knew that he could not be there to do it. Someone who had apparently said nothing about it to anyone else. He stared at the mat beige steel of the tall Gaumont projector and felt the claws tighten again.

July

Say Nothing

Chapter Eighteen

'Gillis,' John Rutter said politely. 'It's a face we know – knew once.'

The stone building of the Westminster Mortuary in Ensell Street smelt of floor polish and formaldehyde. The slats of its venetian blinds were no more than half open, giving the white-tiled interior a winter light in late July. Only at the centre table was there a faint bottle-green tint from a skylight's frosted glass, the cold hygienic light of post-mortem dramas.

Stephenson drew the sheet up again to cover the waxwork mask of the features. The exaggerated hump of the torso beneath the white cloth suggested to Rutter that the dead man had taken in one huge final breath in the path of destruction and held it for eternity. It was only gas, the textbooks said.

'The fingers?' Stephenson asked. 'Any use were they, the finger-stalls we made?'

Rutter watched the contours of Gillis slide back into the darkness of his antarctic metal cabinet. 'The fact that he was wearing gloves helped, Alec. No damage, to speak of, to the fingertips. A perfect match in Criminal Records. But Gillis was nothing much, a small opportunist thief when he was caught. Hardly a burglar even. After that he grew up, of course, but not that we knew of in the past year or so. Better educated than most of our customers. Not an elementary schoolboy. More of a grammar-school reject.'

He followed Stephenson out to the pathologist's office, divided from the public waiting-room by a pale oak counter with a blue-glass vase of dusty flowers. Everywhere in the building the furniture was made of hard green leather and tubular steel.

'Anyone see Mr Gillis and his friend that last hour or so?' Stephenson asked.

Rutter sat down at the desk in the visitor's chair. 'Just a few. The girl in Lawsons, of course. She didn't see their faces, both wearing scarves as masks. But Gillis put a foot to the outhouse door to break it in. Perfect print of a sole and heel on a wet day. Matched his right shoe down to the last detail of wear and tear.'

He took out his cigarette case and offered it to Stephenson. The pathologist shook his head and Rutter put the case away. 'Rayner left his daughter in the shop while he and his man went to the bank. Easier than putting the alarm on. Never thought there'd be trouble in that time. They take the money and valuables down there every week. Sunday's favourite for robbing post offices and pawnshops, while they're empty. Mr Rayner likes to have the best bits off the premises before closing up.'

He looked at the slatted blinds and shook his head. 'Lawsons were far more worried about the Saturday walk to the bank. Much easier target than the shop. Better value as well. The shop made no sense, except to a small-change artist like Gillis. Robbing it with all the cash and gold gone.'

Stephenson took a form from a drawer of the desk

and put it in front of Rutter to sign. 'There's a chance they were seen before last Saturday, on reconnaissance?'

Rutter signed his name and shook his head. 'Not till the girl found them in the back room of the shop. One had a gun. She remembers that both of them spoke. She thought the one with the gun might shoot her but the other told him not to. Not much to go by. Still, she managed to slam the door on them and set the alarm off.'

Stephenson took the sheet of paper back. 'One thing, if it helps, Jack. Gillis was wearing a raincoat all right. Except one side of him, where he hit the road, his jacket and trousers were relatively dry when they picked him up. But trouser legs soaked below the knees, as they would be in that downpour. Nothing in his pockets except money and a latchkey. Not a name of any kind. A precaution, I dare say.'

Beyond the office window there rose the muted but steady roar of traffic from New Oxford Street to Holborn. Rutter stood up and set the chair straight.

'We've got the raincoat, Alec. And Frank Brodie's lined up three doubtful witnesses – apart from the girl – and one boy genius. A waitress saw two men in Lyons Tea shop about ten minutes before the robbery. A woman who lives on the corner of Dalgetty Street thinks she saw Gillis and another man talking to a third who was standing by a car. That was just a couple of minutes before the alarm went off. By the time that started hammering, the men and the car had gone. A chap walking down the next road saw two men run out of the lane behind Dalgetty Street when the alarm was going. Trouble is, they turned the other way. He never got a good look.'

'Who's the boy genius?'

'Door boy,' Rutter said, putting on his hat, 'Arcos Ltd., state-owned company of the Soviet Union that supplies soft timber. They have an office on the first floor of a block off the Hampstead Road. Open till lunch on Saturdays. Two men went into the building on Saturday morning, saying something about an invoice to be delivered by hand. The boy saw them come out again without their raincoats. First he thought they'd left the coats in the office itself because the rain had stopped and they were coming back again. Monday morning, however, there's two raincoats hanging in the shared cloakroom between Arcos and Hillas Rents. Somebody in one of the offices heard about the robbery a few streets away. And Arcos knew that no one had come to them with an invoice. That's when we got a call. The lad on the door picked Gillis out of the photographs right away. He had the advantage of seeing them twice.'

'And the other man?'

'No luck,' Rutter said. 'We might even be dealing with a beginner that no one knows. Or a smart one that's never been caught.'

'Except for the raincoat.'

'Except that,' Rutter said. 'We'll see.'

They stood by the counter that divided the office from the waiting-room.

'What I'd like, Alec,' Rutter said, 'is anything on the car that hit Gillis. The middle of the Hampstead Road on a Saturday morning. So many witnesses and so little agreement. We've had every colour and make. No registration number, of course. It happened too fast. The opinion seems to be that the driver put his foot down to get past another vehicle, not knowing that Gillis was running across the road in front of that vehicle and about to come out on his side. At the speed he was doing, he could have been a hundred yards past before he could stop. When they're that far clear, they very often keep going rather than turn back and face the music.'

'The car,' Stephenson held open the glass-panelled door for his guest, 'apart from injuries caused by it, the car may be another form of expertise.'

Rutter hesitated.

'And then there's the gun. I wouldn't have minded finding that on Gillis. But either he ditched it in the panic or else it's still out there, burning an evil little hole in someone else's pocket.'

Half an hour later, he called Frank Brodie from the sergeants' room. Brodie seemed unusually pleased. 'Two more witnesses, Jack. A man in the New Argyll café opposite Lawsons looked at photos and thinks it was Gillis he saw with another man down the street.'

'How far?'

'About eight houses away, according to our map.'

'And the other?'

'A woman shopping near the Arcos office block. Just thinks she recognized one of the men in the photographs. That makes five who think they saw Gillis and the lad at the entrance to the offices who says he's sure.'

'And the mystery man?'

'No one matches him to the photographs,' Brodie said, 'but one of the ladies picked someone else out of the rogues' gallery. Someone we weren't even asking about.'

Rutter sat up. 'Who's that?'

'Spurgeon. Royston James Spurgeon.'

Rutter shook his head and pulled a face. 'Not a customer of mine, Frank.'

'Twenty-three years old,' Brodie read from a sheet of

paper, 'until March he was in Glasgow, if you believe Criminal Records. Released from Barlinnie gaol in February. A matter of money with menaces. Cadging lifts and sticking it to the men who picked him up. Also robbery at night of taxi-drivers out of the central railway station.'

'We could comb the country for months,' Rutter said abruptly, 'and then find our witness got him wrong. That's the slow lane, Frank. Let's try something faster.'

But Brodie shook his head. 'Spurgeon might be faster. And you don't need to comb the country, Jack. We know where he is.'

'Criminal Records?'

'No, Jack. National Assistance Office. All his life, Spurgeon's drawn the dole. It might have been invented for him. Downstairs, they checked his reference number through Barlinnie. We put it through National Assistance and the answer came back this morning. He's not in Glasgow. He's in Harringay. Harringay division did a check on the address given them, near the greyhound stadium. It's a house let out as rooms. They rousted the landlord and got the names of his other tenants. One of them was Gillis. They're bringing Spurgeon into Harringay for questioning on suspicion of armed robbery. We thought you might like that.'

'Spurgeon wasn't driving the car that hit Gillis?'

Brodie shook his head. 'No, Jack. That's too good to be true. And he seems the wrong size and shape to have been the one with Gillis in the back room of Lawsons. Still, he mightn't have been too far off.'

Rutter shrugged. 'All right, Frank. Ask Harringay to hold on to Spurgeon for as long as possible. Awaiting arrival of officers from Scotland Yard, as the papers say.

Even if he's small fry in all this. We know Gillis, yes. But most of all I want the man with the gun.'

Twice before the end of the day, Rutter telephoned Harringay and spoke to the custody officer and a chief inspector of CID. Spurgeon would say only that he was at home on Saturday morning. But he had not yet demanded a lawyer.

In other words, Spurgeon, bereft of Gillis and the gunman, could not make up his mind what to do and needed a little advice. Rutter asked Harringay CID to let drop in Spurgeon's ear the promise of being put on an identity parade in a case of armed robbery, a crime for which judges were increasingly apt to order the cat-o'-nine-tails. That, he thought, would give the young bastard something to keep him dancing.

But the best news was late in arriving. It was not until the evening of the following day that Frank Brodie came to him and handed over the transcript of a telephone message from Montague Burton Ltd. of Leeds. Rutter read it and saw himself tidying up his case within the week. At the end of the transcript, Frank Brodie had underlined the name of 'the man with the gun'.

Chapter Nineteen

From the iron platform, Sandboy watched a gull rise in a tiny feather of spray, far out beyond the pier and the crowded shingle. The bird rode the warmth of rising air towards the shore like a paper glider, over the men and women in the deckchairs set out along the pale blue promenade rail, the girls in flower-pattern sundresses, the young women in their Martin-White water suits. In strong sunlight, the emerald tide darkened to a black band along its horizon.

Behind him, as he leant on the rail and smoked, the last reel of the morning matinée's Laurel and Hardy, *The Bohemian Girl*, was rewinding on the second projector. No one who had known of their friendship had spoken to him of Gillis. He had bought the London evening papers that came down every day as far as the railway station bookstall. For two days there had been nothing. Then a small paragraph, 'Hit-and-Run Victim. Hampstead Road Tragedy.' It was a superfluous confirmation that Gillis was dead on arrival at the Middlesex Hospital. But, even in death, it seemed that Gillis had been his protection. Gillis had broken a link to McGouran, Samuelson, Pender, even to Sonny Tarrant.

But Tarrant was all right. He had escorted Manders, Yvonne and Nina to dinner at the Garden Royal several days after the newspaper report. Sandboy was there to take them home. As the others went to the dining room, Tarrant had taken him into the bar with an arm round his shoulder.

'You see my young friend has a drink or two,' Tarrant had said to the barman, 'and get the bar waiter to bring him sandwiches and pickle. He needs feedin' up. You see he 'as anythin' he likes.'

The gull had settled now, its feet slithering on the apex of a glass skylight above the brick swimming baths. The wings folded fussily over wind-ruffled feathers. Sandboy went back into sudden darkness after the sunlight. He threaded the second projector again for the afternoon performance and went out for lunch.

He was walking on the pavement beyond the department stores, under the awning of an ice-cream parlour, its polished mirrors reflecting a cool marble interior. A dark-haired man in a blue suit and trilby hat, a face with few but incisive lines, stepped out in front of him.

'Hello, Sandboy,' he said casually. 'You don't know me. My name is Rutter. I'd like a chat.'

At the same moment his upper arms were gripped from behind with firm but increasing pressure. Sandboy felt a spurt of fear at the memory of McGouran and Gillis, the railway tunnel and the speeding car. He knew that he must fight now or never. Once they got him away from the crowded street, it would be too late. He tried to pull himself free of their grip.

'See?' the dark-haired man said sympathetically. 'You'll only hurt yourself doing that. Brings tears to the eyes, doesn't it? Get in here.'

For the first time, Sandboy noticed the dark classic lines of a black Wolseley saloon parked at the pavement

189

beside him. The rear door was already open. He twisted round to the passers-by, his mouth open. But, as in a nightmare, his scream seemed to lack breath. It made no sound. The two men behind pushed him into the back of the car and sat on either side. Rutter took the passenger seat in front, beside a uniformed driver. He turned in the seat as the engine started and showed Sandboy a card. Sandboy caught the words 'Metropolitan Police'.

'Seems to me I'd better have a lawyer, then,' he said, his voice unsteady with shock.

Rutter's face wrinkled with friendly surprise and amusement. 'If you pay a lawyer every time someone wants a chat with you, son, your bill must be the size of the national budget!' He turned to face the windscreen. 'Any case, we're not interested in you. It's your friend, Mr Gillis, we want to hear about.'

'Doesn't mean anything.'

The car had pulled out into the stream of traffic, past the long display windows of the department stores, heading away from the sea towards the long commercial roads beyond the station.

'Don't say that,' Rutter smiled again. 'They tell me that friendship means everything. Let's go back to your rooms and discuss the matter.'

Sandboy thought of his rooms and the gun taped under the loose board. 'There's nothing to discuss,' he said quickly, anxious now to get it all over with. 'I knew Gillis, if that's what you mean. I knew he was dead. It was in the *Evening News* or one of them.'

'Read the London papers here, do you?'

'If someone leaves them around. It's how I knew.'

Rutter said something quietly to the driver and they

turned away from the streets of holiday shops towards the railway bridge.

'Did you also know that Gillis and another man had broken into a cash jewellers in Dalgetty Street off the Hampstead Road about ten minutes before he was killed? Last Saturday morning?'

''Course not,' Sandboy said irritably. 'How could I know? I hadn't seen him for weeks. Months. When he last came down. And I was here all last Saturday.'

'Whereabouts?' Rutter asked, as if it scarcely mattered.

'Home all morning. Then I had to be down the picture-house by half-past two, ready to start at three. I'm usually first one there.'

'That's good,' Rutter said thoughtfully. 'It's good to have an answer like that. Anyone see you?'

'Someone must have done. Ask 'em. I spoke to Mr Manders and Mrs Hallam about three o'clock, checking the sound level in the stalls. Any case, if I hadn't been there in time, the performance wouldn't have started. Would it?'

'I suppose not,' Rutter said.

They sat in silence until the Wolseley pulled up outside the small printer's shop in Queen's Road.

'Keys, if you don't mind,' Rutter said.

Rutter and the two escorts went in with him, past the dark hat-stand and up the dusty stairs. Rutter and Sandboy sat in cushioned chairs while the two sergeants moved from room to room.

'You got a search warrant?' Sandboy asked. Rutter looked surprised.

'No. Do we need one? Mr Brodie and Mr Clarke are just looking. Not searching. We could get a search warrant, I dare say. But then we'd have to do a proper search. If you'd prefer that.'

Sandboy said nothing.

'Raincoats are funny things, you know,' Rutter said. He looked at Sandboy without expression.

'What if they are?'

'Most people button a raincoat before putting on gloves. Not the other way round. We found a raincoat on Monday, hanging in the cloakroom of an office block off the Hampstead Road. Gillis's fingerprints on the buttons. It's what comes of putting the gloves on last.'

'What's that to do with me?'

'Montague Burton,' Rutter said. 'They have a shop in every large town. They make their own raincoats. They make most of the raincoats worn by most people. A huge factory in Leeds. One of their coats was hanging next to Gillis's. Might have been any one in a thousand. No prints on it that we could find. Someone who put his gloves on first perhaps?'

Sandboy stared at the lined, relaxed face. Rutter talked as if nothing could come of the conversation. Sandboy tried to think of a defensive remark but there was none.

'If you take the lining out of a raincoat,' Rutter's tone suggested that Sandboy would find this just as fascinating as he did, 'you find stitched inside what they call a maker's stock number. They have a corresponding one on the manufacturer's invoice. This coat was 8414, a batch of twenty at the end of a run. All of them went to Montague Burton's branch in Southampton, last October. Take those twenty. Nineteen of the people who bought 'em couldn't have known Gillis in a month of Sundays. We checked them, of course. They couldn't know him.'

'So what?' But even to Sandboy his defiance sounded

like the sneer of a sulky child. Rutter smiled, as if he understood.

'Burton's write a receipt when they sell a coat. When it's charged to an account, they have the customer's name and address as well. Very methodical. Customer gets a copy. Mr Manders has an account at Burton's in Southampton. There's a receipt for one Burton Rainwear, stock number 8414, charged to that account in November. Mr or Mrs Manders, I dare say, but bought for you.'

'So what?' It was the best that Sandboy could do in his cold dread.

'So,' said Rutter reasonably, 'now you see why I'm here.'

But at the moment Sandboy saw only that there was a gap. He dived through it. 'You been put on a goose chase, then. Gillis had that coat of mine months ago. He come down here one day in March – I think it was. I promised to show him the picture-house. The projection box and that. It was a sunny day but freezing after dark when he came to go back. I lent him the raincoat that Mr Manders gave me at Christmas. I had an old one as well but that was back home. So he had to borrow the new one I had with me. If you want to know why it was hanging where you found it, you'd have had to ask Gillis.'

Rutter considered this. 'Anyone else see Gillis, while he was here?'

'Mr Tarrant, that's Mr Manders' business partner. He come into the box while we were there and invited us to have a drink at the Garden Royal. Mr and Mrs Manders was in the cinema too and a couple of others. They might have seen him. And the barman at the Garden Royal saw him all right. That enough? I never was in London last Saturday. There's a dozen people could tell you.'

Rutter relaxed as if relieved of an unpleasant duty. 'And how did you first meet Mr Gillis?'

'Two years back he was on holiday down here. We met in a bar and got talking. That's all.'

'And Mr Spurgeon? Roy Spurgeon?'

Sandboy shrugged and pulled a face. 'Don't know the name. Perhaps Gillis lent my raincoat to him.'

Jack Rutter looked a little less pleased. By this time Brodie was walking carefully on the threadbare carpet of the dusty little sitting room with its single sash window at the rear. He stopped near the fireplace where the carpet ended and the boards were black-varnished. Sandboy's heart went cold as Brodie knelt and prised up the end of a loose nine-inch length of board.

Brodie's hand went underneath and touched the surfaces with patient delicacy. His arm was hidden to the elbow. Sandboy watched him. The room seemed to grow darker and colder still. Then Brodie drew back, stood up and opened an empty hand.

Sandboy felt sick with a new fear. Was the revolver not there? Had Brodie not touched it? Were they pretending to have found nothing, as part of a trap? When he could manage a tone of indifference, he asked, 'What happens now?'

'You go up to town,' Rutter said cheerfully. 'A night or two in the care of Tottenham Court Road police station. They'll look after you. Before we go, we shall ask your friends here to confirm your story about Saturday last. Even if they do, as I dare say they will, you'll still have to be looked at by others who think they saw you round the Hampstead Road on Saturday morning. If they did, whatever your friends may say, you got from there to here somehow, even if you sprouted wings to do it.'

By the end of the afternoon, Jack Rutter had pieced together from witness statements a story of Sandboy being at the Luxor before the others arrived on Saturday afternoon. He was not seen entering nor going up the stairs by Mrs Hallam nor Maureen nor even Manders, as he would have been had he come in later. Mrs Hallam had been there by half-past two. The projection had started promptly at three. Sandboy had come down about ten minutes later to check the sound level in the stalls.

There was no car of Manders' that Sandboy could have used to get to London or back. No stolen car had been found within two miles of the Luxor that day. In any case, the journey by car was impossible. To have driven across the congestion of London and down the busy Saturday roads for over a hundred miles, through the centre of several major towns, in little more than two hours, would seem impossible to any jury. A check on the times logged by the Southern Railway suggested that Sandboy had been in the projection box for about half an hour by the time that the delayed twelve thirty express from Waterloo arrived at its destination.

'We'd better hope someone on the home team picks him out, Frank,' Rutter said wearily on the steps of the Luxor. 'If they can't put him near Dalgetty Street that morning, and with Gillis dead, this entire case goes up in smoke.'

Frank Brodie said nothing. He handed Rutter a message. Mr Tarrant had information to give, as a matter of urgency.

Chapter Twenty

Tarrant's tall iron gates were set between fortress walls of rhododendron hedges. Brick pavements along the expensive residential roads, high above the sea, undulated like waves over the roots of the sycamore trees. Rutter's view from the drive lay across the town in a haze of summer heat, to the pale grass of flat fields with steeply sloping banks of drainage channels. The grazing sheep stood motionless as distant toys.

The driver pulled up beyond a sprinkler that cast its arc over the green of Sonny Tarrant's lawn. Rutter and Brodie got out.

'See what you get for persistence in a life of crime, Frank?' Rutter displayed the garden with a wave of his hand. 'He never knew his father. Old Ma Tarrant was a Tivoli chorus dancer when Queen Victoria died. The father could have been any one. Lord Lofty or the stable groom.'

'How long you reckon he's been at the game?'

Rutter shrugged. 'Before he was fourteen, he was round the racecourses with a pail and wet sponge. Nip in and wipe everything off the blackboards where they'd chalked the odds. Caused chaos. They couldn't take bets until they got it sorted. But if they paid him not to do it, Sonny and his mates would stand guard to make sure no one else did it either. Even Darby Sabini never ran a protection racket on his days off school.'

'Mr Rutter!'

The distant call was like a parade-ground command to attention, as Tarrant came down the steps from the French windows to the lawn. To Rutter, he seemed to carry his age and weight badly. Tarrant's preference was for expensively tailored suits in a style long out of date. The result made him look like a middle-aged razor-boy. Where the grey waistcoat buttoned tightly, his stomach swelled hard under the cloth like some ominous deformity.

'Mr Rutter!' As he crossed the lawn, Tarrant sounded a second trumpet note of bluff insincerity, learnt from the racetrack tipster and the three-card trick. Yet the insincerity had been finely tuned. It had the confidence of a rogue who appeared to make common cause with his dupes. It exhilarated them by the adventure of having a man of no scruples on their side against the world.

'Mr Rutter!' The call softened apologetically. Rutter found himself shaking hands without intending to and introducing Frank Brodie. 'Let's go and sit somewhere quiet,' Tarrant said.

He led the way through the French windows into a broad lounge of silver-grey curtains and pearl-tinted hangings. There was a crystal-pendant chandelier and a Steinway grand piano polished to the colour of liquid honey. Tarrant gestured them to square modern arm-chairs, upholstered in chocolate-brown leather.

Rutter glanced at his watch. 'Just a matter of your statement, Mr Tarrant.'

Tarrant smiled. 'More like information really, Mr Rutter. Only, when they phoned me from the picture-house, it seemed the young lad that works the projectors might be in trouble for not bein' there last Saturday. All it was, I seen him there. Not to speak to. He must have come out of the gents on the circle balcony, seein' he hadn't been downstairs where the rest of us were. I just saw the back of him goin' up the little stairs to the projection box. I can't be sure I said hello. But he was there. I do hope that helps you.'

'When did you see him? What time?'

Tarrant made an effort of recollection. 'Well now, Mr Rutter. What I can say for sure is I had to pick up wage packets from the Garden Royal and take 'em back down the picture-house. Up the Royal, I passed the time of day with Charley Archer that takes care of security for me. And Mr Thorp, the contractor for maintenance. Quarter to three, I should say, needin' to be back down the picture-house by three. You'd be welcome to ask. In all conscience, I couldn't leave the picture-house less than ten or twelve minutes before I got to the Garden Royal. So whatever time I saw our young friend goin' up the projection box couldn't be later than about half-past two. Might be a little before. You want it written down?'

'If a witness statement is needed, you'll be informed. You saw Sandboy from the back. You don't think he or you spoke . . .'

Tarrant gave him a grin and a sniff. 'Come on, Mr Rutter! I got no axe to grind. I see someone goin' up the projection box stairs, about the time Sandboy comes on duty. Wearin' his clothes, looks like him. We know he was up there because he come down later to speak to Mrs Hallam and Mr Manders, as I been told. And whoever was goin' up them stairs knew how to handle the Gaumont projectors. Pardon my French, but who the fuck else was it likely to be? And don't tell me I saw him on my way back later from the Garden Royal neither. I hadn't got the wage packets. I was on my way out. Just come from Mr Manders' office.'

'All right,' Rutter said, but the drawing back of Tarrant's lip from his teeth had lost the pretence of a smile.

'No, it's not all right, my friend. It's far from all right. I told you what I saw. Just a minute. We'll get this straight.'

He reached out to the wall and pressed the white nipple of an electric bell in its brown bakelite surround. Rutter waited uneasily for the trap to spring. A tall girl came in, wearing a plain grey dress, her pale blond hair down to her shoulders and her eyes an odalisque green. Tarrant laid his hand on her arm as she stood by his chair.

'You phoned the Royal, my sweet? Asked if anyone saw me quarter to three last Saturday?'

She nodded. 'Mr Archer, Mr Thorp and Billy on the door. All the same time.'

Rutter felt his face beginning to warm with anger at Tarrant's ambush of the investigation. But Tarrant got in first. 'Right.' He looked up at the girl. 'Just a minute.' Then he looked at the two policemen. 'Either of you two gentlemen 'ave a drink?'

'No,' said Rutter sharply, 'thank you.'

The girl went out.

'What I would like,' Rutter continued, 'is to question witnesses for myself. Without interference.'

Tarrant shrugged. 'Fair enough. Nothin' against that. I just 'ad to be certain I wasn't makin' a mistake as to time. Not leadin' you on. I got a great regard for the work you and your colleagues do, Mr Rutter. There's Charley Archer and two more that used to be in area division. On the force, same as your good self. All of 'em workin' for me now. I was glad to have 'em and they was glad of the work. But that lets our young friend out of it, does it?'

Rutter stared at him. 'No, it doesn't. Whatever you claim to have seen, Mr Tarrant, there's reason to suppose that the young man may have been seen in London at midday on Saturday.'

Tarrant shook his head as if in disbelief. 'You're never takin' him back there?'

'He'll be assisting with inquiries,' Brodie interposed quietly.

'Oh, yes!' Tarrant's mouth opened in silent humour. 'One of these identity parades that either picks no one or else the wrong man! Which police station?'

Rutter felt his face growing warm again. 'What's that to you?'

'What it is to me, my friend, is simple. We need to know which station to send the lawyer. He'll be there before you get back to London, that's a promise.'

'Why?'

Tarrant had now abandoned all pretence of amiability. He looked at Rutter with his upper lip curled in contempt. 'To my own satisfaction, I seen that boy here, in the picture-house, about half-past two last Saturday afternoon. Savvy? In that case, wherever else he might have been, he must have been in this town soon after two o'clock. I should say so, wouldn't you? He wouldn't just pop up on the projection box stairs from nowhere! You tell me you're going to prove he was in London at midday! He couldn't get from there to here in that time. Sir Malcolm Campbell in *Bluebird* couldn't do it in that time. But you're going to try and prove otherwise, aren't you? Meaning, he's going to be sewn up. I been around,

Mr Rutter, as you well know. I seen a bit too much of that in my time, especially young lads that's no match for you and your lot!'

'If there are witnesses who saw him in London . . .'

'Listen,' Tarrant said furiously, 'who's more likely to be right? Me, that's seen him a hundred times or more and would recognize him, or witnesses that never knew him from Adam and perhaps only saw him for a few seconds and never knew it mattered until now?'

'If it comes to a choice,' Rutter stood up, 'a court will decide.'

'Stannie Bowlett,' Tarrant said quietly, 'he's our lawyer. You've heard of him? I don't stand by and see one of my employees in trouble and let him sink or swim. Especially not a lad with no one to look out for him. Still, I'll do you one favour. Make sure Stannie knows which station his client's at. We had this fandango before. Stan Bowlett had a superintendent in your lot done for obstructing his client's access to legal representation. He had the Commissioner of Metropolitan Police out of bed and a writ of habeas corpus drawn up. You had one of those yet?'

Rutter wanted only to get out of Tarrant's sneering presence. 'Mr Bowlett is your solicitor, not Sandboy's,' he said coldly.

Tarrant stood up. 'You think again, Mr Rutter. That young man works for me and Manny Manders. Helps out, time to time, up the Garden Royal. As such, my firm's legal representative is at his disposal. Goes with the job, like a pension or free grub up the Circle Café.'

Rutter turned to the French windows and then looked back. Tarrant had irritated him so deftly that he had almost forgotten his final question. 'Do you know someone by the name of Gillis?'

Tarrant appeared lost for a moment. Then he said, 'Yes. Yes, of course I do. I met him once, about six months ago. He came down to see Sandboy. They were in the projection box, looking at the new Gaumont projectors. I told the two of 'em to go and have a drink up the Garden Royal, on the house.'

'Was he wearing a raincoat?'

Tarrant looked lost again. 'Not that I recall. No, I'm sure he wasn't. Is that it, then?'

'For the moment,' Rutter said.

Tarrant's lip moved in a final characteristic smile. 'Good,' he said. 'Remember me to old Stannie Bowlett when you see him, won't you? He's just your type.'

Chapter Twenty-One

A dusty sun was settling over Fitzroy Square and the park trees beyond. Sandboy held the woven thong beside the back window to steady himself as the Wolseley turned sharply off the Tottenham Court Road, short of Goodge Street Station. The brick front of the new police station was marked off by a modernistic blue lamp at either end.

The car turned again between the open rear gates of the yard and drew up by a flight of steps. Half a dozen uniformed officers were leaning on the rail of the metal walkway above, watching the suspect's arrival. Three more uniformed men stood on duty down either side of the yard as the car came to rest. One of them opened the rear door and two more escorted Sandboy up the steps to a door in the blank stone wall. The case might be Rutter's but police-station etiquette belonged to the uniformed branch of 'E' Division.

Rutter and Brodie sat in the car and watched the uniformed officers escort Sandboy through the doorway.

'Two chances to pot him, Frank,' Rutter said quietly. 'One tonight, when he's questioned. Another in the morning when he's put up for identification.'

'Charge him?' Brodie asked.

Rutter shook his head. 'No. The minute we do that, Bowlett will close down the questioning. Any case, the longer Sandboy thinks he's got a chance of getting clean away, the harder he'll struggle and the tighter he'll tie himself.'

'You know this lawyer of Tarrant's? Stan Bowlett?'

'Seen him at work in the police court.' Rutter glanced at his watch, giving them time to document Sandboy. 'Sharp as a ship's rat. Night-school boy. On call to every chancer round Stepney, Limehouse, Wapping. Talks like it too. Still, him being sharp is what might just sink Sandboy for us. And Bowlett being lawyer for Tarrant's company tells you all you need to know about Sonny Tarrant as a man of business!'

'And Manders.'

Rutter shook his head. 'Manders lost his rights to Tarrant in a fire sale, they tell me. He's there as a name. Pensioner only.'

They got out of the car and walked up the steps.

'The plan is simple,' Rutter said. 'We let Sandboy dig himself into his alibi tonight. So deep that he can't dig a way out tomorrow. Don't try and stop him. Let Bowlett coach him if he wants to. We'll have it all on record. All it needs then, tomorrow, is two or three eyewitnesses to pick him out. Or the girl in Lawsons to recognize his voice. From then on, he's shot himself. Stuck with a bent alibi that he can't alter and fingered by several respectable citizens.'

'Except for the witnesses at the Luxor.'

Rutter stopped and held out a hand to his sergeant. 'Bet me five quid, Frank. Say we get two or three solid eyewitnesses to Sandboy being with Gillis in Dalgetty Street last Saturday. All of a sudden, the three witnesses in the cinema are going to remember they never actually saw Sandboy until well gone three o'clock.'

'Except Tarrant.'

'And Sonny Tarrant's going to have a Damascus Road conversion. He'll think that perhaps he made a mistake about the time. Later than he thought. After he'd been to the Garden Royal Hotel, not before. And, perhaps, he only saw what he thought was the back of Sandboy going up those stairs to the projectors.'

'I'd feel bad about taking your money, Jack,' Brodie said, but Rutter was not to be put off.

'Sandboy could find himself in front of a jury without a friend in the world. He'll be stuck with a story he can't prove and with witnesses to show him a liar. That's why we let him have his head tonight. The bigger the lies now, the quicker a jury convicts him. Whatever he says, Frank, we have to look as if we half believe him.'

They walked into the linoleum-floored vestibule where Sandboy was now sitting on a chair in the waiting area with a uniformed man beside him.

'Just take him to an interview room and sit with him,' Rutter said to Brodie.

He turned towards the duty sergeant at the desk. Another voice called out to him, 'Mr Rutter?'

He had not seen Bowlett in the doorway behind him. But the voice had a self-confident abrasive twang, like the resilience of a steel spring. Stan Bowlett was spruce and slim, neatly suited in brown herring-bone, a dockland defender exuding a faint but pervasive perfume of West End barbering.

'Mr Bowlett?'

'Stanley Bowlett,' Bowlett said, shaking Rutter's hand with a display of white shirt cuffs held precisely level. 'You going to interview him already?'

'Only to check a few times and dates, Mr Bowlett. I think he'd like the chance to put himself in the clear.'

Bowlett's thin, tanned, trimly whiskered face remained impassive. 'Young man not been charged with any offence, I take it?'

'No,' said Rutter reassuringly. 'It hasn't yet come to that.'

'Nor will it,' Bowlett said. 'Not been cautioned either?'

'No.'

'Good.' Bowlett slipped a gold pencil and a small note-book from his pocket. He found a page and touched it with his pencil point. 'Then you won't have asked him any questions as yet?'

'Only to establish his identity and whereabouts . . .'

'And to take him back to his rooms, to interrogate him and search the premises without authority?'

'Your client made no objection.'

'My client, Mr Rutter, is not expected to be familiar with *Moriarty's Police Procedure and Investigation*. Specifically, the section on procedure in summary and indictable cases. You, on the other hand, Mr Rutter, are expected to show such familiarity. Shall we take it from there?'

Rutter had dealt with too many of Bowlett's kind to allow his irritation to turn into blistering rage. It was the old defender's trick of bowling a bumper or two at first, to take the shine off the questioners.

'And before we begin,' Bowlett went on, 'I'd like to confer with my client.'

'By all means use the interview room.' Rutter led the way and then returned with Brodie to the charge room.

'You reckon our suspect could be Tarrant's bum-boy or something?' Brodie asked. 'An alibi for half an hour

206

before the rest! Smart-pants lawyer waiting the minute he gets to the station! How does he rate that?'

Rutter shrugged. 'Ask Tarrant.'

'You see Sandboy as next boss of the underworld?'

Rutter chuckled and relaxed. 'No, Frank. But then I didn't foresee the last ones. And they were dafter and uglier than Sandboy. I'd say it's time we gave old Bowlett a nudge. Sandboy's got the right to be fed and watered before we go any further.'

In the heat of the closed room at half past ten, Bowlett sat down on the far side of the table next to Sandboy, Rutter and Brodie faced them. Above the bare table, the white china shades cast a bleak glare through the haze of cigarette smoke. Rutter noticed that the summer night had brought beads of perspiration to the young man's dark hairline.

While Bowlett opened his notebook again, Rutter went through the formality of informing Sandboy that he need not say anything unless he wished to do so, but whatever he did say would be taken down in writing and might be given in evidence. Then he relaxed.

'What we're giving you, Sandboy, is the last chance you're likely to get to put yourself in the clear before the wheels get set in motion. A chance to tell your own story in such a way that we believe it. Fair enough?'

'I am in the clear,' Sandboy said. 'I don't need putting there.'

Bowlett looked up with a quick smile. 'May we get this straight, Mr Rutter? Are you inviting Mr Sandboy to tell a story or to make a formal witness statement? You can't do both. Which is this?'

'Neither,' Rutter said. 'We ask questions, he answers

them. Fair enough? If he does so to my satisfaction, he can go home any time.'

'He can go home anyway,' Bowlett said crisply. 'A matter of judges' rules. Unless you charge him with a specific offence. Mr Sandboy tells you that he is in the clear. Mr Manders and his business partner Mr Tarrant, and the cashier Mrs Hallam, and the circle usherette, all saw him at various times between half-past two and just after three o'clock last Saturday afternoon. If that is so, there is an end to this investigation, so far as my client is concerned.'

Beyond the half-open metal slats of the blinds, a hawkmoth pattered insistently against the glass, the branches of a tree shifted under a weight of leaves. Blue smoke continued to spiral into the glare of the white china shades. Rutter stared at the ill-concealed smirk on Bowlett's narrow face.

'Mr Sandboy can best decide himself what he thinks important. And he'd be well advised to decide now. A young man by the name of Gillis was knocked down and killed by a car at eleven fifty-five on Saturday morning, shortly after attempting an armed robbery on Lawsons Cash Jewellers in Dalgetty Street. A waitress in Lyons Tea shop on the Hampstead Road saw Gillis and another man – answering your client's description and wearing your client's raincoat – about ten minutes before the attempted robbery.'

'We know it was his raincoat, do we? We identified it on him, did we?'

'A raincoat which Mr Sandboy admits to being his was found hanging with Gillis's in a nearby office block on Monday. With your experience, Mr Bowlett, what would you expect a jury to conclude?'

Bowlett shrugged, as if it was not of great concern to him. 'My information is that the raincoat in question has not been in my client's possession the last five months. May I ask you, Mr Rutter, what you would expect a jury to conclude from that?'

Rutter ignored this and turned to Sandboy. 'How well did you know Gillis?'

'Quite well.' There was a slight movement of Sandboy's eyes which suggested that he had not expected this line of questioning again.

'When did you first meet him?'

'A year or so back. He was down on holiday. We met and got talking. Had a few drinks. Picked up a couple of girls. Usual things.'

'You met often after that?'

Sandboy took a cigarette from a packet of Capstans. He sprang the flame from a tarnished silver-coloured lighter. 'He came down a few times. I met him in London, last year. Matter of fact, we went to the Windmill together. Saw Dicky Dash.' He stopped suddenly, his eyes moving, as if he felt he had gone too far.

'And the last time you saw him was when he came down to visit you in March and you lent him your raincoat?'

'I don't recall that I seen him since then.'

'Ever go out to his rooms in Harringay?'

Another line of sweat was glimmering, this time along the clean-shaven upper lip. In his need to respond promptly he stumbled in the answer. 'I might have done. Yes, I did. Only he wasn't there.'

'How long ago?'

'Not lately.'

'Before or after last Christmas, for example?'

'Before,' Sandboy said, nodding affirmatively. 'Quite a bit before. Definitely.'

'All right,' Rutter sounded satisfied.

There was no mistaking the relief as Sandboy relaxed again.

'Do you know Roy Spurgeon?'

Sandboy tried the furrowed brow of honest recollection. Then he sat back. 'No. Can't say I do. Not that I know of.'

'That seems odd,' Rutter said slowly. 'If you went to Gillis's rooms and someone told you he wasn't there, surely that would have been the other tenant in the house.'

Sandboy shrugged. 'If you say so.'

'Roy Spurgeon.'

'If that's who it was. I got no idea.'

'You think he might recognize you again?'

'Mr Rutter!' Bowlett laid his gold pencil neatly down the centre of his open notebook. 'This is a preposterous line of questioning! Only Mr Spurgeon can tell you whether he would recognize my client.'

'Fair enough,' Rutter said reasonably, ignoring Bowlett and concentrating on Sandboy again. 'You saw Mr Spurgeon and he saw you. Would you know him again?'

Sandboy was looking scared now, sailing into uncharted depths, sitting so upright on the hard chair that his thin neck stuck up rather absurdly from the white collar of his shirt.

'I suppose I might.'

'So if Roy Spurgeon says he could pick you out of a line of men, you suppose he might be right?'

Bowlett seemed about to say something but thought better of it.

210

'I suppose he might. How can I say? It's only you says it was him I saw.'

Rutter took a small head-and-shoulders photograph from his pocket and laid it on the table. 'That him?'

Sandboy's eyes moved halfway to Bowlett, searching for the right answer. There was none.

'I suppose it might be him. I think it was, as I recollect. At the house in Harringay. Yes.'

'Well before last Christmas?'

The expression on Sandboy's face was that of the pinioned man who feels the first creak of the trap opening under him. He said nothing.

'Would it interest you,' Rutter asked gently, 'to know that until this March Spurgeon was in Glasgow? That he was, in fact, a prisoner in Barlinnie gaol until February?'

'Then it wasn't him at Harringay!' Frank Brodie listened as Sandboy's voice jumped a semitone higher.

'All right,' said Rutter in the same reassuring voice. 'So if Roy Spurgeon can pick you out, it must be because you and he saw one another on a later occasion. Right?'

'If you say so.'

'Such as last Saturday morning. Near Dalgetty Street at about eleven thirty.'

'Mr Rutter,' Bowlett's voice was quieter this time but the steel-spring twang was tauter, 'I shall advise Mr Sandboy to answer no more questions of this kind. They are not directed to matters of fact but attempts at conjecture. You must employ your evidence or witnesses as you think best. However, the use of photographs in an interview of this kind puts an end to any possibility of Mr Sandboy being asked to identify Mr Spurgeon or vice versa.'

'I don't doubt it,' Rutter said indifferently. 'If anyone

identifies your client as having been in Dalgetty Street last Saturday, it won't be Mr Spurgeon.'

'Then I can't see the point of this,' Bowlett said sharply.

'I don't doubt that either,' Rutter said, 'but later on you may.'

'Saturday!' Sandboy now seemed to be making a direct appeal to Rutter's good nature. 'What more do you want? Saturday morning I was in my rooms, Queen's Road. Had a bath, washed some clothes. I have to do it then, not being back till after eleven at night. No one saw me in the bath. How would they? I had some sardines on toast there for lunch. Just after two, I went out, walked to the picture-house. I was the first one there. I usually am, having to thread the projectors and get it all set up. Just about half-past two, I got there. I went up to the circle and then stopped for a piss. I came out and went up the stairs to the projection box. Must have been when Mr Tarrant saw me.'

Rutter clenched his teeth lightly. Bowlett's 'conference' with his client had clearly been the point at which Tarrant's 'evidence' was revealed to Sandboy.

'I knew someone passed across behind me,' Sandboy said, 'only I never turned, needing to get the projectors threaded up. Doors open ten to three. After we got started at three, the main film came on about ten past. The sound seemed a bit boxy. They got Western Electric Reproduction, so it shouldn't be. I went down to the stalls to check. I saw Maureen, Mrs Hallam and Mr Manders. And I spoke to them all. That was what happened on Saturday. I went home about eleven.'

Bowlett had made no attempt to interrupt this appeal. Now he turned to Rutter and Brodie. 'Whereas your suggestion, gentlemen, is that Mr Sandboy somehow equipped himself with a car and came to London. That he was on foot in the Hampstead Road at about noon. From there he got to a car, perhaps five minutes later. He drove twenty miles across London. There's a speed limit of thirty miles an hour. There's traffic lights, traffic jams, road junctions. In case you need to know, your people reckon a properly trained police driver couldn't do it under an hour in such conditions. So it's now after one o'clock. Then he's got a hundred miles and more through busy Saturday traffic as well as through several major towns or cities. I spoke to your people about that too. They reckon another two and a half hours minimum. So it's gone half-past three and he's still got to get rid of the car and walk to the Luxor Picturedrome. Mr Tarrant saw him there an hour before that. Three other people saw him there almost half an hour before that.'

'Your client knows about cars . . .'

'Listen,' Bowlett said, 'anyone that knows about cars would never try a drive of that sort in that time. He'd need to be a professional trained driver to get there by three thirty, let alone two thirty. As for the railway journey, you know already what I found out today. The next train after eleven thirty on Saturday morning left Waterloo at twelve thirty-five. It ran late and arrived at five minutes past three, half an hour after Mr Tarrant saw my client going up to the projection box. Why don't you wrap this whole thing up?'

'There's an identity parade in the morning,' Rutter said coldly. 'That's why.'

Bowlett shot his cuffs and folded his hands.

'I thought your object was to clear up the details now and end the matter. Sitting here listening, I'd say you'd got even less of a case against my client now than you had half an hour ago. You might be well advised to let it drop and look elsewhere.'

Rutter got to his feet. 'We'll talk about that in the morning, Mr Bowlett, if it's all the same to you. After our witnesses have had a look at him.'

Despite Rutter's confidence, when he and Brodie were alone in the police station's CID office, Frank Brodie sipped his canteen tea and looked across the desk. 'Tell you what, Jack. About our bet. I'd say there's five quid in your wallet that's making eyes at me.'

Chapter Twenty-Two

Merson, the uniformed inspector of 'E' Division in charge of the parade, blocked Rutter's path. The vestibule of the police station was filling with volunteers to stand in line at five shillings each.

'Bowlett wants coats,' Merson said dispassionately.

'He wants what?'

'Raincoats. According to all your eyewitnesses, Gillis and the man seen with him were wearing coats and hats. If you put Sandboy out there bareheaded and in a suit, Bowlett's going to enter a complaint. If I was you, Jack, I'd give him what he wants. What I hear about this case, these parades could be your last throw. You let him get a complaint in, I doubt it'll ever go to a jury.'

Rutter glanced at the wall clock above the desk.

'We're on in fifteen minutes, Len. Where do we get twenty raincoats to fit this lot?'

'Half of them had coats anyway on a cloudy day like this. Almost all had hats. We borrow the rest from lost property and, if necessary, the duty watch's civvy wear,' Merson said. 'And Mr Bowlett's very keen on hats. That's what the little bastards were wearing, I hear.'

'Do what he wants,' Rutter said, as if no longer caring. 'I just don't want to see Sandboy's hat pulled down to his nose.'

'Thanks. And another thing. Bowlett's going to exercise his privilege of being present. I have to play this by every rule, Jack. So you stand outside, look through the glass in the door if you want. You can hear every word on the intercom. But you don't come into the room and you don't communicate with anyone that's running the parade. Sorry.'

'I don't suppose Slippery Stan would like to take over the investigation of the case for me?'

'He wouldn't touch it,' Merson said pessimistically. 'I can't say I'd blame him.' He turned on his heel and walked away to make the final arrangements.

Frank Brodie was waiting to speak as Merson turned away. 'Merson's sergeant wants to know what we're doing about Spurgeon. Does he go in a line-up or not?'

Rutter watched half a dozen of the volunteers as they formed a shuffling queue to be handed out coats and hats. 'What a fiasco! No, we're not putting Mr Spurgeon in a line-up.'

'Shall I tell them it's definite?'

'It's got to be definite, Frank. Our only witness is the old lady looking from her window. The one who saw two men talking to a third by a car. She was looking for a photo of one of the other two and she actually saw one of Spurgeon. That's all we've got on him so far. But her seeing that photograph compromises any identity parade in which she takes part. Judges' rules. Where'd they get this bunch from?'

'They mostly work in the department stores down the road.' Brodie turned and looked at them. 'Maples and Heals. It's their lunch hour. Five bob and a free meal. Plus standing in line with an armed robber. A story to thrill the lady wife back in Bromley or Orpington tonight.'

Rutter continued to stare at them morosely. 'Not good news, Frank. Bowlett's scared the wits out of Merson. We're not to be in the room when they hold the parade, nor speak to anyone. Just watch it all through the little windows in the swing doors and listen to the intercom.'

'Where's that?'

'Top floor,' Rutter nodded towards the main staircase. 'They're going to use the games room that belongs to the section house. Only place where you can stand twenty people in line. Can't use the yard outside. Too much coming and going.'

'Where's Sandboy?'

'Learning his lines from that sod Bowlett.'

Ten minutes later the last of the volunteers had gone up the stairs. Merson appeared at the landing. He beckoned Rutter and Brodie. 'You've still got Sandboy's raincoat.'

'It's been busy down the fingerprint department,' Rutter said mildly. 'Not much joy, though. Looks as if it might have been untouched by human hand it's kept so clean.'

'We had to find one for him. Mr Bowlett wouldn't have it any other way. I'm leaving Inspector Jordan to keep you company.'

The games room on the top floor had been cleared of apparatus, so that its narrow boards ran uncluttered from the swing doors through which Rutter and Brodie watched to the far end where the suspect and witnesses came in. Merson and his sergeant stood at a small table by the further doors. Nineteen men in hats and raincoats were at their places, a triangular metal number plate on the floor in front of each. Rutter watched as Sandboy was brought in at the far end.

'Look at that!' he said helplessly. 'Bloody raincoat doesn't even fit him. Halfway up his arse.'

'This is a working division,' said Jordan just behind him, 'not Simpson's of Piccadilly.'

'If our witnesses get a whisper about the volunteers being kitted with raincoats for the parade, Sandboy will look exactly like one of them in that rig.'

Jordan was unimpressed. 'He's supposed to look like one of them. Anyway, it's the faces they come to look at, not the arses.'

Rutter gave up. Sandboy, hands in the pockets of the borrowed raincoat, chose the second position from the far door.

'He's cool,' Jordan said. 'Usually they want to lose themselves in the middle. He'll be second on view.'

There was a pause, then Merson went back to the far door and opened it again. Rutter recognized the waitress from the Hampstead Road tea shop. She was wearing a light summer coat and a jaunty beret. She stood in front of the first man, looked him up and down, paused, and moved on. Sandboy, next in line, was tall enough to stare straight above her head.

'Come on!' said Rutter softly. 'Come on!'

The waitress looked Sandboy up and down. She looked at his face again, let her eyes travel down, looked up again and moved on to the third man.

'She saw him on and off for twenty minutes!' Rutter murmured for Brodie's benefit. 'She can't not pick him out!'

'Early days, Jack. She might go back when she's seen the others.'

'If she can't pick Sandboy after twenty minutes with

218

him, Frank, she's likely to be God's gift to the defence. It's that bloody raincoat!'

'I shouldn't think so.' Jordan was watching over Brodie's shoulder, breathing a light air of peppermint humbug. 'As I say, it's the face they go for.'

The waitress was almost at the end now. She looked at the last man and walked slowly back.

'Told you,' Brodie said. 'She's going to pick someone out.'

As they watched her, she touched the shoulder of a man two places short of Sandboy. Rutter shook his head. 'Why?'

'Perhaps,' Jordan said reassuringly, 'because your man wasn't in Lyons Tea shop last Saturday morning after all. How do you know he was?'

'I know,' Rutter said tersely. 'Let's just leave it at that.'

The petite grey-haired woman whom Merson was leading in now had chosen to wear a veil over her face.

'At least she was smart enough to pick Spurgeon's photo out of the album,' Brodie said helpfully.

But the veiled woman walked slowly up and down the row of men, came to the far end, looked at Merson and shook her head. She was followed by the neighbour who had seen two men in raincoats and hats running from the lane behind Lawsons into the road at the far end. Rutter's heart beat faster as the witness made his way down the row, walked back and stood in front of Sandboy. He stood looking, first at the face, then down and up again. Something about the mackintosh had caught his eye. He turned round and made a comment very quietly to Merson. Merson asked him a question and the man shook his head.

Rutter stood back from the little window in the swing doors.

'He thinks it might be Sandboy but he can't be sure! I could write the speech for him.'

'More or less what he told us at the time,' Brodie said philosophically. 'They were too far off.'

The last eyewitness was the boy from the Arcos office block. He walked down the line, walked back and hesitated in front of Sandboy.

'He thinks it might be him,' Rutter said wearily, 'but he's not sure. I can't believe this. He saw the bugger twice! What more does he want? This keeps up, we'll all begin to think Sandboy must be telling the truth.'

'He's not,' Brodie said. 'You can smell him a mile off. That alibi is exactly the sort of thing someone would invent but never happens in real life.'

Jordan leaned forward again, looking over Brodie's shoulder. 'You couldn't get anything from the guard on the train, ticket inspector, anyone travelling?'

'No,' Rutter said irritably. 'Anyway, if you believe his witnesses, he was in that projection box about twenty-five minutes before the train got in. We'd have to break that first.'

'Wasn't there a woman who saw them outside the Arcos office and a man in the New Argyll cafe?'

Rutter snorted at the absurdity of it. 'They turned turtle at the second interview. Memory fading already. Couldn't be sure. Wouldn't like to say. That was them. Two of the nation's finest.'

Merson's sergeant was walking towards them.

'Inspector would like to know if you still want Miss Rayner from Lawsons to try identifying the voice.'

'Yes,' Rutter said sourly. 'You brought her here, so you give her something to do.'

Before Rayner's daughter was admitted, the sergeant went down the line distributing scarves which the volunteers were to tie round their lower faces. When the girl came in she looked even younger than Rutter remembered, almost like a schoolgirl with her fair curly hair and blue dress. She walked up and down the row of masked men with their hats on. Each in turn said, 'If you don't act stupid, you got nothing to worry about.' The voices were flat, inept, barely distinguishable from one another. They all sounded to Rutter like out-of-work actors reading from a card at a last-chance audition.

'The emphasis, everything about it, is wrong. No one talks like that!'

But now they were on the second recital. 'Don't fire the bloody thing.' The performance was as useless as the first.

'What was the bloody thing, by the way?' Jordan asked. Rutter shrugged.

'Small-bore revolver, so far as we can make out. She looked through some pictures and picked out about half a dozen likely weapons.'

Merson was ushering the girl out.

'End of case,' Rutter said. 'All this evidence has to be handed to Bowlett now. Judges' rules. This goes to trial, every one of those witnesses is going to be called by the defence. Plus four people to say he was in the Luxor picture-house. Five more to say they don't recognize him as the man who was in London.'

'Except there won't be a trial, will there?' Jordan's peppermint breath was close behind him again. 'This lot wouldn't get past a magistrates' court.'

Brodie pushed open the door as the volunteers were thanked and began to disperse to their canteen lunch. 'You reckon he's clear, Jack?'

'I reckon he's a bloody little liar, Frank, with Slippery Stan Bowlett behind him. But short of Sonny Tarrant sobbing brokenly on the charge-room desk, we're shafted. I've never know an ID parade go so wrong.'

They went back downstairs and found Merson.

'Where's Sandboy?' Rutter asked.

'Mr Bowlett's making arrangements to return him home. Oh yes, and your lot will be getting the bill for his travel. You'd better come and do some paperwork, Jack.'

Brodie waited for about twenty minutes. Then he looked up to see Rutter coming from the direction of Merson's office, his face flushed with anger.

'Frank! We've been set up, not shafted! By Bowlett!'

Brodie stared at him.

'Out here,' Rutter said, leading the way to the metal gallery above the yard. 'Did you know that Sandboy had a paper in his pocket?'

'What paper?'

'Christ! A newspaper, of course! In the pocket of his raincoat! Merson's sergeant saw it as Sandboy walked out at the end. He'd had his hands in his raincoat pockets when he walked in. Dead easy to cover a newspaper that way. Take your hand out, even move it a bit, and it's there for anyone to see who's standing directly in front of you. As each of those witnesses was! Not you nor me at one end. Not Merson, seeing him from one side, on the slant. Just the witness standing in front.'

'But what newspaper?'

'Only today's *Evening Standard*. That's all. Lunchtime

edition, which they put on the streets about ten in the morning! Who gave it him? How the hell did it get there?'

'I never saw it, Jack.'

'Nor did anyone until the whole thing was over.' Rutter looked about him as if he might spot the culprit. 'No one saw it until the parade was over, except the witnesses. And what's more those witnesses had been in a room with a chaperone beforehand to make sure they never saw Sandboy by accident.'

'Still not with you, Jack.'

'What do you bet some woodentop puts his head round the door and says sorry for the delay but they just have to fit the volunteers out with raincoats. So there's Sandboy in a coat that's up his backside, making him look like he's a volunteer just come in.'

'They couldn't be sure . . .'

'And what's a thousand times worse, there's a newspaper that could only be got by a man that was on the streets in the last hour or so. The witnesses knew yesterday, when they were asked to come in, that the suspect was already under arrest. So it couldn't be him if he'd got today's *Evening Standard* in his pocket! What a skate-arse trick!'

'Bowlett . . .'

'Of course it's bloody Bowlett. Sandboy just says the paper must have been in the pocket when he put the coat on. Bollocks!'

'Perhaps it . . .'

'No, it wasn't! Worse luck, any investigation of how the parade was run would have to be by Merson's lot. And, as Merson says, it's not against the law to attend an identity parade with a newspaper in your pocket.'

'So what now?'

Rutter studied his polished toecaps. 'I don't know, Frank. One thing, though. You don't go this far to spring a no-hoper like Sandboy unless there's a bloody sight more to him than appears so far. Bowlett!'

Brodie studied his polished toecaps. 'Bowlett's only the monkey, Jack. Tarrant's the organ-grinder. The only person who could have an interest in Sandboy like that must be Tarrant. He can save him or bury him, or both.'

August

Olympia

Chapter Twenty-Three

Yvonne moved on all fours, the sheet draped over her, like a child romping in bed. The auburn hair was loose and disordered. In the warmth of the afternoon, a thin strand of it clung to the side of her face.

'A bad boy,' she said severely. 'I think I always guessed it. They must have had a good reason to come for you.'

She lowered herself on to him and began moving like a slow swimmer against the water.

'And they let me go for some reason,' Sandboy said nonchalantly. 'Such as, I didn't do what they thought I'd done. Walk into a shop in London with a gun? I was here. Even Manny saw me.'

Yvonne stopped moving and looked up at him, her chin touching his breast bone. 'You could be a vicious little bastard,' she said, as if encouraging him. 'I can quite believe it.'

He could see that the idea warmed her. 'They reckon women get excited by vicious bastards,' he said casually. 'The gentle touch don't work half as well. It's true. You only got to look around you. You ever see some big-time gangster without a cutie on his arm? They get the hots from how he lives.'

She laughed, scrambled up and sidled towards the sunlit window. Concealed by the edge of the net curtains,

she drew them across the wide panes. In the warm afternoon, Sandboy heard the fountain playing across the lily
pool.

'Don't close the curtains!' he said wearily. 'It's bloody
stifling. You need some air in here.'

She sprang back to bed. 'Though love may be blind,
Sandboy, the neighbours aren't. Where does "Sandboy"
come from, by the way? Something you've never told me.
Real name? Just a nickname?'

He folded his hands behind his head and let her
sprawl naked across him. 'It's a trade, that's all it is. A
name from a trade. When they cast iron or brass in a
foundry, they make a mould to pour the metal in. First
they make it in sand. Whoever does that is a sandboy.
They start at fourteen.'

'Happy as a sandboy?'

'Because it's a good number. Not like being a boy
down the mines. Not like trundling hot metal all over the
place in a moulding shop. More of a skill. You never told
me about this business with you and Nina, while we're
on about secrets, went all shy.'

'What business?'

'Holding hands in the movie show, when all the lights
are low? That night we had the Ivor Novello downstairs.
I never seen you do that before. Something going on, is
there? You never answered when I asked before. That
why Sonny Tarrant whacked your face for you?'

He felt the tension in her and saw her blush. But it
was the memory of Tarrant, not Nina.

'Little Madam needs her hand held. That's all. Like a
little girl. Reassurance. She's not half grown up yet. Useful
to have around sometimes, but no competition.'

'She's seventeen,' Sandboy said thoughtfully. 'That's

grown-up enough. I still dream about her sometimes. Don't mean to, just happens. Like kissing goodbye after a party, only suddenly it's her mouth and her tongue. Or we're alone, kissing and cuddling. That's all. Not screwing her or anything like that.'

Yvonne pulled the sheet clear. 'Sounds to me like a waste of a good dream.'

Sandboy shook his head. 'I never thought about her until the first dream. The tongue in the mouth after a party. Then I had about a dozen of them. Like thought waves in the night.'

Yvonne slid off and lay beside him. 'Every so often there's a man that thinks he can get Little Madam's knickers off. The look of her. They think she's dying for it!'

Sandboy laughed. 'Isn't she? You think I should try?'

'Not unless you want frostbite on your cherry.'

'Sorry?'

'What she's got between her legs, young man, is like the icebox in the frigidaire. Try it, if you think it's worth it. It's not worth it, I can tell you.'

'I suppose you'd have to think that. If you reckon she's the competition.'

Yvonne propped herself on an elbow.

'Listen. They all walk into it. They think she's like Madame Moscovich, the Moscow witch in the George Formby song.' She turned her head and looked at him, fingers drawing down the corners of her eyes. 'That's what they want. Those green Slav eyes, pale blond hair like a bloody Garbo. Those glances of mysterious passion. Nina and her look of exotic sensuality.'

Sandboy wished, too late, that he had kept his thoughts to himself. Yvonne laughed.

'You know where our exotic little Madame Moscovich was born? In a street at the back of Wandsworth Common station. Somewhere in Balham. Name of Smith. And she wasn't christened Nina. She made that up. Nora. Nora Smith. You'd need a lot of Greta Garbo to live that down. Nina Manders sounds much more fun. As for mysterious passions, have you ever bothered to listen to her? She's no interest in you or anyone else. She doesn't even pretend she has. Try changing the subject and two minutes later we're back again. Nina thinks this and Nina wants that. I found out something else not long ago. Our mystery princess's father was a plumber in Balham. Arnold Smith.'

Sandboy stared at the ceiling and said nothing, daunted by the sudden bitterness of Yvonne's outburst. Then the bed began to shake with her muffled laughter as she giggled. 'She was only a plumber's daughter, but she knows how to tighten your nuts . . .'

Sandboy laughed as well. The worst was past. 'What about Manny and her? Perhaps he should give her one.'

Yvonne looked at him and put on her official BBC announcer's voice. 'Manny isn't, shall we say, active in that department any more. She's just his little girl – rather an elderly little girl. But that suits Nina fine. Manny gives her everything she wants. And she doesn't have to bestow her favours on him in return. Not burdened with the social niceties is our Nina. Just a graceless little baggage. What she needed long ago was a good whipping.' Yvonne paused and leant over him. 'I say, Sandboy! That might be your way in. Who knows? It might cure her. She might love you for it!'

Sandboy took Yvonne by the hair, pulled her face down and kissed her.

'This London trip . . .' he said presently.

Yvonne tickled his nose with a strand of her hair. 'That's just you and me. And Freddie can look after Little Madam if she's around. Bookings at the Strand Palace. There'll be Larry Samson's party with Jack and a supper with Ivor. Manny's not on for it, of course. Too busy keeping tabs on Sonny.'

'And Nina comes?'

Yvonne now began to sulk. 'She can come if she wants to. Up to her. But we keep her on a leash. Nora Smith meets Jack Buchanan? Nora Smith seen sharing a joke with Ivor Novello? I don't think so, somehow, do you? We're going to have some fun, though, you and I. Aren't we? Unless you want Naughty Nora in your dreams, of course, freezing the living daylights out of you.'

She tickled his nose again and Sandboy brushed the hair away.

'The build-up you give her,' he chuckled, 'she sounds bloody irresistible. You got some spite for her.'

'Don't be a fool. It's just the truth.'

Then, as he watched her, Yvonne yawned and rolled on to her back.

'Lady Blue is waiting to rehearse,' she said.

The garden was in shadow when Sandboy moved from the bed. Yvonne was already sitting naked on the dressing stool before the oval mirror. He came round and kissed her on the side of the neck. The full light of the August afternoon had faded from the curtains as the sun moved round behind the house.

He laid his finger beside a hard red bump on her

upper arm. 'You been bitten,' he said gently, 'that's a whopper.'

'So it is,' she said quickly, and blushed at him unaccountably in the glass.

Chapter Twenty-Four

'Got a match?'

Tarrant turned from the blank shutter of the projection box, eyebrows raised in anticipation. Sandboy hesitated. Despite the orange safety triangles on the blue boxes, smoking among the reels of film broke the Luxor's first rule of security. Tarrant read and understood his silence. The lip rose a little.

"'S all right son. I'm goin' out the escape platform. Your boss won't mind. This bloody epic goes on a couple of hours yet.'

Sandboy slipped his hand into his jacket and offered a slim squat lighter, a silver-coloured Ronson Cadet, its clean shape as squat and slim as the conning tower of a U-boat. Tarrant took it and turned back to the projection shutter. Then he looked round with a twist of his mouth. 'This thing's no good. Makes the tobacco taste of petrol 'aven't you got a strike, for fuck's sake?'

Sandboy felt in his pocket and handed over the box.

Several hundred children, gathered from schools and youth clubs, filled the auditorium for the morning matinée of *Olympia*. The title said everything to them. On the screen the athletes were now running the marathon, well spaced out, plodding resolutely along forest paths near Berlin.

Then the music changed and the camera cut to a sparkle of bright water, the starting gun, the sails of little yachts skimming across the Havel or the Wannsee. But always it came back at last to the great white oval of the new Olympic stadium with its square modern towers, rising among the chimneys of Berlin's industrial zone. The curve of the arena was now black with the tense crowds of spectators, as a roar greeted the lone Japanese runner returning first from the long race.

Tarrant opened the fire door and stepped out into a glare of noon sun. Beyond the promenade rails, a slack tide sparkled in dancing flashes, like lozenges of flame, the waves meeting and recoiling in jagged flashes of brilliance.

The long Olympic film had become dull to him. Tarrant cared nothing for its endless races and field events. It was the ceremonial of the games which had swept his thoughts along. A Wagnerian theme unveiled the misty remains of ancient Olympia. The runner with the flaming torch passed across the map of Europe, through Athens, Belgrade, Budapest, Prague, entering at last the long modern avenues of Berlin, hung with the banners of a new imperial order. Sonny Tarrant's heart was quickened by the searchlight displays in the stadium at night, the pagan hymn of the uniformed squadrons, the roman salute of the leader.

The camera, like his own thoughts, returned again to the figure in the imperial box, the god of life and death. It was a commonplace profile, less remarkable than Tarrant's own. Yet it might stamp out the insect existence of a man's life in a twist of anger or spare him with a tight smile. The cut of the military cap, the smoothly gloved hands and the belted tunic showed a man who would conquer through blood. Even a fool like Manny had seen that. No Loon of Lossiemouth. No pig-faced, pig-breeding Stanley Baldwin. Once, on the screen, the close-up lens had caught a pulse beating in the leader's cheek, beating in time with the excitement of millions.

The god of millions. The phrase came to Sonny Tarrant, as he stared across the roofs and chimney pots towards the crowded beaches and the summer sea. The film played again in his mind. The thrill he could not explain, even to himself, came from the image of this god, or rather from this god who was also a gangster. Was it the same excitement which drew so many women to admire the plain-faced little man? The thrill, the threat of the gangster-god?

Tarrant recalled an adventure not many months before. The newsreel on the screen of the Luxor had called it THE NIGHT OF THE LONG KNIVES. Men who thought themselves safe and favoured for years to come had all been put to death in a few hours. No trials and no appeals were needed. Generals, commanders, loyal confederates of the gangster-god had been destroyed by him like so many summer flies.

Some woken from sleep, some taken even in the act of love, they had found themselves surrounded by armed troopers. No explanation was given, no protest answered. Only a command to get up, to be taken into the courtyard and shot the next minute. Some had argued, all had pleaded, not understanding, demanding an audience with the gangster whom they had raised to be their saviour. The newsreel had shown the written answer: a stone wall, its surface chipped or shattered by bullets and marked by the darkness of blood.

Not a man nor a woman whom Tarrant could remember had thought the worse of their god. Not Manny. Not Yvonne. None of their kind. His mouth tightened at the humour of it. There were shudders, of course. Of terror? Of pleasure? Of both? Once it was done, there were newspaper stories of women with money and position who had gone to put themselves at the disposal – at the mercy – of their beloved tyrant.

He lit his cigarette and watched the crowds unwinding along the promenade and through the gardens. His mind had returned to the story of the long knives in the past months, because he saw himself at a similar stage in his career. Stern justice had been necessary in the progress of the gangster-god. A new leader was in no danger from his defeated and terrified enemies. Those who had assisted his rise were the men who might destroy him. Sooner or later, they would claim a debt of gratitude. Only the god could judge the dangerous moment when their demands gathered strength. Then it was necessity, not callousness, which required that the astonished protests and the appeals for justice should fall silent among fusillades that rattled and rang within the walls of ancient courtyards.

Thinking of this, Tarrant threw the cigarette end away, watching it fall and burst in a dozen sparks on the tarmac below. There was too much else in his life that called him to action. Even his brief worship of the gangster-god must wait its turn. The last marching hymn of the black-uniformed legions had fallen quiet in the auditorium. In its place, the soundtrack of the Monday newsreel was running on the Bell and Howell projector: 'The loveliest of a hundred girls! . . . No wonder she's smiling. Wouldn't you be, if you had been chosen as beauty queen from a hundred entrants in the Modern Venus Parade . . .?'

He pushed open the iron door and stepped into the dusk of the projection box. Sandboy was rewinding the last reel of *Olympia* on the Gaumont Kalee. The screen was now filled by the image of a white, modern, swan's neck high-diving board, rising above a walled bathing pool with pink-tiled promenades surrounding its green water. The six finalists were parading on an open-air cat-walk before holidaymakers in deckchairs, each of the girls in a thigh-length bathing tunic and high-heeled shoes. Beside them was Dicky Dash at a compère's microphone on a tall stand. There was striped bunting, a sign advertising a licensed bar and tea-room.

Tarrant watched through the next shutter. The three blondes and three brunettes turned, walked, and walked back again, pausing and posturing. Such young women were an irritation to him, reminding him of much that was best forgotten. In the world that was to be, they meant less than a set of child's dolls, taken out of their boxes, played with and put away again. Ignoring the vapid commentary, he turned to Sandboy.

'They buried your friend Gillis yet?'

'They said so. I never knew him that well. Saying I did was down to that ponce Rutter.'

'Don't call him that,' Tarrant said affectionately. 'He's a good man, Mr Rutter is. Decent enough fellow. He's got a job to do, like we all have. If he was lookin' for work, I'd take him on up the Garden Royal any day. So what'd your friend have to do that for? Runnin' across in front of the traffic? Someone after him, was there?'

'I couldn't say, Mr Tarrant.'

''Course you couldn't!' Tarrant said heartily. 'You

wasn't there! And a good thing too. Else it might have been you went under that limo.'

Sandboy took the rewound reel of film and slid it into its box. Tarrant grinned. 'Still, that's behind us now.' He looked about him at the projection box. 'Bloody old miser, Manders is. He got no reason. He's well-lined now, with all the money put into his business for him. We'll make him do somethin' better for you than this. He could get you a rewind boy for a start. Give you some time to play.'

Sandboy murmured his thanks. Tarrant, in general, disliked physical contact. All the same, he let his hand drop on the young man's shoulder. 'Somethin' better'n this shithouse,' he said confidently, and went out.

Sandboy waited until the footsteps had cleared the stairs down to the circle lounge. Then he drew from his pocket the two-inch column of newsprint which had come to him through the post that morning in an otherwise empty envelope. There had been time to read it more than once before the matinée but after a single reading he seemed to know it by heart.

Royston James Spurgeon (23) of Hamilton Street, Glasgow was remanded in custody to Duke Street prison by the Sheriff's court yesterday on five counts under the Larceny Act 1916. The accused man is charged with handling property knowing it to be stolen. Inspector Craigmyler, in evidence, told the court that Spurgeon had been apprehended following attempts to sell three fur coats and two mink stoles to garment factors in Saltmarket and Gallowgate. Inspector Rutter told the bench that the Metropolitan Police also wished to question Spurgeon in the matter of

several thefts from retail premises in north
London . . .

The death of McGouran had been reported to him in
the same way, by a news clipping sent through the post.
But that clipping had come from Gillis. Sandboy supposed
that this one was cut from a Glasgow paper. Whether it
was or not, it had been sent by someone who had known
his address. Someone who must have known that the
furs had been in the possession of Gillis. Someone who
perhaps knew that he, Gillis and McGouran had robbed
Pender.

Tarrant? It was possible, but Tarrant had saved him
from Rutter. Tarrant could have destroyed him twice over
by now, if that was the game. Perhaps it was a kindly
warning, just as someone had taken the Walden Safety
Revolver from under the floor of his room before the
police could get there. That had saved him, as Tarrant
had saved him. He dared not ask Tarrant, but surely it
added up to a near certainty that Sonny or one of Sonny's
friends had put him in the clear?

He looked at the clipping. Who else? Was it Rutter?
It was not beyond that bastard to stampede a suspect. But
he was free of Rutter and Dalgetty Street. Thanks to
Sonny Tarrant again. Could it be Pender? But there had
not been a squeak from Pender since the night of the
robbery, seven months ago. And how could Pender know
Spurgeon?

Spurgeon himself had done it! Who else in Glasgow
would send it? Even Sonny Tarrant had no reason to
connect Sandboy with Glasgow. Spurgeon had got bail at
the next hearing. Or else Spurgeon had put someone else
up to it. Spurgeon could have got his address from the

papers Gillis had left. Somehow Spurgeon had managed to tip him off.

It made complete sense. He stared at the gaunt metal dinosaurs of the projectors. Spurgeon was no hero. He was looking out for himself, of course. But if Sandboy was implicated now, it might go against Spurgeon. It would put Spurgeon in Dalgetty Street when Lawsons was burgled. It might even tie Spurgeon to the Pender robbery and the old woman dying.

Who else was in Glasgow but Spurgeon? Who else had so much to lose if Sandboy was caught? Who else might know his address? Sandboy sat down and knew that the worst was over. What lay ahead was a week squiring Yvonne in London with Freddie looking the other way. Parties and theatres of the kind that the movie screen showed. Yvonne's friends. Cocktails with Jack Buchanan. Supper parties with Ivor Novello. Dicky Dash and the song Yvonne had written for him. The Strand Palace with Yvonne naked all night in Sandboy's bed.

There was only one thing to be done with Spurgeon, Gillis, McGouran, Pender, the whole bloody business. It was history now. Over and done with. Even the press clipping was a liability.

He reached for the lid of a floor-polish tin, which served him as a surreptitious ashtray. He picked up the Ronson Cadet, which Tarrant had left on the table. The flint sparked with a faint metallic smoke, failed and then flared at the second attempt. It needed more fuel, that was all. Its tiny starved flame touched the two-inch column of newsprint and caught it. Sandboy dropped the scrap of paper into the metal lid, watching it writhe in fire until it flaked into ash.

September

Strand Palace

Chapter Twenty-Five

The midnight-blue Chrysler Airflow, white-walled tyres like a Chicago battle wagon, belonged to the business partnership of Tarrant and Manders. Outside, it had the lines of a Brooklands racer or a Coniston Water speedboat. Inside, it was fawn-coloured leatherette and chrome, a miniature smoking room on wheels. Sandboy drove with Yvonne beside him and Freddie in the back seat.

On the road to London, Freddie and Yvonne cried with laughter and excitement. Through the streets of Southampton they reminded each other of the funniest bits in the new Jack Buchanan movie. Yvonne flung herself round in the seat to shout at Freddie above the noise of the traffic. Freddie obliged her as the good-natured tweed-suited buffoon, moustached and pop-eyed, red-faced from drink. Yvonne's eyes glittered at him but it was only the pitch of her voice that made her seem drunk at ten o'clock in the morning. Sandboy smelt no drink.

'There's the first bit in India, where Jack's a subaltern,' she shouted at Freddie, 'and the old colonel always says, "What! What!" and Jack says, "Why? Why?"'

They laughed at this until Freddie began to cough. Through the busy streets, he cried, 'What! What!' and Yvonne shouted back, 'Why? Why?' – 'What! What!' ...

'Why? Why?' . . . 'What! What!' . . . 'Why? Why?' Sandboy glanced sideways. He had never seen her like this. She had become a vulgar sharp-eyed little animal or perhaps an hysterical child.

'Oh, he's so wonderful!' she cried. 'And then he's a knight in the middle ages and one of the other knights comes up and says, "What's afoot?" and Jack says, "Twelve inches, I think!" '

They howled together. Yvonne noticed Sandboy's silence.

'What's the matter with you, Sandy? Lost your tongue?' And they laughed again, as if it was the best joke of the morning. Sandboy turned the wheel a little on a curve beyond Eastleigh.

'I never saw the film,' he said lamely.

'Some projectionist,' Freddie bellowed and they began a game of 'She was only . . !' which lasted through the ancient streets of Winchester.

'She was only a postmaster's daughter,' Yvonne sang, 'but she knew how to handle the male . . .'

'She was only a cow-keeper's daughter,' Freddie shouted back, 'but she sure could tell one from an udder . . .'

'She was only a magistrate's daughter, but she knew what to do on the bench . . .'

'She was only a bandmaster's daughter, but she couldn't resist a beau fiddle . . .'

'I say! I say! I say!' Yvonne shouted at Freddie. 'I know a girl whose assets are immense!'

'So she's got class with a capital A!'

They stopped at a mock-Tudor roadhouse for coffee, after which Yvonne got into the back seat with Freddie. Sandboy listened as they talked more quietly of the week to come, of night clubs and supper clubs. The size of somebody's dinner bills at Ciro's and the amount of the tips the waiters earned. To Sandboy, they were like two believers discussing their places in heaven. Heaven for them was with King Edward and his party, dancing at the Embassy Club. With Noël Coward at his habitual place in the Monseigneur Bar before the curtain went up on another *Cavalcade*. In the Empire Room at the Trocadero. At the Bon Viveur in Shepherd Market or the Marquis de Casa Maury's new cinema in Curzon Street, where the patrons sat in blue armchairs to watch the film.

'Talk of Edward,' Freddie said. 'Chap I know that was in New York says he's got a new one. American. Something different. In all the papers over there.'

'Good for him,' Yvonne clapped her hands.

Then the two of them played a game with cards marked by questions or answers, shouting out their bids: 'Is your soup spoon a musical one?' 'Only in my bath.' 'Are your teeth your own?' 'Would a nudist colony accept you?' 'Only in the mating season.'

The last answer was so neat that Yvonne accused Freddie of cheating and they fought playfully over the rest of the cards on the fawn leatherette of the back seat. Sandboy drove on towards Waterloo station, where Nina would be waiting.

'Little Madam doesn't travel by car!' Yvonne had said sharply. 'First-class rail for Little Madam.'

As he drove, Sandboy calculated that he had not dreamt of Nina since the night he had stayed in Gillis's rooms, before the attempt on Lawsons. Perhaps, since Yvonne's denunciation of her, he was cured of Little Madam. Or perhaps, as Nina, she had gone deeper into his dreams, deeper than he could remember when he woke. It was Yvonne, with a dancer's figure that most girls of sixteen might envy, who had changed more than Little Madam. She showed a brittle excitement on the threshold of London, as if this was her triumphal progress. She no longer seemed to hear or check herself, her laughter uncontrolled, like a farmyard snort.

He glanced in the driving mirror and saw the auburn head bowed over the cards in her hand. She was still beautiful to him but suddenly loud and vulgar. Why? There was no more reticence, no subtlety, in her. Had the bright and brittle coarseness always lurked, unnoticed until others sparked it into life? That night, in her room at the Strand Palace, he noticed a hard insect-bite redness, this time on the other arm. But he said nothing.

The foyer of the hotel put even the Garden Royal to shame. There was a new staircase walled by modernistic panels of opalescent glass, like squares of onyx lit from within. The new rectangular pillars might have framed the ceremonial way to a pharaoh's tomb.

Yvonne had made the arrangements for their stay. She and Sandboy would have adjoining rooms on one side of the bedroom corridor, Freddie and Nina on the other.

'Freddie's safe,' she murmured softly as they lay in her bed on the first night. 'Anyway, he knows the first time he got his hand in Little Madam's knickers, she'd have his arm off at the shoulder. Outrage or gratitude.'

But during the hours that followed they both seemed to sense that the nights of pleasure so carefully prepared for had begun with indefinable disappointment. All the same, there was laughter and quiet teasing in the car next morning on their way to Simpson's in Piccadilly, where he was to be fitted with a new suit at Manders' expense. On her own account, Yvonne bought him several new shirts to be worn at the week's parties.

Apart from gatherings at Manders' or Tarrant's, Sandboy knew nothing of parties. Now he talked with men and women who seemed far more interested in him than he could account for. He smoked unfamiliar cigarettes with names like Lucky Strike, Philip Morris, Caporal, and Markovich in a black and white striped box. He drank new drinks. They met casual friends in the marbled landscapes of the cocktail room at the Coventry Street Corner House or at the Criterion in Piccadilly Circus.

The next evening, from a distance, he watched Yvonne talking to Jack Buchanan in a group of his admirers. Sandboy knew now that he had seen the actor on the screen. There was no mistaking the black gloss of hair groomed to perfection, the wide forehead, high brows, dark mobile eyes. The profile was fine and intense, like a famous lawyer or a politician. But the mouth had the easy engaging smile of a romantic clown. Sandboy remembered Buchanan on the screen, tap-dancing on the snow in white tie and tails.

The star was talking to Yvonne with the exaggerated courtesy, the chivalrous smile, of a man who was not quite sure who she was. And the greedy little face with the glittering eyes was looking up at him like a docile and adoring schoolgirl, breathing the same air as her idol.

'He couldn't have been nicer,' she said to Freddie afterwards. 'We talked about the last show. Jack says he'd like nothing better than to work with me again. Not dancing, necessarily. But something in a new production. They won't start casting for a month or two. He's taking it on tour in the spring with Elsie Randolph.'

Her words were bright and confident, only the tone of her voice and the weariness in her face were wrong.

Their supper party was at the Strand Palace, after the Drury Lane performance of *Careless Rapture*. The man with the fine, shy, thoughtful face was pointed out to Sandboy by Freddie as Ivor Novello. There was always a crowd about him. It was impossible to see whether Yvonne spoke to him or not. Afterwards she said, 'Ivor's doing a new one in the spring as well, *The Crest of the Wave*. They'll all need supernumeraries and under-studies. It's as good as a promise.'

When the doors on the other side of the bedroom corridor had closed, she turned to Sandboy. 'Not tonight, Sandy. Tomorrow. Must sleep. Tomorrow, definitely. We'll make up for lost time.'

But as she kissed him, the lighting of the hotel corridor made her skin seem tighter and yet finely wrinkled. For the first time since he had known her, she looked much older than he. 'Old enough to be his mother.' The words came to mind unprompted, but she was certainly not that. Perhaps she was ill.

Alone in his room, he stood before the mirror and drew the end of his tie clear. Yvonne had shown him how to fasten it in the bold square knot that the late Prince of Wales, now the 'Bachelor King', had invented, so that it stayed firmly in place. Because it was the fashion at Fort Belvedere, it had been called the Windsor knot.

Next morning, she still looked pale and her voice was dull, as if she had not slept after all. Sandboy felt fear for her and pity. Yvonne had been so decisive in her preparations, so confident of success. She talked of a career that was only just beginning. But he saw only that the week of planned triumph and pleasure was to end in humiliation.

That afternoon, he, Freddie and Nina went to the new Chaplin film in Leicester Square, without Yvonne. She said nothing about the appointment to be kept and none of them asked her. Sandboy guessed she had gone to a doctor. That night she slept alone again, appearing next morning with the glitter almost restored to her eyes.

The evening was set aside for Dicky Dash in a supper cabaret, at a table reserved for Sandboy and the two young women by the comedian himself. This time it was Freddie who had a dinner date of his own. Sandboy watched the black polish of the dancing shoes twinkling, the silver-topped cane tumbling and twirling effortlessly in the fingers, as Dicky Dash tapped and sang through his opening number.

'Thank you very, very much, ladies and gentlemen. You are all ladies and gentlemen, aren't you? Only you got to be so careful nowadays, haven't you? Yes. Yes, you have. What? What me? Like that? No! I'm not! No, I'm not! Definitely not . . .!'

Sandboy watched him and thought of Gillis. Sitting with Gillis through the afternoon watch of non-stop *Revue-deville* on a February day. A boom of fog signals in Piccadilly. The Edgware Road tram. Samuelson's cold ill-lit shop in Praed Street. Now Dicky Dash had a violin in his hands, torturing the strings between each sentence.

'Listen, listen! Are you listening? . . . You get some fun with a fiddle, can't you? If you know where to put your fingers . . . Listen . . . Sad story. All the great violinists are dead . . . Paganini is dead . . . Joachim is dead . . . I don't feel so good myself . . .'

And Gillis was dead. And McGouran was dead.

Sandboy listened inattentively to the comic patter, repeated from the fog-bound afternoon that seemed as remote to him now as his childhood.

'And last of all, ladies and gentlemen, I mustn't say anything too rude tonight, not here. They made me promise. So, last of all, a brand new number entitled, "She may be a classy dresser, but you should see her stripped for gym . . ." No wonder they have to carry poor old Jim everywhere on a stretcher . . .'

The diners at their tables clapped and Dicky Dash grinned back at them. Their laughter and applause almost drowned his exit. Bowler-hatted and marble-eyed, he opened his arms to embrace them all.

Yvonne stood up and walked across to the waiter who had shown them in. They spoke for a moment, their heads bowed together. Then the man unhooked a red velvet rope and led her to a pass door at one side of the revue stage. Sandboy found himself, almost for the first time that week, alone with Nina. People were queuing for tables among the silk-swags and crystal mirrors of the foyer. Sandboy broke the silence. 'I seen him do her song, last winter at the Windmill. The one she wrote.'

Now that he studied her more closely, Nina's pale blond Greta Garbo hair and the green Slav eyes were spoilt by a pallid schoolgirl pudginess, absent in his dreams of her. Even in the supper club, she seemed to give off a wholesome adolescent air of soap and toothpaste.

'What song?'

'The one she wrote for him.' He began to hum it and then gave her the words. 'Who do you think you are? All the swank and la-di-da . . . I don't remember it all.'

'You are a proper fool,' she said, with no affection to

soften the words. 'She couldn't write a song, not if her life depended on it.'

Sandboy stared at her, across the little table with its neatly arranged cloth, the silver plating of the cruet and ashtray. Little Madam took a gold-coloured Christmas-present cigarette case from her bag and flipped the wheel of a matching lipstick lighter. She blew out smoke, snapping the lighter and the case shut.

'She wrote it for Dicky Dash,' Sandboy explained. 'Everyone knows that.'

'A proper fool!' Nina said again. Sandboy looked at her and knew that he was arguing with an obstinate child. 'She couldn't write a tune nor a lyric. All that happened was Manny went somewhere with her. Somewhere like this. They were introduced to that man on the stage. And she said to him or someone, "Who do you think you are?" as a sort of joke. I dare say she was a bit drunk or worse. When she said it, he laughed and said that it wouldn't make a bad title for a song. Write it? That's a joke! Any case, people like him have full-time writers working for them. Did she tell you she wrote it?'

He stared at her. Little Madam fidgeted on her chair and rearranged the folds of her skirt.

'I thought she did.'

Nina glanced up at him, as if studying him for the first time. 'It was Manny that knew Dicky Dash and Jack Buchanan. He introduced them to her. Same as Ivor Novello. They wouldn't know her otherwise, any more than if she just walked in off the street. That's how well she knows them!'

'She's gone to see him now.'

But Nina made no reply.

'Anyway,' she said at last, 'I'm glad she didn't write a

song for him. I think he's disgusting. Those jokes he tells and those rhymes.'

Sandboy continued to stare. The green-eyed mistress of his dreams with the promise of their embraces, the words in his ear, the tongue that sought his own and turned an innocent kiss into simmering lechery, was unveiled as a plain young prude. The air of perverse passion in her eyes was nothing but his own creation. And, if Yvonne was right, he was not even staring at Nina Manders but at Nora Smith from Balham.

In his anger, he decided she was not going to get away so easily. 'You've got it wrong,' he said irritably. 'She said she wrote that song.'

'Suit yourself,' Nina turned her head aside. 'I suppose you like that sort of thing. The dirty jokes and songs. I know she does.'

'They're not that bad!'

Little Madam turned to face him. 'I don't suppose they are to you. Not if you don't mind going into her bedroom behind her husband's back. Far as I'm concerned, you deserve each other. Not that you'll get away with it much longer, I dare say.'

The curtains of the revue stage opened on the next act, a black-haired woman in an ice-blue spotlight, holding a microphone close enough to her mouth to kiss. The melody glided, hesitated and glided again: 'Love is the Sweetest Thing'.

Yvonne had left him completely unprepared for Nina's hostility to them both. She had sworn to Manny's indifference. And Manny had showed no sign of curiosity, let alone jealousy, over what she did with her friends. They had taken their freedom so much for granted that Sandboy was caught without an answer. Nina made no attempt to watch the singer. She said, 'You'd believe her, wouldn't you? That man's only being nice to her now because he met her with Manny once before. You think she's ever going to be in a show? With what she drinks and everything else she sticks into herself? Don't make me laugh!'

'Everything else?'

'Hop!' Nina spoke it in a muttered whisper. 'Dope! You tell me you didn't guess? There's always a doctor in Harley Street or some clinic that will chance giving it when it's someone who can pay. She's careful, but not as careful as all that. There's marks. She tells Manny she has to go away and see a consultant about her womb or her nerves. Nerves! That's a joke!'

'She's not here to see a doctor, is she?'

'She's here to spend his money. Two years ago, he threatened to put one of those notices in the papers, saying that he wouldn't be responsible for her bills. Then they patched it up, somehow. Then there was you. You can't live in the same house with her and not know what's going on.'

'There's nothing going on!' Sandboy knew he had to say it, whether it sounded right or not.

But Nina seemed no longer to care about adultery or deceit. 'Fool!' she said again. Folding her skirt and turning sideways to him, she began at last to watch the stage. Neither of them spoke again until Yvonne came back through the pass door.

'He's a scream!' she said, sitting down again, 'and so nice. It's all put on for the act. Once he's off-stage, he's a natural gentleman.'

Nina turned her head. 'Ask you to write a new song for him, did he?'

Yvonne hesitated and glanced at Sandboy. 'Oh, you know, we talked about it. What counts is getting the right idea. The first line and the rhythm. Once they're fixed in your head, you can go on forever.'

'Some people can, I suppose,' Nina said, and looked away from them.

Sandboy felt a brief fear that Little Madam might accuse Yvonne in front of him. But Nina had again lost interest in everyone except herself. A waiter was approaching them between the closely placed tables, carrying glasses and a bottle in an ice-bucket, with Mr Dash's compliments.

Alone in his room on that last night of the visit, Sandboy listened, dreading the sound of Yvonne's tears. The week of her little triumph had turned to despair with ominous ease. The idols who were to bring her back into the circle of their favourites had been courteous, friendly and indifferent. Like a thousand others, she had waited among the admirers of the stars until hope and promises had withered. He felt anger on her behalf, fear for himself of the wretchedness that might affect them both, and an emptiness in his arms.

He heard no weeping. Perhaps her actress's vanity would hide the mortal truth from her. She was certainly vain enough to take their smiles and courtesy as binding agreements. Vain enough not to see that whatever interest these people might have had in her once was gone for ever. To them, she had been only Manny's wife.

With one hand behind his head on the pillow, he smoked and stared at the ceiling. With Gillis gone, McGouran gone, Yvonne was the last person in whom he might have trusted, to whom he might have spoken. Their afternoons together were his last refuge. As she weakened and failed, so did he. There was no other person in the world who owed him the least loyalty. Every man and woman might now as easily betray him as not. Once he understood that, Sandboy knew what it meant to be utterly alone.

October

Wanted for Questioning

Chapter Twenty-Six

'Hello, Mr Pender,' Rutter said cheerfully. 'You'll start thinking you'll never see the last of me.'

He stood in the doorway of the detached suburban house, unannounced. The trees of the short driveway were touched with a scattering of autumn red. Beyond them he heard the laughter of children playing rounders on the common.

Pender stared at him. 'Today? Sunday afternoon? What you want?'

'Nothing much, Mr Pender. A few details to clear up on a day when I'm on duty, you're likely to be home and we can sit quietly. I'd prefer not to come to the workshop during the week. I expect you'd prefer that too.'

He had edged his foot forward a little, so that Pender could no longer shut the front door without pushing him off the step.

'It's hardly convenient.'

Rutter smiled. 'I think you'll find it is, Mr Pender, when you hear what I've got to say. I believe we've found some property belonging to you. May I come in for a moment? I shan't keep you long.'

Pender looked uneasy at the mention of property. But he could hardly refuse to discuss it without a lawyer present. Rutter smiled at him again.

'You come alone?' Now there was caution but also relief in the old man's voice.

'Quite alone, Mr Pender, so it can't be as bad as all that, can it? You'll be pleased to know we've at last made progress in your case.'

But Pender did not look pleased. 'What case? I haven't got a case.'

'The reported robbery.'

'I thought I said . . .'

Rutter now stood in the hall. The door to the sitting room was open, two long chesterfields in blue leather arranged back-to-back before the tall stone mantel of the Minster fireplace. There was a white bearskin rug and a copper screen before the empty hearth. The cocktail cabinet, the baby grand, the silver-framed photographs on occasional tables were still in place. He followed Pender and sat down on the first chesterfield without being invited. He noticed that Pender read *Reynolds News* on a Sunday: 'MR BALDWIN AT FORT BELVEDERE. PRIME MINISTER IS KING EDWARD'S WEEKEND GUEST'. He also saw that a section of Pender's picture rail had been replaced and painted over.

'How're you getting on, Mr Pender?'

Pender stood with his back to the copper fire screen. The large eyes and the jowls gave him a sullen look at the best of times.

'I been bereaved. How d'you suppose I'm getting on? You come to pay your respects or what?'

Rutter took a sheet of paper from his pocket and pretended to consult it. 'I'm sorry about that, Mr Pender, but this time I might have a bit of welcome news for you. You know a man called Roy Spurgeon?'

'No.'

'He seems to know you, in a manner of speaking. Spurgeon was arrested in Glasgow with three coats and two stoles that seem to belong to you. He's a known thief with two longish prison sentences behind him. I don't see how he could have come by these articles honestly. He insists, of course, that he knows nothing about you. He was certainly in Barlinnie gaol at the time when Mrs Pender was taken to hospital.'

Pender sat down in the fireside chair and stared at the copper screen, keeping his face away. 'So what you keep bothering me for?'

'He claims that he came by these articles honestly. According to your records, that must be impossible.'

'I don't know what you're on about.'

'Just say that again to yourself, Mr Pender, and think how silly it sounds. And if you have to say it to a jury, think how silly it's going to sound to them. You know what I'm on about.'

Pender looked up, the eyes staring behind the lenses of his horn-rimmed spectacles. 'What jury?'

'The jury that hears the case against Spurgeon. Possibly a jury that hears charges brought against you.'

'What charges?'

'At the best,' Rutter said gently, 'concealing a felony. What's technically called misprision of felony. You can get two years for that. At the worst, being an accessory after the fact in a theft and possibly in the death of Mrs Pender. Not up to me to say. Still, if that happened, you might just as well be charged with the substantive crimes themselves.'

Pender stared at his shoes. 'It's all just nonsense.'

Rutter inched forward to the edge of the chesterfield,

as if in a change of heart he was about to take the old man's arm to comfort him.

'Nonsense? Listen to me. Ask yourself why I came alone today. No Sergeant Brodie. No one else. Just my word against yours. Right?'

Pender looked up at him. The large eyes showed a hesitant hope. 'This isn't official?'

Rutter cocked his head apologetically. 'It's official, Mr Pender. It has to be. I can't talk to you on any other basis. But what I'm trying to tell you is that I am not interested in you. Not in arresting you nor charging you. I will if you make me. But you're not the man I want.'

Pender returned his gaze to his shoes.

'These coats and stoles in Glasgow,' Rutter went on. 'Someone'd cut out the bit of the pelt that had your trademark pricked into it. Spurgeon I dare say. Whoever it was thought they'd done a clever job by getting rid of the marking. We know better, don't we?'

Pender stared at him again. 'Do we?'

'Mr Pender,' Rutter smiled to show his patience, 'you and I both know what's under the lining of a fur coat or stole, even if the customers don't. A thief like Spurgeon or his friend Gillis wouldn't have a clue. First thing I did with those coats, not knowing whose they might be, was to take them to the Furriers Association in the City of London. I expect you belong to it. Those garments were unpicked by one of their very best men. The lining was taken out and put back again so that you'd never know. I don't have to tell you what they found, do I?'

Pender shook his head.

'No,' said Rutter gently, 'every pelt that goes into a coat like that has a code number dyed into it before it's shipped, let alone bought. Our man was good. He even

262

picked some of the skins apart in the back of the coats to get the numbers. You know, don't you, that the whole batch with those numbers on was sold to you, as a manufacturing furrier, and that the coats and stoles were made up in your workshop? I got the numbers here, if you want them.'

Pender said nothing.

'I'd like to get this settled, Mr Pender, I really would. As much for your sake as anyone's. You don't want me and Mr Brodie coming back and back, bothering you. Do you?'

Pender sat hunched and abject. In the face of the evidence from the numbered pelts, the last sign of fight had gone from him. 'What happens now?'

'You tell me the truth, Mr Pender. That's what happens. Tell me what took place that night. That's all I want.' Pender nodded. He began with an effort.

'All right. We was upstairs in bed. I heard a sound or two, being half asleep. I thought it was outside or somewhere. Then I could swear there was a bump down here. I got the torch and come down the back stairs. You can't see them from the front of the house. I came in through the kitchen to this room. First I couldn't see a thing. They'd used torches to save turning lights on. Smell of it, they been striking matches as well, to find their way. Then I put the lights on 'em. They hadn't bargained for that. Never seen me nor heard me till then, eh? They'd kept the front door open ready and there was some car outside. But by then they'd bloody half burgled the place. Two of 'em with raincoats, hats and scarves round their faces.'

'They saw you when you came in here? Not before?'

Pender's eyes brightened. 'Too bloody true. I got a

263

walking stick and went for 'em, Mr Rutter. I suppose they thought I might rip the scarf off of one of their faces and see who they was. Anyway, they never stopped to argue. Just run for it. Pity of it was I hadn't come down a bit previous and put a stop to it all before they could take anything outside. Anyway they made a run for their car. Except one of 'em turns, somewhere in the garden, and there's this crack. Not a lot of noise but it was a fucking bullet went over my head, if you'll pardon the language.'

'What did they take?'

'They'd been in the dining room. And under the stairs where the coats hang. Under the stairs, they took Mrs Pender's coat and mink stole. In the dining room, they found a coat and stole in a flat tailoring box, ready to give her sister on her birthday. And there was another coat that was for a young lady. And I'll go to prison before I'll say who she was.'

Pender favoured Rutter with a droll grimace, as one man of the world to another. Rutter winced at the lie. But after the next question it was hard to stop the old man from talking. 'And what did you do?'

'Before I could do anything, Mr Rutter, she called from upstairs. She sounded bad. It was the fright of what she'd heard going on. She'd had a dodgy pump for years. I mean, we knew it was only a matter of time before it gave out, but all this set her off. I phoned the doctor and got a few things ready for the hospital, in case.'

'And you never called the police?' Rutter heard himself speaking in the tone of an old friend who has been disappointed.

'How could I just then? I'd got a dying woman on my hands, as it turned out. I hadn't time to wait here for the law nor sit around to make statements. Have some sense,

Mr Rutter. As for her, last thing I wanted was Mrs Pender being bothered in her state.'

'And in all the time that followed, you still said nothing? Not even when I came here with Sergeant Brodie after Mrs Pender died?'

'Listen!' Pender leant forward as if they might be overheard. 'I couldn't have Mrs Pender questioned nor bothered in the state she was. Don't you understand? I knew she was dying. I couldn't have that.'

'All right. But later?'

'And the matter of this other lady. I wasn't going to have all that come out. Nor I wouldn't now.'

'But after Mrs Pender died . . .'

'It was a bit late, wasn't it?' Pender said sourly, 'as you'd have been the first to point out, Mr Rutter. Not to mention that taking the coats for Vi's sister and the young lady out of stock might be made to seem irregular. Oh yes, and the fact that I had two phone calls telling me what would happen to my private bits if I went to your lot.'

Rutter studied the rippling pattern of the copper fire screen. But Pender had not finished with him. 'Mr Rutter, I'd just lost my wife. What the fuck did I care about three coats and a couple of stoles? I could replace those easy. I could never replace her. You think that's an odd way to look at it? It's not. A lot of thieving don't get reported for good reasons. A lot of people get robbed and can't face having the police all over 'em. No disrespect, but I wanted it all behind me. Can't you see?'

'Yes,' Rutter said thoughtfully. 'I can see.'

'And the longer it went on, the further behind me it was, the less I wanted to know. And the cleverer you'd have come it, if I'd told you months later.'

There was a long pause. Then Rutter came to the main point. 'What interests me most, Mr Pender, is evidence. This shot that was fired. You know much about guns?'

Pender shook his head. 'Not a thing. I never was in the war. Too old by then.'

'If the gun was fired in the garden, the cartridge case would be ejected there. On the base of the metal case, there'd be the imprint of the hammer that fired the round. You can identify a gun from that imprint, Mr Pender. Then there's the bullet that came in here. Unless it's badly damaged by impact, you can identify the gun from the marks left on a bullet by the barrel that fired it. The man who's been identifying firearms for ten years past is a good friend of mine. I'd be surprised if your intruders could have found the cartridge case in the dark, the hurry they were in.'

'The shot hit the picture rail,' Pender said. 'The piece that was damaged, I had took out and repaired. I dare say the bullet was in it.'

'What happened to the piece that was cut out?'

'No idea,' Pender said, 'but I dare say the cartridge case you were on about might be in the garden somewhere. Could be lying there, or dug into the soil by now, or anything else. They might even have left something else behind. As you say, dropped it, or not had time to pick it up before they ran. Something could turn up, I suppose.'

'It often does,' Rutter said, 'not usually this long after the event, but still it does. And if you should get another of those telephone calls, threatening you, please tell me.'

'So you can put a tap on the line?' Pender asked sceptically.

'If it will help you. It could only be done with your agreement.'

Rutter stood up and Pender, from his chair, looked round the large silent room. He blew his nose.

'It's nothing, is it,' he asked mournfully, 'without a woman's touch?'

'Have you no family?'

'What the fuck they care?' The words came in a half choked squeal. Then, to Rutter's embarrassment, the old man began to weep noisily into his handkerchief.

As the door closed behind him, Rutter turned and walked through the autumn sunshine down Rooks Lane towards the main road. Just before the junction, he opened the passenger door of the Wolseley.

'How was Mr Pender?'

Rutter considered the question for a moment. 'We had a talk, Frank. Man to man. A warm, understanding, candid, friendly talk. By the end of it, we each knew the other better than ever before. He can account for the three coats and the two stoles that Spurgeon had in his possession. Not convincingly enough to satisfy the Inland Revenue or Customs and Excise, but he's got a story about them being presents for his lady wife, the wife's sister and Pretty Polly Perkins of Paddington Green.'

'So they were never sold?'

'You got it, Frank.'

'And someone thieved them before the sister-in-law and Polly could be given them?'

'In a nutshell. You might almost be his ventriloquist.'

'So how was he?'

'He was as you'd expect, Frank. He was Pelly Pender. Lying and congenitally dishonest. Proving it would be the trick, however.'

'That difficult?'

Rutter sighed. 'I had him blubbing for sympathy. Inconsolable old widower. I've a fair idea of the performance he could put on in the witness box. Especially once he's been coached. I'd say he's been coached already.'

'Meaning?'

'Meaning that so long as he's more frightened of the people that he owes favours to than he is of us, Pender would cut his tongue out before he told the truth.'

'Wouldn't you?' Brodie asked philosophically, putting the Wolseley into gear.

Rutter ignored the suggestion. Opening his copy of the *Sunday Express*, as Brodie drove back to Whitehall, he saw that Ambassador von Ribbentrop had assured the Anglo-German Fellowship of his government's peaceful intentions in the Rhineland. Elsewhere, Mrs Wallis Simpson, 'a popular Baltimore socialite', had been granted a decree nisi in the Ipswich divorce court.

Rutter shook his head. The royal romance, which the middle-class British press had agreed to keep 'secret', had filled the front page of the Communist magazine *The Week* in every issue since the beginning of November. Therefore, Special Branch knew it. Therefore most of Scotland Yard knew it. By next week the entire country would probably know it. But the press would still be keeping the 'secret'.

He folded the paper, bowed his head and wondered what he might be hearing if only there was a tap on Pender's telephone line already.

Chapter Twenty-Seven

When it was quiet in Mr Samuelson's shop, he could hear the underground trains. They ran on the shallower line between the main railway at Paddington and King's Cross. Their rumbling came up to him like a long peal of distant thunder. It was quiet in the shop now as he held the earpiece of the telephone to his head and waited. Because of the way that the sound carried in the soot-crusted tunnels below him, if he listened hard he could sometimes hear the rumble of the wheels rise to a keening of steel as the train pulled into its platform at Edgware Road.

Beyond the shop window, winter rain was blowing in gusts down Praed Street. Men and women hurried past, mackintoshes shining wet, clutching their hats to their heads. Water streamed down the red metal flanks of the London Transport trams and gleamed on the dark coats of the draymen's horses.

"'Ello? . . . 'Ello? . . .'

Mr Samuelson's voice was apprehensive but impatient. A steam lorry shook the plate-glass window, smoke and sparks rising from its metal chimney behind the driver's cab. Naphtha flares on the hawkers' barrows dripped fire along the kerb, the fogged gas lamps shining on hard chequered pavement.

In the late afternoon of the autumnal day, a dark

London sky glowed purple with the reflected light of the city. A last streak of crimson in the west lay over the porticoed houses of Craven Hill and Leinster Gardens, the bridge clubs and the apartments of doll-faced prostitutes who solicited the length of the Bayswater Road. The old man stared at the scene of greasy brilliance beyond his window as he clutched the phone tighter. This far back, the cavernous shop stank of mice. Somewhere in the world there were frigidaires and electric cookers, silver grilles and dance bands in evening dress, but not in Mr Samuelson's, Praed Street.

''Ello? . . . Mr Rutter? . . . 'Ello . . .?'

At last there was a click and a voice said, 'What's the news, then, Sammy?'

The old man's wet lower lip trembled briefly before he spoke. 'Mr Rutter? You still interested in old Pelly Pender? That business last January?'

'I'm always interested in everyone, Sammy. That's my job. Why?'

'I got a name for you, Mr Rutter. Come my way last night down the drinker. You remember I had a visitor with goods to sell? I got a name for who it was. Seems I wasn't the only one he went to.' He hesitated, the edge of his unsteady hand brushing gathered spittle from the lower lip.

'Go on,' Rutter said.

'McGouran. A jock. Big fellow. Seen in several places trying to place similar goods. That's who come to me. A jock that they reckon been in gaol once or twice. That any good to you, Mr Rutter?'

Rutter clicked his tongue. 'Whether he came to you or not, Sam, I can't ask him now. I know who McGouran was. He's been dead a few months.'

'Oh, has he? Well, I'm sorry about that, Mr Rutter. All the same, it's the name I heard. McGouran. Definite.'

'You alone in the shop, Sammy?'

''Course I am, Mr Rutter. I don't make a call like this with a shop full of customers.'

Rutter covered the mouthpiece with his hand and looked at Brodie. He spoke very quietly, with exaggerated motions of his lips, as if expecting his sergeant to lip-read. 'Get a car from Paddington Green down to Samuelson's in Praed Street. Quick as they can. See who's in the shop with him. It might just work if they hurry. Now. Fast.'

As Brodie went out, Rutter said, 'All right, Sammy, describe your McGouran for me. Everything you can remember.'

'I don't remember that much, Mr Rutter. Almost a year ago now. Darkish, quite a good build. I'd know him again. I tried to be 'elpful at the time. You'd have his picture I dare say.'

'You were helpful, Sammy, you were. And if something were to turn up now, there could be a drink or two in it for you. What I need to ask you first, though, is how this description of yours that you remember now matches what you had to say then . . .'

'All right. But I'll have to stop for a bit, Mr Rutter. I got two ladies just come in the shop. I'll give you a call in a jiffy. Soon's I got rid of them.'

He put the phone down without waiting for a reply. The young man who had been standing beside him put his hat on. He reached up and patted Mr Samuelson's withered cheek, while the old man looked back at him in dog-like affection.

'There's a good boy,' the young man said and patted the patina'd flesh again, a little more sharply.

Then the visitor opened the flap in the wooden counter, unbolted the door and turned the card hanging in the glass panel. Instead of saying 'Closed', it now read 'Open'. He drew up the collar of his raincoat, and tilted the hat down a little to protect his face from the wet. Without looking or speaking again to Mr Samuelson, he stepped out into the sweeping rain. A second man had been scanning the peg-board window display of the neighbouring Book Exchange, a row of paperbound volumes with red and blue picture covers, *White Slaves in a Piccadilly Flat* and *The Road to Buenos Aires*. The man who had just left Mr Samuelson spoke to him. They turned away through the storm, whose drops bounced high on the paving stones and against the dark-glazed bricks of the public house across the street.

On Rutter's instructions, the squad car from Paddington Green collected Mr Samuelson and brought him to Scotland Yard. By eight o'clock that evening he was sitting at a table in the interview room near Rutter's office with two photograph albums before him. Brodie stood by the narrow casement window as the old man turned the stiffened leaves, their rows of expressionless faces staring from the pages.

Rain was still sweeping through the city, fogging the lights of County Hall across the flood tide of the river. The newspaper stand on the Embankment was deserted early, the placard wet and wrinkled in the lamplight as it moved with the wind: ' "FOR HE'S A JOLLY GOOD FELLOW" – EX-SERVICEMEN CHEER THE KING. MRS SIMPSON IN FRANCE.'

'That's him!'

Brodie turned round. Samuelson was looking up at him, his eyes bright with triumph, his finger under one of the faces in the album. Brodie looked.

'Just wait here a moment, Mr Samuelson.'

Brodie tapped on Rutter's door, waited and entered. 'McGouran. He's picked McGouran.'

Rutter got up from his desk, tight-lipped. 'Then some-one's shown him a picture of the bastard. He gave us a description In January. It wasn't McGouran. It couldn't have been McGouran.'

'He says it was.'

'Sunday we go down to Pender and hit him with the evidence that he was robbed and we know he was robbed. He comes up with a half-cock story about chasing off gunmen. Two days later – after all this time – Samuelson comes crawling out from under his stone with a story of just having found out that the man who came to him a year ago was McGouran.'

'So that's the end of Samuelson? No more treats from the reward fund?'

'Too true. Still, his grief is only just beginning. Half a minute.'

Rutter opened a drawer and took out a photograph. It looked like the work of a promenade photographer, full length and full face. Sandboy strode past the sea-front kiosks, the angle of his eyes not quite directed to the hidden camera. Rutter led the way back to Samuelson.

The old man was on his feet, ready for them, eager to please. 'Same as I said on the phone, Mr Rutter. I got that name for you. Been mentioned to me twice, what's more. McGouran. I knew his face in the photo the minute I saw it.'

The intense honesty of Mr Samuelson's gaze intensi-fied Rutter's distaste. 'Shut up and sit down again, Samuelson. Look at this photograph. Don't say anything yet. Look at it carefully.'

'I picked a face already, Mr Rutter.'

'Shut up. What I'm wondering, Sammy, is how many people there are who you've grassed up and never knew you were a grass. What I wonder is how some of them might feel if it got about that you had this little sideline. That you'd been informing on half of Paddington for years past . . .'

The old man looked up from his chair and his lower lip steadied with indignation. 'I don't deserve that from you, Mr Rutter. It's not – not – ' he sought the word, 'honourable.'

'Honourable!'

'Yes, Mr Rutter. Honourable. I always been honourable with you.'

'Look at that photograph! Who is that?'

Samuelson studied the image of Sandboy striding towards him in the summer light. He shook his head. 'Don't know him from Adam. Never seen him. You tell me, 'cause I can't say.'

Rutter felt his face growing warm but Samuelson had not finished. 'You don't want me telling untruth just because I might be frightened of you, do you, Mr Rutter?'

Rutter turned to Brodie. 'Put him in the car and take him home.'

But Samuelson had still not finished. 'If it's all the same to you, Mr Rutter, there's Charing Cross tube just down the road. Straight through to Paddington or Edgware Road on the Bakerloo. I'd rather make my own way. If you don't mind. If that's agreeable. And as for the other business of information I might have passed to you, you can say what you like to who you like.'

They watched him go. Brodie picked up the two albums of photographs and closed them. 'No one's going to touch Samuelson, Jack. You heard him good as tell us to fuck off. He's being looked after by bigger people than any he's informed on.'

'I'm counting on that, Frank.'

'You really thought he'd identify that snap of Sandboy?'

Rutter looked surprised. A tram rattled below the window, sparks trailing from its conductor rail. 'I didn't show him the photo for that, Frank. I knew he wouldn't identify it. He couldn't after picking out McGouran. But he'll sure as hell go scurrying back down the rat-hole to tell someone that he's been asked to identify it. The way things stand, that might light a fire under Sandboy.'

'And that way you get him?'

Rutter shook his head. 'In most cases, Frank, I get what I'm given. Like everyone else. Especially when it's Tarrant or Bowlett on the other end of the line. In this case, someone gave us Spurgeon. Someone took McGouran and Gillis off our caseload. A little voice whispered to me the other day that the lovely Mrs Manders is taking dope. The needle, not just a sniff or a smoke. Now, someone might try to give us Sandboy and come a cropper in the attempt.'

'Or else?'

'I suppose someone might take him off our caseload as well. I don't think I would mind that very much, Frank. Spurgeon, McGouran, Gillis and Sandboy. Then let Customs and Excise have Pelly Pender. A tight little gang gone to glory – and a nice clean slate.'

'And Tarrant?'

Rutter looked down at the wet pavements and the flooding river. 'He's been wiping slates clean since he was a nipper of fourteen on the racecourse. Ten bob not to wipe off a bookie's chalk from his blackboard with a wet sponge, bugger up his day's takings and put him out of business. He wouldn't do it for ten bob now. Even Sonny Boy came cheap in those days.'

November

Red Flowers for Lady Blue

Chapter Twenty-Eight

Charley Archer walked quickly ahead. 'We left it as long as we could, Mr Tarrant. Getting no answer, on and on, we had to use the pass-key. It was only then we found them.'

The two men turned the corner of a bedroom corridor in the west wing. Below a window arch lay the evergreen walls of the hotel driveway, framing a flash of blue water. Tarrant's face was marked by an uncharacteristic expression of concern.

'I hadn't been home from London half an hour, Charley. Dinner for the Lord Mayor's charity do last night. Crippled kiddies. Duchess of Kent's good cause. Stayed up at the Waldorf, where the function was held. Come down this morning on the seven thirty Pullman from Waterloo. How the hell did this happen? Where's the police? You called 'em first, of course?'

'They're on the way,' Archer said, counting the bedroom doors. 'I rang Superintendent Landis when I rang you, only I rang you first. Knowing they'd want you here. And knowing you'd want to be here when they arrived, or in case you wanted to be the one that called them.'

'Appreciate that, Charley. You're a good scout. What's the score on all this? What happened last night?'

Archer slid the pass-key into the bedroom lock and paused. 'Mrs Manders rang from London just about teatime. Strand Palace. She'd been up in London half the autumn. This time with Mr Manders. Christmas shopping, I suppose. They were coming back here for a few days as usual, the hotel not the house. Made the booking weeks back.'

Tarrant stared at him. 'Why not the house?'

'Not in a fit state. They have painting and repairs done inside this time of year. Workmen redecorating upstairs and downstairs. Has to be finished before the holidays. Mr Manders gave the maid and manservant time off, the house being upside down. Just Miss Manders and an old housekeeper with an eye on the place. The Manders usually treat themselves to the Strand Palace and the Garden Royal while that's going on. After all, it's free for them here.'

'They bloody lived in hotels . . .' Tarrant began. He stopped. To complete the sentence to his own satisfaction he needed to say that they had bloody died in one as well. But it would have sounded like an hysterical joke, hardly to be spoken without laughing. He had a moment of panic that he was going to laugh in front of Archer at the mere thought of it. He steadied himself by thinking of more solemn moments then their deaths.

'How many in the party?'

'Mrs Manders booked three rooms. Mr Manders, Mrs Manders and Sandboy, who did the driving down from London. They got in just after ten. Cold supper. Drinks all round. I don't like saying it, Mr Tarrant, but a lot of drink was drunk. All three of them. And him and her had quite a drop already.'

Tarrant watched the door swing open. His pulse now beat with dread and longing at what he must see.

'Not in the best of moods neither.' Archer was still talking in the quiet tone of controlled shock. 'I can't swear there'd been a quarrel between Mr and Mrs Manders before they got here but it had that feel about it. Like thunder in the air.'

Someone, the chambermaid presumably, had opened the scarlet curtains of the bedroom before discovering the tragedy. Bright winter sunlight shone back from the walls in their two shades of white. There was a chair in red leather and another in cream. The bed with its cover of cherry-red silk had not been slept in. A large flat evening bag lay by the pillows. In the far corner, a tall silver and black standard lamp on a slim metal stand was still burning. Perhaps Archer thought that an important clue might have been lost by switching it off before the arrival of Landis and the CID.

On the dressing table, Tarrant noticed two silver-backed hairbrushes, belonging to Manders, among a litter of combs and the implements of a manicure set that must have been Yvonne's. A bottle of Guerlain's Shalimar stood beside an open tin of Gibbs Dentifrice.

There was nothing in the adjoining dressing room to identify its occupant except a black silk dress on one hanger and a green coat with an ermine collar on the other. Archer walked slowly into the bathroom beyond.

The brilliance of the winter morning was mirrored on the polished chrome of towel rails and fittings, spangling the walls and the ceiling with prismatic lozenges of light. The early sun cast a glaze over Yvonne Manders and the reflecting water in the large oval of an amber bath. She seemed to lie motionless and naked in a bowl of golden syrup, curled on her side as if asleep. Perhaps the level had drained down a little in the hours since her death. At any rate, her face was now half-in, half-out of the water, her hair floating like darkened weed.

For Tarrant, the sight of such a death held no mystery or horror. It was an unreality, detached from sense and feeling. A waxwork display in the chamber of horrors was more lifelike. He glanced quickly round to see what might have been overlooked. But someone had prepared Yvonne Manders in death as gently and carefully as a nursemaid might settle a child. So far as was possible on such an occasion, the body had been decently composed. He was glad of that, glad to be spared the grossness he had seen after other deaths, even those attended by the medical profession.

Nothing else seemed out of place. Tarrant glanced over the room with a hotelier's eye. A red rubber shower cap hung on a hook over the end of the bath. There was a pink nightdress folded on the stool and a pair of pink mules on the cork bath mat. A hypodermic syringe lay on the far ledge of white enamel.

'That's the worst of it,' Archer said, following Tarrant's gaze. 'There's needle-marks from the past week or so. She hadn't much idea about injecting herself, though. Red lumps on her arms where the point went in.'

'So when d'you reckon this happened, Charley?' It was the first question they would expect him to ask.

'She must have been in the water for hours, sir. Outside of the bath was stone-cold when I came in. More than that, I don't know.'

'Where's he?'

Archer turned and led the way back out.

'And Sandboy?' Tarrant asked.

'In his room and told to stay there. Billy Corder, duty porter, gone in there with him to make sure he does as ordered.'

Tarrant nodded, as if approving that all had been done correctly and with tact. Archer unlocked the adjoining bedroom. It was a match for the first with its scarlet curtains and the walls in two shades of white, the two leather chairs and the standard lamp. But this time the cherry-red silk coverlet had been drawn down the bed. Manders lay on his back, the colour still in his cheeks, as if sleeping deeply. Only the awkward angle at which his arms were spread and his head turned aside suggested otherwise. One of the pillows was by his feet and a single oatmeal-coloured carpet slipper lay at a distance on the rug.

'What happened to him?' Tarrant asked quietly. 'He looks all right. What the fuck happened to him?'

Archer shook his head. 'The colour of him, he could have been gassed. Seeing that pillow by his feet, though, he was more likely smothered. Blood in the mouth. There's muck on the pillow too.' Then he said, 'I think I can hear Mr Landis.'

Leaving Tarrant alone with Manders, he went out. Tarrant listened and heard him talking to the superintendent. Best to remain aloof until he was called for.

'The governor's here already, Mr Landis. Charity dinner in London at the Waldorf last night. But fortunately he'd already come back by the seven thirty Pullman from Waterloo this morning. He's free when you want him.'

The voices faded as Archer and Landis, a veteran of area CID, two years from retirement, went into the other bedroom. When Tarrant came out on to the main staircase, there were already two uniformed constables standing with a proprietorial air in the lobby below him. He looked about him.

'There's no necessity for advertising trouble like that. Someone tell Mr Landis.'

No one seemed to hear him. He began to walk back towards the room where Manders' body still lay. By the time he reached it, there was no one available to speak to him. Before the door closed, however, he glimpsed a uniformed sergeant and a young CID constable standing by a low screen which now surrounded the bed. Behind it, wearing a surgical mask, was the figure of the duty pathologist. He was waiting while the magnesium bulbs of the police photographer, his box camera on a tall metal stand, popped and flashed above the canvas.

Tarrant turned and found Archer beside him.

'Never known Ray Landis move so swift,' Archer said confidentially. 'I dare say he must reckon this is his last big one. Nice for him to retire on a chief super's pension, if it all falls right.'

Tarrant clapped him on the shoulder. 'I'll only be in the way here, Charles,' he said graciously. 'You take charge. They'll find me down in my office when I'm needed.'

Alone in his room, the unreality of the drama still hung like a mist about him. McGouran and Gillis had been nothing, names of strangers that he might have read in a press report of a distant plane crash or a colliery explosion. But now he was part of a drama that might fill the pages of the *News of the World* or *Sunday Pictorial*: 'TWO SLAIN IN HOTEL LOVE-NEST MYSTERY.'

He had expected to feel greater agitation than this and was a little concerned that he did not. The aftermath of the death scenes was like a boyhood memory of swimming underwater in the municipal baths, slow moving, the sounds of the outer world far removed, its objects not clearly distinguishable. Perhaps it was what they meant by shock. But shock was something that had never touched him.

He sat down in the revolving chair. A copy of the *Daily Express*, left on his desk by a page-boy, carried its lead story in thick black type: 'GRAVE CONSTITUTIONAL CRISIS'. Underneath was a pale grainy photograph of a man with a placard by Hyde Park railings: 'GOD SAVE THE KING FROM MR BALDWIN'.

Tarrant picked the paper up and put it down unread. The sight of Manny and Yvonne had neither moved nor shocked him. Even the man in the newspaper photograph was more real to him now. The sight of the placard was light breaking already in the upper world at the end of the underwater swim. Sonny Tarrant thought that he would have done what he could to save the king from Mr Baldwin, but he had been too busy with Manny and Yvonne. Even that was finished. In the odd way of death, they were now less real than the stranger in the newsprint photograph. Death diminished their lives to monochrome images projected on a screen, a celluloid fiction to be wiped out or altered by rewinding and editing the film.

In all honesty, Tarrant could not say exactly how they had died. That was the business of men whose names he was never told. Perhaps Foxy knew them. Such angels of death came not in billowing flame but in anonymous Burberry raincoats and trilby hats. The mysteries which they left behind them were no more profound than morning-matinée puzzles for Mr Moto or Charlie Chan.

But only in the clever world of screen detectives were such puzzles designed to be solved.

He sat back against the yielding leather of the chair. Someone had left a sample calendar for the new year of 1937 beside the newspaper. Brandons Garages. Manny would have no part of Brandons Garages now. The façade that carried his image would be gone in a few days. Gone in as short a time as it took for Bowlett to write a creditor solicitor's six-and-eightpenny letter, exercising an option on Tarrant's behalf. Revealing the reality of Sonny Tarrant within.

In lemon sepia, the twelve calendar photographs caught the light of warm days last summer. The months were represented by the finalists of August's 'Modern Venus' parade. Tarrant turned the leaves of photogravure. A shimmer of sun scorched the hillocks of scooped sand. Sharp rectangular shadows were cast by the cream-washed stone walls of the bathing pool. The modern grace of the high-diving platform rose against a sky that lay pale in the afternoon heat.

The seasons of 1937 were heralded by smiling goddesses with bare unblemished thighs, the suggestive sleekness of swimwear and water suits, the breasts a little flattened by the elastic pressure of the material, the bottoms demurely tense. Caught in the moment of their perfection, the contestants had only the impersonal desirability of shop-window mannequins. In the camera's eye, it was the men and women watching from the deck chairs who showed expression and character.

Tarrant studied the girls and their admirers, like a winter ghost haunting the lost hours of that August afternoon. Most of the men and women in the deckchairs were elderly, a few of those at whom he looked might be dead by now as they smiled back at him. The smiling welcome of the dead. The bathing beauties would be seen and desired by someone or other until the glossy leaves of the calendar shrivelled and faded. Would they be less desirable because the beauties themselves were dead by then?

The images held no secret from him, no mystery. His hands could sense, as though he touched them, the softness of each breast, the sleekness of the thighs and backsides, the slight rise of warm flesh moulding itself to his caress. He knew them for what they were. He knew Manny and Yvonne, who were now united with the calendar photographs in some Valhalla of the past.

Outside his window, the white glare of the sun cleared the undulating branches of the tall monkey-puzzle, shining directly across his desk. He put the calendar down. Then, with a shock of true pleasure, surprised that he had forgotten her for so long that morning, he remembered Nina Manders. The bonus!

There was no twinge in him of humdrum sexual desire for Little Madam. What enticed him was more exquisite and promising, more precisely controlled. Bereft of Manny and Yvonne, still beholden to their paymaster, Nina was to be his possession. The Greta Garbo hair, the green Slav eyes. Little Madam must be pampered, refused, indulged, taught a lesson, rewarded, commanded, even caressed in the most innocent way.

There would be little rebellions, he hoped, answered by implacable reprimands. Brief defiance, even hysterics, followed by tears – always tears – paving the way for gentleness, reconciliation, gratitude, loyalty, reward. There was no end to the images which ran through Sonny

Tarrant's mind, each more potent than any trick of the photographer's art . . .

He had no idea that an hour had passed when Archer tapped at his door. Tarrant had expected a summons but this seemed too soon. Archer himself looked uneasy.

'Mr Landis wants to take fingerprints. All of us. Just for elimination. They've got the kit here now and they can use my office. Would you have any objection, he wants to know.'

Tarrant smiled with relief. 'No objection at all, Charley. I'll be first in, in case anyone's feelin' nervous. I been in every room in this hotel, somewhen or other. Odds-on they might find my pinkies in there, for what that's worth to them.'

Chapter Twenty-Nine

After the prints had been taken, Tarrant followed Archer back to the warm office. He guessed that Charley Artful would have been pressing his former colleagues for information.

'Any whispers, Charles, as to how long this might go on or what the thinking is?'

Archer turned from the window. 'Bit early, without post-mortems,' he said cautiously. 'Still, they all seem to be singing the same tune.'

'About Manny?'

'Looks like he'd drunk enough and been dosed enough to put the Brigade of Guards to sleep. There must have been so much, it makes them wonder if he was slipped a dose without knowing it. Pills in his drink too, perhaps. No sign at all that he put up a struggle. Probably he was suffocated in a very deep sleep, the doc thinks. It's how it looks. What he drank might have been spiked to make sure he was stone-cold, but not necessarily. Not with the state of his heart. They'll need to open him up to tell.'

'And her?'

'Looks like she topped herself about half an hour later,' Archer said. 'Being in a bath of water that went cold makes the timing difficult, of course. But she did it after

DONALD THOMAS

a good few drinks. I saw her putting them down. Also, in her case, a certain amount of heroin or cocaine taken by needle, and there's an empty bottle of Nembutal or something of the sort.'

'But why? And why in the bath?' Tarrant tried to sound puzzled, veiling his excitement to know the last and most intimate secrets of Yvonne Manders.

Archer shrugged. 'Anyone that far gone, who can say? Some of them, mostly women, want to be found clean and decent. There was one lady in my time who said as much in a note she left. That was a bath too. With running water. They're not very pretty if they die that way in bed. Not like on the films. In Mrs Manders' case, it was what she took that killed her. Whether she'd been in the bath or not. The police surgeon reckons she was gone when the water went into her nose. The sting of it never woke her.'

'Seems a waste,' Tarrant said thoughtfully, 'with looks like hers. They got a time? Or a reason?'

'They reckon there could have been a row of some kind. I told them what I told you. I swear they'd had a ruck before they got to the hotel. Whether he put himself to sleep or she spiked him, who can say? About two o'clock, they think, he was lying on his bed. She was there presumably. Looks as if she'd had her fingers on that pillow. The stiff edging. She could just have put it over his face and held it. Sat on it even. Not likely he'd give much trouble in his state. And it wouldn't take long. Thirty seconds or so, if he'd just breathed out. Sixty if he'd just breathed in.'

Tarrant felt a sense of growing calm as Archer told his story. The pieces of the puzzle were locked too tight for Mr Moto or Charlie Chan ever to break it open. But

290

so much still depended on his own performance. For a start, he must not understand Archer too easily.

'Why d'they think she'd bother to kill him, Charley, if she was going to top herself anyway? Why bother with him?'

'Other way round, Mr Tarrant. That's the guess. She killed herself because she'd killed him, perhaps never really meaning to, or not in her right mind. But I suppose she realized there'd be no witnesses to say she hadn't been rational at the time. Then she must've guessed what was going to happen to her and took her own way out. That's how it fits. Funny thing: I can remember her once, talking about that Thompson and Bywaters case.'

'Woman that made her lover stab her husband?'

Archer nodded. 'She was going on about Edith Thompson off her head with terror for weeks in the death cell, till they drugged her. Having to be doped and carried to the gallows on a chair. When Mr Manders was dead, however it happened, seems like Mrs Manders must've thought she'd rather do it herself than have months of that. Without any drink or dope to help her through.'

'They reckon more people who kill actually kill themselves than live to be arrested. Did you know that, Charley? More people actually . . .' He shook his head and broke off, as if overwhelmed by the thought.

Archer said quietly, 'Mrs Manders really meant to make a good job of it. She couldn't have known anything at the end. They guess she was dead soon after four. Say half an hour to decide she'd got to do it. Then an hour to do it and die.'

Tarrant watched the angle of the sun glittering on the windows. Men and women worried so much over what might go wrong with their plans for killing one another.

They never thought how much easier it might prove to be than they imagined. Here was another bonus from the blue, for instance. Yvonne Manders talking to Charley Archer about the Thompson and Bywaters murder case. Of course, it was a story women liked to talk about, the beautiful terrified heroine going to the rope. A young woman like Yvonne Manders relished play-acting, the thrill of fright, as keenly as any shopgirl. Putting herself in the condemned heroine's place, shivering, imagining . . . handing Sonny Tarrant an unexpected bonus.

Presently he shook his head, the good friend emerging from shock into grief. 'Who'd have thought it'd end like this, Charley?'

Archer ignored the platitude. 'There's something else you'd better know, Mr Tarrant. While I was up there, they found a gun, under the nightdress on the bathroom stool. That's what makes them prefer the story of Mrs Manders being involved in her husband's death and then her own. If she'd had a gun on her all the time, she meant business. If the pillow didn't kill him, a bullet would. Premeditated. I suppose that's how she knew she'd get the rope.'

Tarrant looked up, genuinely startled now. He had assumed that those who had taken possession of the gun would use it to implicate Sandboy, not Yvonne. 'What the fuck'd she want a gun for, Charles, if you'll pardon my French? Going to use it on him and tell some yarn about an armed intruder? Never! She hadn't got it in her!'

'That's what they're asking, Mr Tarrant. Perhaps she was hoping just to frighten him to get something she wanted, not to kill him. Might be what she was going to use as a last resort. Might be she wasn't going to do anything with it until she thought she could use it on herself if nothing else worked. If she came round from the dope after all.'

'But a gun?'

'Walden Safety Revolver, more for target-shooting than anything. She could have had it for that. Holds twelve rounds but only .22 calibre.'

Tarrant frowned more deeply, as he thought Archer would expect. 'They're not sayin' someone else been shot?'

'No,' Archer went back to the window. 'Any case, something that small, you'd have to be very close and very accurate to be sure of killing. As close as a woman might be to a man without him suspecting. There's not much penetration to those bullets. Probably have to be through the heart or in the head at very short range. Mind you, she could have shot him through that pillow, if she had to. And they can see there's a print on the frame of the gun. So far, all they can say is it looks like a woman's. Not much doubt whose, if it was found under her nightdress.'

Tarrant thought about this. 'One thing, Charley. Are they thinking she was in this alone?'

Archer looked uneasy. 'They won't when Miss Nina Manders says her piece. And she will, I reckon. About Sandboy sleeping with Mrs Manders. Even to me, that's stale news. But it'll put Sandboy in the line of fire. He was in a room on another corridor of the hotel. But he could have been at the Manders' rooms in three minutes. He's got the prime motive.'

'And where's that leave him?'

'Sweating on whether they'll find out about him and Mrs Manders.'

Tarrant avoided Archer's gaze. An arrest of Sandboy on its own, would be acceptable. The Walden Safety Revolver, on its own, need cause no alarm. But put the two developments together . . . They brought Vi Pender and Dalgetty Street, therefore Gillis, perhaps even McGouran, into the Garden Royal Hotel. Tarrant did not think he was being set up by those whom he had paid. He could break too many people if that happened. It might hang a man just the same.

But he had cut himself free of his enemies before, by doing the very thing that seemed most likely to destroy him. When he looked at Archer, his face was untroubled. 'Sandboy and Mrs Manders. Mr Landis has to be told about them now. For the lad's sake. I'd have to tell Mr Landis, in all honesty, if I was asked. So would you. Or I'd have to tell it in the witness box, if questioned on oath. So would you.'

Archer looked at him, not understanding. 'No help for that, Mr Tarrant.'

'That's where you're wrong, Charley. I'm going to do that young man a good turn. There's one thing always helps in this life. Honesty. Bein' straight with people. I learnt that a long time ago. If Mr Landis finds out about Sandboy and Mrs Manders, days from now, he's going to know it was hidden from him. And where's that leave Sandboy? With a guilty conscience, that's where. Suppose a jury was to hear that he'd tried to hide his slap and tickle with her from the police? Had to have it forced out of him?'

Archer said nothing.

Tarrant shook his head. 'I'm right, Charles. It needs Sandboy to own up now. Nothing to hide. See? If it ever got to a jury, he's been open and honest. From the start.'

Archer's eyes narrowed. 'He won't do that! You know him, Mr Tarrant. He'll just hope they never tumble to it. Like anyone might.'

A tooth gleamed in Tarrant's smile. 'Then those that got his interests at heart must do it for him. I'll have a word with Mr Landis. Say that Sandboy wanted me to mention it to him, being embarrassed himself. How's that?'

'Sandboy hasn't quite got a clean sheet to start with, Mr Tarrant.'

'All the more important to put that right, Charley.'

'Evidence like this would have him in the cells before tonight.'

Tarrant wagged a finger and grinned. 'Still, what's worse, Charles? First one in the cells and first one out? Or last one in the cells and never seen again?'

Archer watched Tarrant reach for the telephone. Then, for a moment, he held his hand over the mouthpiece.

'Sandboy's green, Charley. Green as a bloody leek. He needs puttin' straight. I mean to do that for him.'

'But you don't need the phone for Mr Landis,' Archer said quickly. 'He's still here. I can find him.'

'No, Charles. It's not Mr Landis just yet. I'm givin' old Stan Bowlett a rattle. He's the one to do the talkin'. If my staff's in bother, they get the best that Stan Bowlett can give 'em.'

By the time that he had spoken to Bowlett, the deep-carpeted, pastel-hung lounge of the hotel was open for drinks. Over its glass-topped tables, there was a wide view of the sea from long, elaborately curtained windows. The hired pianist was rippling through a selection from *Top Hat* as Tarrant passed. Its melody filled the lounge and the vestibule, the notes carrying ever fainter to the upper floors where the body of Yvonne Manders, curled cold and naked, was being lifted from the oval bath.

'Me and Mrs Tarrant,' he remarked to Archer at the desk, 'we'll have to find someone else to play our old Steinway to us now.'

He meant it as a man of the world's acceptance of fate but the tone of his voice missed its mark. Archer looked at him as if uncertain how to take the comment. Tarrant abandoned the attempt and nodded towards the sound of the pianist in the lounge.

'Business as usual, Charley. That's just how it should be. That's how we'll keep it.'

He almost added that it was what Manders would want. But, on reflection, who gave a fuck what Manders would want? Being dead deprived a man of the right to an opinion, among other things.

It was twelve thirty as he crossed the vestibule, from the serpentine elegance of the grand staircase towards the central revolving door. Sunlight through Victorian-coloured glass patterned the marble paving. The imperturbable piano selections. Business as usual. Behind the dwarf palms in their copper urns, both chairs of the hotel barber's shop were occupied. At the florist's kiosk, an elderly man in plus fours was writing a cheque for roses in a cellophane sheath. His face bore a mauve cardiac flush, like the bloom on ripe grapes.

Of course, there would be funerals. Red flowers for Lady Blue. The phrase came neatly to mind. The biggest and the richest to brighten her winter burial. It was no more than she deserved.

He was pleased to see that the lobby was busy with arrivals for lunch. Some hurried to keep their appointments, others stood at their rendezvous. The sound of voices and shoes on the polished marble echoed in the glass dome like the rhythm of surf.

He stepped out into the glittering air of the December seaside. A custard-yellow tram rumbled past the gardens, its side placarded with slogans for Tolleys Ales and the *Empire News*.

Though he felt nothing for them personally, it pleased him that a measure of justice had been done to Vi and Pelly. In his way, Tarrant valued justice. Justice was a shattered body by a railway tunnel, a huddle of clothes in the Hampstead Road, as surely as it was a body hanging under the execution shed.

Justice to the Penders was more than the law could have done. And even McGouran and Gillis had reason to be grateful. Foxy and his kind brought death in the same merciful moment as judgement. Which left Sandboy. Sandboy might have taken the same train as McGouran or crossed the same road level with Gillis. But not now. As matters stood, it was only the law who could safely be persuaded to put Sandboy to death. Even then, Sandboy, waiting in a cell for the hangman, talking his head off to win a reprieve, was too great a liability.

Therefore, Sandboy must be saved, for something more useful than the six-foot drop beneath the execution shed. The drop was always there, if it was needed. Tarrant smiled. The thought of saving Sandboy had been unwelcome at first. Now it warmed him with the self-approving glow of a crusader. Sandboy had yet to feel the loyalty of pure terror.

A dark van paused at the exit of the drive, then turned towards the centre of the town, picking up speed. Tarrant was surprised that it had taken so long to remove the bodies. He assured himself that he had never felt true animosity towards Manny and Yvonne, scarcely a moment of real ill will. It was not their fault to be out of place in the new order. They were harmless in themselves. A bar to progress, nothing more. A bar to progress. The epitaph struck him as accurate and neat.

He stood on the lawn and watched the tranquil November tide. Above the Channel, the sky was a shell of perfect blue. Now that the pieces of the puzzle he had set for Mr Moto and Charlie Chan had locked into place without a flaw, the great calm returned.

Sandboy and Yvonne. Landis, the heavily moustached and weary veteran, might be lured into sympathy for the lovers. With luck, the matter of sexual motive could be stone-dead before Rutter heard of it. He would come sniffing, of course, Tarrant had counted on that. It was why Stannie Bowlett had been slipped into gear. But now that Sandboy need give no cause for concern, a door closed in Sonny Tarrant's mind on the figures of Manny and Yvonne in their waxy chamber of horrors.

At the edge of the lawns, he turned away from the cold green water. He would order flowers for Mrs Tarrant. Not red roses, under the circumstances. But something just as nice. Hothouse daffs, from the girl at the kiosk with her usual smile for him. Put her to a bit of trouble. She liked that, from him. He smiled at the sea. In its lunchtime brilliance, it was a day that made one glad to be alive.

December

Eight O'Clock Jump

Chapter Thirty

Sandboy took a last glimpse of the winter afternoon as the procession paused on its way from the detention block. Beyond the glass doors and wide entrance steps of the police headquarters building lay a road of bare winter trees and red-brick villas with cream gables.

Two heavily built uniformed constables stood either side of the swing-doors, as if expecting him to make a dash for freedom. A duty sergeant watched from behind the reception counter. On the far side of the lobby, a windowless strip-lit corridor led to the interview room.

As they moved on, Detective Superintendent Ray Landis reappeared from his office. He stood briefly in the doorway. His heavy eyes and abundant Edwardian moustache marked him as one whose great cases were long in the past. The two men who stepped out from behind him were Rutter and Brodie.

Stan Bowlett, waiting with Sandboy, looked undismayed. His neat courtroom suiting had been exchanged for a tailored out-of-town blazer and grey flannels. The whiskers of his thin face were trimmed and the dark hair pomaded.

'Afternoon, Mr Rutter, Mr Brodie. Paths cross again. Must be in our horoscopes this year.'

Rutter's mouth tightened at the shrewd nasal twang

of the night-school graduate and police court professional. He nodded to Bowlett without replying. Bowlett turned to the superintendent. 'This take long will it, Mr Landis? Only Mr Sandboy's been locked up far too long already, considering the lack of evidence against him and the help he's already given you.'

'Depends entirely on your client, Mr Bowlett. Give us straight answers to the questions, it'll be over all the quicker.'

Bowlett gave him a brief smile, on and off like an electric torch.

They followed Landis to an interview room that was long and narrow, part of a late-Victorian villa incorporated into the police headquarters building. It had been carved out of a rear dining room by white plasterboard partitions. At one end, the metal venetian blinds of the sash window were open to allow a glaze of winter light, like a dentist's surgery.

Landis sat at the far end of the long table with Sandboy facing him, Rutter and Brodie on one side, Bowlett next to Sandboy on the other. Next to Bowlett, a uniformed constable kept a record of the interrogation.

'For the book,' Landis said, 'Mr Rutter and Mr Brodie will be present at this interview. There may be evidence common to this and another investigation still in progress.'

'What other investigation?' Bowlett was leaning aslant on the back of his chair, one arm draped casually over it as he turned to face Landis. 'What other investigation?'

Landis coloured a little round his moustache and side whiskers. 'You know quite well, Mr Bowlett, that I can't discuss such details here or now.'

Bowlett raised a hand slightly, giving a glimpse of

white cuff and a diamond stud in its gold link. By the cold light his face was tanned the colour of soft unlined leather. 'Mr Sandboy is here, of his own free will, to give what information he can as to the circumstances surrounding the deaths of Mr and Mrs Manders. He is not here to be questioned or harried over any other investigation. At the first attempt to introduce any other case into this, I shall advise him to answer no further questions of any kind and to leave this building.'

Landis made no attempt to reply. He looked up at Sandboy, as if Bowlett had not spoken or was not even present. 'You were cautioned yesterday. That still applies.'

'I was hit round the head yesterday. Does that still apply? You going to do that again with Mr Bowlett here? Or wait until he's gone?'

Landis ignored this as well. He turned to Rutter. 'Mr Rutter?'

Rutter looked at Sandboy, the graven lines down his face gave him a thoughtful, concerned look. He lowered his voice, like a man who could be trusted with a confidence, 'This statement of yours. Let's talk about that. You know who I am, so we'll omit the introduction.'

'Horoscopes,' Sandboy said expressionlessly, 'like Mr Bowlett said. 'Less there's any other reason you keep bothering me. I told Mr Landis everything yesterday.'

Bowlett looked at him sharply but Rutter nodded, as though he understood the young man's frustration.

'I'd like to get the times in the statement right, for a start. The sequence of events. You were with Mr and Mrs Manders when they returned to the Garden Royal Hotel from London at about ten thirty on the night of the third of December?'

'I told Mr Landis that. About half past ten we got there.'

'Never mind what you told Mr Landis for the moment. Had there been an argument of some kind between the Manders before you reached the hotel? In the car perhaps?'

'I never heard one. Definitely not in the car.'

Sandboy was relaxed now, as if this was much better than he had expected.

'By the time you saw them downstairs in the hotel, after you'd been up to your rooms, did you think they had been arguing?'

Sandboy was about to reply when Bowlett leant forward. 'He says he heard no argument, Mr Rutter. What he thought isn't material. He can't answer a question like that.'

Rutter stared at Bowlett for a moment. 'Please don't interrupt.' Then he looked away at Sandboy again. 'Very well. What did you do on your arrival at the hotel?'

Sandboy relaxed again. 'We all went to our rooms for a minute. Then we had sandwiches and something to drink.'

'How much to drink?'

'I had a glass of beer. They had shorts. I can't say how much they had. I went to bed first. Left 'em in the lounge. Never saw 'em again.'

'What time was that, when you went to bed?'

Sandboy hesitated.

'Don't look at Mr Bowlett!' Landis said sharply. 'He can't help you.'

'Half past eleven, I should say. And don't bloody interrupt me neither!'

He had shown that bugger Landis where to get off!

Sandboy felt his confidence surging. Now he need only tell the truth to knock Landis stone-dead. As Rutter continued to ask his questions, Sandboy felt like a batsman playing himself in. Jack Hobbs. Don Bradman. Soon he could judge the flight of the ball even before it left the bowler's hand.

'You were in your room all night?' Rutter asked.

'Of course I was, except for a few minutes once. I woke up about four. It was hot in there with the radiators on, that's what woke me. I had to go down the lavatory, just down the passage. When I got back, I opened the window a bit. Like I told Mr Landis, there was a man walking towards the cars outside. Wearing a raincoat and a hat. When I heard what had happened, I thought at first he was one of your lot, come to investigate. He was dressed like CID. Then I heard that you hadn't been called until much later in the morning, so he couldn't have been police unless he was there for something else.'

'Could you make out the man well enough to tell whether you had seen him before or would recognize him again?'

Sandboy shook his head. 'Not dressed like that. Not from the back almost, in the dark.'

Rutter examined his fingers and spoke quietly, not looking up at the young man. 'What time did you leave your room and go downstairs next morning?'

'Just before half past eight.'

Rutter folded the fingers into his palm and looked up. 'According to your statement, there is no one who can corroborate your story of being in your room all that time. Half past eleven at night until half past eight in the morning, except for the visit you say you made to the lavatory at four a.m.'

Bowlett was about to intervene but Sandboy answered first. 'How could there be anyone? I was given a room to myself. There must have been dozens of people in the Garden Royal who wouldn't have a witness if they were in bed and asleep.'

Rutter inclined his head sympathetically. 'Of course there must. But there were not dozens of people who were having an affair with Mrs Manders.'

For the first time, Sandboy felt a thin chill of sweat along his hairline. But the confession already made on his behalf by Bowlett robbed the question of its force.

'Affair? I wouldn't call it that.'

Rutter held his eyes steadily. 'Very well. Let's say there were no others who had spent nights, or more often afternoons, alone with Mrs Manders in her bedroom. Unless you choose to deny that you had ever done so.'

Sandboy gave a short gasp and a faint smile, appealing to the others, at the absurdity of the allegation. 'I already said that I did. But that's all it was. It wasn't an affair. It only happened occasionally. It was just a tumble. She wouldn't be likely to run off with me, would she? Where'd we go? It'd be ridiculous.'

'Adultery, then,' Rutter said gently. 'Let's call it adultery. A court will call it that. You had been committing adultery with Yvonne Manders under her husband's roof. Correct?'

'If you say so. I told all that as soon as I heard what happened to them. You know that from Mr Bowlett. I got nothing to hide.'

'Adultery and sexual jealousy. Your jealousy for Mr Manders, his for you.'

Sandboy assumed the same look of exasperated amusement. He leant back in his chair. 'It only happened between us because he'd stopped being interested in her, in that way. Long ago. She was years younger than him. What's she expected to do? He couldn't have cared less about me, nor me about him. I liked him, as it happens.'

Brodie took over, at a glance from Rutter. 'Miss Nina Manders tells me another story. At odds with the touching picture you paint us. Mr Manders had told his step-daughter that he intended to dismiss you from your employment and divorce his wife.'

'She's lying.'

'Did you ever discuss the matter with Mr Manders?'

'Of course I didn't.'

'Then how do you know that Miss Manders is lying?'

'How do you know she's not?'

'Why should she?'

'She never liked me, nor Mrs Manders, come to that. And she's a great one for making things up. Don't take my word for it. Check. Even her name's made up! I bet she never even told you that she's not Nina Manders. There's no such person. Her real name is Nora Smith. That's how much you can rely on her telling the truth. If you got a false name on her statement, it won't look very clever, will it?'

Bowlett watched Rutter and was sure that neither he nor Brodie had ever heard of Little Madam's past.

'She gave you a false name!' Sandboy was leaning forward, almost grinning in his triumph. 'And you were dumb enough to believe her! And now you come here and accuse me of lying because she must be telling the truth. I do hope all this is going down in the notes!'

'It will certainly go down in mine,' Bowlett said quietly.

Rutter came to Brodie's rescue. 'I hope you can prove

that the young lady is lying in the matter we're discussing. Prove it to the satisfaction of a court. Most people will find it easier to believe that Mr Manders resented your seduction of his wife than that he was indifferent to it. Especially in the light of other evidence to be produced.'

'You may find it useful to remember, Mr Rutter,' Bowlett said, 'that it is you who have to prove that this young lady was telling the truth. My client does not have to show that she was lying.'

Rutter conceded the point. 'Very well. Let's turn to something else.'

Sandboy had done well on this topic, now he was being taken into the dark again. He glanced at Bowlett, trying to guess the 'something else'. Pender. Gillis. Lawsons. But Bowlett was lounging back in his chair again, leaving his client to himself, as Rutter took a cellophane package from a briefcase and laid it on the table.

'Seen this before?'

The cellophane showed the neat silver shape of the Walden Safety Revolver. Sandboy stared. But there was no time to think and only one possible answer.

'Not that I know of.'

Rutter put the gun away.

'Quite sure?'

'I think so.'

'Don't you know? Do you see so many guns that you can't tell?'

'Wait a minute!' Bowlett was now sitting upright again. 'That's well out of order! You want to ask questions on material evidence, you do it. Otherwise, you stop trying to rubbish this young man's defence by allegation and innuendo.'

'All right. Let's try something else again. On the night of the third of December, Mrs Manders, her husband and her lover – who admits he was her lover – stayed at the Garden Royal Hotel. During the night, Mr Manders died. Someone suffocated him . . .'

'But I was never in either of their rooms,' Sandboy said fiercely. 'You know that. You took everybody's fingerprints.'

'Mr Landis certainly took them,' Rutter said.

'Then you know I was never . . .'

'Your prints were in those rooms.'

Bowlett's eyes were still as marbles. Sandboy stared at Rutter. It was impossible. As crazy as if the late afternoon sun had fallen out of the sky.

'My prints can't have been in those rooms. Unless someone put them there. I could prove I was in my own room, if you could find who that man was, walking to the cars. I couldn't have seen him, if I wasn't there.'

Rutter looked at him dispassionately. 'Even if this mystery man could be found, it proves only that you were in your room at four a.m. Your employer and his wife were dead by then.'

'My prints still can't be . . .'

Rutter took out the little gun again in its cellophane sheath.

'This was found in the bathroom, where Mrs Manders died. Her fingerprints are on the frame of the gun . . .'

'My prints can't be on it!'

But they could be, of course. The sweat was now cold on the back of his neck. Sandboy sensed a sickness of fright. That small ugly silver shape in the cellophane was the one thing that might hang him after all.

'No,' said Rutter, unexpectedly accepting the point, 'that's true. Your prints aren't on the gun.'

'I told you! What . . !'

'They're on the cartridge cases.'

The shock was like a noose that choked off speech.

'You'd be surprised,' Rutter continued conversationally, 'the number of people who take great care to ensure that their prints aren't on the gun, but never think about the cartridges. Look at me, not at Mr Bowlett. He can't give you the answers.'

Christ! Had they found the case of the cartridge that McGouran had fired at Pender's picture rail? Had he left a print when he loaded it? But in that moment, it seemed to Sandboy, the shock of fright cleared his confusion, like a wave of icy water. For the second time in his dealings with Rutter, he saw his escape and sprang at it.

'Is that all? She had a little gun. How should I know it was that one? All she had it for was target shooting. That's all.'

'When had you seen it?'

'One day, some time back. She might have just got it, perhaps. Anyway, she asked me to show her how to load it with these little bullets. I hadn't seen it before but I managed to do it for her. That's the simple truth.'

Bowlett watched the faces of the policemen. After witnessing so many interviews of suspects, he knew that the fingerprints on the cartridge cases were intended to knock Sandboy flat and allow Rutter to finish the kill. But Sandboy, after so much stupidity in fighting for his life, had brought the attack to a halt in the one way possible. Now it was only Little Madam's uncorroborated story of the young man's dismissal and a Manders divorce that remained. And Little Madam might be proved a liar in other things.

Rutter hung on, like a weary terrier to the neck of a rat. But perhaps it was only for the benefit of the transcript. 'So when you said that you had never seen the gun until I showed it to you, you were not telling the truth?'

'Well, I certainly wasn't lying,' Sandboy said aggressively. 'You never said which gun it was, nor where it had come from. Hardly surprising I didn't realise. Easy enough not to know or make a mistake. That was definitely down to you, Mr Rutter.'

'But when, as you say, Mrs Manders first showed it to you, you knew at once how to load it.'

'No,' Sandboy said, 'as it happens I didn't. But I fiddled around with it until I found out how. I get to know how to work things by trying them: cars, wireless sets, cinema projectors, all sorts of things.'

'And when did Mrs Manders show the gun to you?'

'Months ago. I can't tell you exactly. I'd no reason to remember the date, had I? I never knew it was going to be important.'

'Was it before or after you were last questioned by Sergeant Brodie and myself?'

Bowlett pulled his dark blazer cuff down over the gold link. 'I'm not having this, Mr Rutter. You're trying to put words into his mouth. He doesn't know. I'm not having him forced to make guesses – and that being put in as evidence against him if he gets it wrong. There's an end of it.'

After his fright, Sandboy had recovered and was answering again with the assurance of a man who was innocent. He seemed confident, certain of his direction, like a driver on an open road.

'The fact remains, you cannot establish that you were in your hotel room all night,' Rutter said. His words were combative but his tone was flat.

'The fact remains,' Bowlett intervened, 'that you can't prove he wasn't. My client could have loaded that gun for Mrs Manders anywhere at any time. It's not evidence. Before we get any deeper into this, there's something I'd like to say for the record of the interview. So that it may be heard by any jury . . .'

Landis, who had been sitting silently, like a mourner at the reading of a will, took command again. 'What's that?'

'A House of Lords decision in the Woolmington case last year, Mr Landis. The man who shot his wife. You were involved in the investigation, I recall. Not one of your best results. There were certain observations their lordships thought should be passed on to investigating officers such as yourself. Forgotten already, have you?'

'I'm not having this,' Rutter said.

But Bowlett began to speak, as if by invitation, leaning back in his chair and studying the ceiling. 'Throughout the web of the English criminal law, one golden thread is always to be seen, that it is the duty of the prosecution to prove the prisoner's guilt . . .'

'I'm not having it either,' Landis said.

'Which is no doubt why you saw Woolmington walk free on appeal at the end of your case. You may have forgot already, Mr Landis, but I haven't. My client doesn't need to prove he was never in the rooms where Mr and Mrs Manders died. You have to prove he was. So far, you've offered no kind of evidence except nonsense about cartridges, which proves nothing, and the fact that he spent time with Mrs Manders, information which he volunteered to you as soon as this investigation began.'

Rutter tried to resume the questioning. 'There's another matter.'

'No.' Bowlett folded his hands on the table. 'No, Mr Rutter. This interview has gone as far as it's going. You had your chance. You asked him to prove he was in his room all night. You know he can't do that. No one could. You asked him to prove Miss Nina Manders was lying. He can't prove a negative. However, it seems we could prove she lied about other matters. Even her own name is false. You accuse him of having been in the Manders' rooms with a gun that night, when all he did was show Mrs Manders how to load a target revolver weeks or months earlier. Her prints are on the gun, not his, as they are on the stiff edging of the pillow with which Mr Manders was suffocated.'

'She could have touched that pillow when it was on her own bed in her own room,' Rutter said furiously. 'Someone could have used it to suffocate Mr Manders and then switched it with Manders' for us to find by the body. Pillows in hotels are all alike.'

'Then you prove it,' Bowlett said contemptuously. 'I don't envy you. My client's here to give information on specific and material issues. Not for you to throw all the mud you can find in the hope that some of it might stick.'

Landis glowered at him. 'You know what obstruction of justice is, Mr Bowlett?'

'Better than you seem to know what my client's rights are, Mr Landis. Seeing the turn this interview has taken, I'm advising him to answer no more questions. You'll find that's not obstruction of justice. It's judges' rules. You break them at your peril. You got a case against him? You prove it. You want to charge him? Charge him. He's been detained without charge quite long enough. You charge him now or he goes home with me.'

There was a silence. Landis and Rutter seemed each to wait for the other to answer. But it was Bowlett who spoke first.

'Two other things, gentlemen. First, I'm informed that while detained by Mr Landis and another officer of this division yesterday, my client was cuffed round the head by Mr Landis who was standing behind his chair. Second thing, if he's not charged or released half an hour from now, I'll be going to a judge in chambers for a writ of habeas corpus to set him free. And when I do that, I'll want to see a charge of assault on him preferred.'

Another silence followed. Rutter noticed that Ray Landis, the 'Iron Man' of area CID, was more deeply flushed than seemed good for a man of his age and build.

Bowlett relaxed again. 'Now, if I might be pardoned a cliché, gentlemen, am I to take it that silence equals consent?'

Chapter Thirty-One

Rutter watched the white path of the headlights cutting a tunnel back to London through the winter night. Brodie braked sharply on a downward curve.

'You could beat Bowlett,' Brodie said loyally. 'I dare say you could beat Landis. Between the two of them, they're lethal. Why the hell did Ray have to hit Sandboy when he took him in?'

'It's a custom they have down there.' Rutter yawned at the chalk and flint ridges, rising on either side of the road in the headlights. 'Coppers' perks. Anyway, Sandboy's a cocky little shit. Needs a slap.'

'Between the two of them—' Brodie began but Rutter talked him down.

'I can't blame old Landis. I wrote the script for his interview, he agreed it and it flopped. I'd counted on Sandboy saying at the start that he was never in the Manders' rooms that night. He'd have to say that, true or false. I was also sure he'd say that he'd never seen the gun before. What else could he say? Get those two denials and then let him have ten or fifteen minutes of winding himself into the web. Then we'd spring his prints on him – to show he must have handled the gun that was found on the stool next to Yvonne Manders' body. If she had it

315

with her when Manders died, then Sandboy's prints were there as well. And perhaps Sandboy too.'

Brodie turned the wheel. 'You put him on the back foot there, Jack. But he came round so fast with that story of loading the gun for her. Almost sounded true.'

'Sounded bollocks! If he ever did load it for her, he could have done it in her room the night she died. Just in case the pillow over Manders' face wasn't enough. Still, you're right. I should never have handed him that chance.'

'Anyway,' Brodie said consolingly, 'it was her prints on the gun itself, not his.'

'Easiest thing in the world, Frank. No need to press a dead hand round the grip, in her case. All someone had to do when she was alive was hand it to her. Ask her if she'd ever seen one like this. Or ask her if she'd like to take a pot shot at a tin can. Anything. A few drinks and she'd have her hands all over it. Then he takes it back by the point of the barrel and keeps it safe. Her prints on the grip. All others dusted off.'

Brodie touched a foot switch and dipped the head-lights as a car took the bend towards them. 'Not your fault, Jack. Bowlett's right about the lack of motive, though. Sandboy was screwing Yvonne Manders. Manders might or might not care. But what's in it for Sandboy, if he kills the old boy? So long as Manders was alive, Tarrant might keep him afloat. The minute he was dead, the creditors would close in. That's the information, anyway. For her it might be different. Young widow. Some of the cash might come her way, even with the debts. She could pick someone better than Sandboy. He was strictly there to service her. No other future. He'd got everything to lose when Manders died.'

'You even talk like bloody Bowlett!'

'Better get used to that, Jack. If this had gone to court, you'd hear a lot of people talking like Bowlett. A couple of QCs for a start. Even the judge. I'll grant you Sandboy's a cocky little shit but there's nothing to hang him by. Not a print not a whisker. Plus, if the Manders finale was a set up, it's a hell of a sight too smart for Sandboy. He's all cock and mouth.'

They drove in silence through the south-west suburbs until Rutter fell asleep. He woke again as they were crossing Vauxhall Bridge. Beyond Buckingham Palace Road, a girl working through the night in a Victoria Street display window was arching tinsel over a collection of winter fashions.

'Stan Bowlett, Frank. That's twice we've had him sitting there holding Sandboy's hand.'

'You can't screw Bowlett,' Frank Brodie said reasonably.

'I don't want to screw Bowlett. I'm just thinking of the bill for his services.'

'Legal aid pays it, for a no-hoper like Sandboy.'

'Not that bill, Frank. Sandboy has Sonny Tarrant to pay for Bowlett's services. A small-size sneak thief that thought too big. You think that bill's not going to be presented? Before Tarrant's finished with him, Sandboy might be pleading to be back in the cells with comfy old Ray Landis smacking his head and the local gendarmerie using his solar plexus for boot exercise. I suppose that's justice, of a kind.'

The car drew up under the turreted height of Norman Shaw's opera house design. There was a telephone message waiting on Rutter's desk. It was marked 'urgent'. He opened it and looked up at Brodie.

'That's it, Frank. Ray Landis. Bowlett came on heavy

about habeas corpus and a judge in chambers. Not to mention the slap round the head that could have been embarrassing to Landis's remaining eighteen months. So Ray's let the little bastard go. I hoped he mightn't, but I knew he would.'

'Arrested him too soon,' Brodie said, 'and therefore had to let him go too soon. Broke two rules in one.'

Rutter put the message on his desk. 'Ray Landis has been treading water for the past five years. Everyone knows that. Waiting on his bungalow and rose bed. And a super's pension. He's got the rank but he's lost the taste. Sandboy was handed him ready for the oven – and handed back again almost before we had a foot in the door. Sonny Tarrant could show that he was just the concerned citizen who came forward and put Sandboy on the spot. We try to prove that he was pulling old Landis's strings from the start, it could bring down their area CID in ruins. Ray Landis knows that. He'd stop it even before it started. His Chief Constable would stop it anyway. So far as Landis is concerned Yvonne Manders suffocated her comatose husband with a pillow and then topped herself. Overdose and alcoholic poisoning, while unconscious in the bath.'

Brodie shrugged. 'Which could be true, Jack.'

'Which could also be bollocks, Frank.' Rutter reached for his briefcase and turned out the light.

Brodie paused in the corridor. 'Which leaves Tarrant and his team still out there. This keeps up, Jack, that's five quid you'll be paying me.'

On the following day, Sandboy earned only four lines at the foot of a column in the southern counties evening paper. An unnamed man who had been helping the police with their inquiries into the deaths of Yvonne Manders and her husband had been released. Suicide had not been ruled out but the area CID team were still following several leads.

Chapter Thirty-Two

'Got a match?' Tarrant stared across the desk at Sandboy in the leather chair. Then he touched his pocket. 'No,' he said, 'you wouldn't 'ave, would you? I still got 'em.'

Beyond the window of the hotel office, the winter tide rolled steadily ashore in long gathering breakers. With great elaboration, Tarrant lit his cigarette, shook the match leisurely, so that the flame guttered before it died, and dropped it into the bakelite ashtray.

'You been lucky, Sandboy, all things considered. You got a lot to be thankful for. Home Office could have been gettin' a grave ready for you now by Wandsworth wall, if truth be told.'

Sandboy said nothing, staring at his tormentor, waiting for a sign of condemnation or reprieve. Tarrant resumed. 'Take that business at Lawsons. You was nearly put in Dalgetty Street the morning of that break-in. You don't even know how close, do you? Near as anything. But not quite. Still, they don't hang you for a break-in. But then you was an inch from bein' mixed up in that nasty business of Pelly Pender's furs and the poor old lady. Not quite. But you still could be. And then you was on the hot spot for poor old Manny and his missus. But not there quite long enough to burn. And all you could give Mr

Landis was some cock about plain-clothes men. Lucky? I'd say you'd been lucky!'

'I saw . . .'

Tarrant's lip moved in a waggish sneer. 'You'll tell me next you saw plain-clothes men round Dalgetty Street. Only, of course, you weren't there, were you? I'm not sayin' you never saw any of them in the Garden Royal, only no one believes you. So what's it matter? If you was to see 'em again, it wouldn't be for very long, I don't suppose. Hardly time for you to ask, 'Why me?' or say, 'Goodbye.' Bit like your friend Gillis and that car. I dare say he didn't even have time for a little piggy-squeal of fright. He was too busy dyin' in the Hampstead Road.'

They sat in silence, which Sandboy lacked the courage to break. Gillis. McGouran. Manny and Yvonne. The 'plain-clothes men'. Sandboy understood them all.

Tarrant looked at him thoughtfully. 'Mind you, son, fair's fair, that was a swift dodge about the gun and your prints on the cartridges! Sayin' she asked you to load it for her. You sure about that?'

'I told them,' Sandboy said. 'Didn't I?'

'All right,' Tarrant said reasonably. 'Only perhaps you don't know everything about .22 ammo.'

'Meaning?'

'Meanin' this,' Tarrant said contemptuously. He drew his hand from his coat pocket and opened it. A little cylinder of gunmetal lay in his palm.

'They pack 'em in such silly little boxes,' he said understandingly. 'They rattle around. You can't hardly lift a box of .22 ammo but one of 'em falls out. Some smart-arse hides 'em under a floorboard, say. He thinks no one knows. But there's always one or two slips out in time. With the box bein' lifted and put back. They roll out of sight under the boards, of course. But all it takes is a whisper in the right ear. A good search with all the boards up. Cartridges come to light, even months after.'

Sandboy had supposed that someone on Tarrant's orders had searched the rooms in Queen's Road and taken the gun after Dalgetty Street, before Rutter's arrival. But he knew by instinct that he dared not admit to Tarrant what they both had in mind. Tarrant had saved him – for what? The cackle of a gull landing on the hotel balustrade ended their silence.

'Fair enough,' Tarrant said, changing the subject. 'So you want to know what's going to happen to you now? First, think about what you've done. You've shat on some important people, if you'll excuse my French, and you got to be smacked for it. You're not the first, of course. There's others I've had in here, in that chair, pleadin' to know how much they got to be hurt, as if they couldn't wait for it. Or they're beggin' to have it done and over with and start again fresh.'

Sandboy stared at him, the rabbit before the stoat, unbelieving in the face of Tarrant's casual savagery.

Tarrant took the cigarette from his mouth. 'You been up to one or two things best not spoke about outside this room. Right? If you ask me, Mr Rutter and his friends let you off a bit light. Mind you, someone could still hand you over as a gift. Pelly Pender could, if he made you one of his three robbers. Or a bum-boy called McGouran could have done. He was a little bird that squeaked a note or two before he stopped singing. Not squeaked to the law, naturally. Good enough, all the same. Bum-Boy seemed to recall my good friends Pelly and Vi tied in a couple of chairs. His memory was jogged for him, good and sharp. And now there's that fat fairy Spurgeon might speak a piece. He doesn't know he might as yet, but he would, if it was put to him proper, same as McGouran. You think Spurgeon's a hard man? Him bein' in prison, there's one or two could be moved in to share his cell, have him cryin' his eyes out after an hour or two. Then there's that old fake Samuelson . . .'

'All right,' Sandboy said, as bravely as he could. 'What exactly do you want?'

Tarrant took the cigarette from his mouth again, slowly. 'Fuckin' shut up,' he said quietly. 'I'm talkin', you're listenin'. There's two might put you in London that other day when Lawsons was broken into. Dalgetty Street with Gillis. You think you got an alibi for that? 'Course I saw someone goin' up them stairs to the projectors. That what you're thinkin'? Thinkin' you're safe? Don't bother. Naturally, when Mrs Hallam and Manny said they seen you in the picture-'ouse at ten past three, I thought it must have been you I saw from the back on the stairs. But if you was definitely seen elsewhere . . .' He exhaled a thin stream of pale smoke from his nostrils. 'Manny knew how to run them projectors at three o'clock, if you wasn't there. And he must have done. Rather than leave the public sittin' there with nothin' on the screen. Anyone could do it. Especially if the machines had been loaded in advance. And Manny ain't here any more to deny the suggestion, is he?'

He looked at his cigarette with distaste, holding it out, then crushed it in the bakelite ashtray. 'You still say you never met my friend Pelly Pender?'

'No,' said Sandboy shortly. The pretence of innocence was all that lay between him and the worst that Tarrant could do.

Tarrant shrugged. 'You'd be wettin' yourself with

fright now, if you had the intelligence to do it. You never twigged what Rutter's really after? Pelly's had our Mr Rutter at his house twice, over that business in January. He was robbed, of course, but that's not what Rutter's there about. You ever hear of a thing called constructive murder?'

'No.'

'Time you did. It's when some prat like you goes out, with someone else, to do somethin' quite ordinary. Just a bit of thievin'. Only you, or the someone you're with, hits whoever's bein' robbed. Or hits a bit harder than was meant. And whoever is hit dies. Right? Killin' was the last thing you wanted, likewise the man you're with that struck the blow. And you, yourself, never even touched anyone. Now then. If you hadn't been thievin' or robbin' it might just be called an accident in court. Perhaps manslaughter at the worst. Ten years banged up and then out again with your cock in your hand, ready to make up for lost time. Only, if you was up to no good, when this accident happened, they call it constructive murder against you. Just because you was there when it happened.'

Tarrant had positioned the plank meticulously. Sandboy would walk it now, inch by inch. Tarrant drew his lip above his teeth in another sneer.

'What's all this to me?' Sandboy had to say it, but he watched the end of the plank come closer.

'Nothin' much.' Tarrant took a monogrammed handkerchief from his pocket and blew his nose for effect. 'Except they hang you for it. Eight o'clock jump, in other words. Constructive murder. You was there thievin' when it happened, even though none of you meant it to happen. Even though you wasn't on the scene when it happened. It's murder by you just the same. Ask old Stan Bowlett to tell you.'

There was a pause.

'What I hear,' Tarrant said, 'some little bastard tied up poor old Vi Pender and held her face in water so's she couldn't breathe, knocked her about so's she died of it later in hospital. That's another thing Stan Bowlett could tell you. She don't have to die that minute for it to be murder. Year and a day, she can take. And police don't give up on a case like that. Not even years later. They keep comin' back and lookin'.'

'It wasn't me,' Sandboy said firmly. 'I never was there.'

'Good,' Tarrant said encouragingly. 'Only I'm against hangin' for crimes like that. It's too easy. If I was to find that someone had done Vi Pender, he'd be pleadin' for the rope before I'd finished.'

Sandboy said nothing. Tarrant changed the attack, as if he might believe his suspect. 'I hear from Mr Rutter that they're still there at Pelly Pender's. They're missin' a matchbox one of the little bastards left in the house. And there's a missin' bullet. One of 'em fired a bullet right by the old lady's head. Imagine that! Can't wonder the poor soul died of heart failure.'

He paused, looked out of the window as if to control his grief, then turned. 'If there's a bullet found, then they reckon there's got to be a cartridge case somewhere nearby. If they could find that or the bullet, they'd identify the gun. Cartridge case or bullet would do it. Just like fingerprints, they are. No two sets alike. Base of the cartridge case has the imprint of the hammer. Bullet has the marks of the barrel. If it's a gun the law should happen to have in its hands already, they'd identify it in ten minutes. Still you know all that, I'm sure.'

'I was never there.'

Tarrant's mouth tightened in a grimace of impatience. 'Don't keep on like that, not if you want any help from me.'

At the mention of help, Sandboy wondered if he had misunderstood Tarrant's aggression after all. Tarrant lit another cigarette and said, 'Right. You can forget what happened at that old villain Lawsons – whether you was there or not. You can forget McGouran and Gillis, even Spurgeon. You can even forget Pelly Pender. What you can't forget – never – is a matchbox or a bullet or a cartridge case. Things you could hold in the palm of one hand. Things that might go anywhere to anyone by the next post, for matchin' against any gun the police already confiscated and got in their collection. Got it?'

Sandboy waited. Tarrant's lip rose a little. 'You got bloody earwax? I said, got it?'

Sandboy nodded. Then he saw an opening for a clever answer and went for it. 'Matches and bullets could have come from anywhere, if they wasn't found until now. Or they could be planted there.'

Tarrant seemed unexpectedly pleased by this small burst of defiance and the pleasure of crushing it. 'If it was only them things you'd be right, my son. But the world's full of amateurs like you. Right? Vi Pender was killed by amateurs. Every young skate-arse thinks that once he puts on a pair of kid gloves, he won't leave prints. Right?'

Sandboy said nothing, unable to imagine what lay in store.

'I said right?'

'If you say so.'

Tarrant leant across the desk, the bland face suddenly

flushed with outrage. 'If I say so? Who the fuck you think you're talkin' to?' Then he was abruptly calm again. 'You look at a pair of kid gloves next time. There's a vent and little amber-coloured button at the top where the gloves do up. You got that on yours?'

Sandboy nodded.

'So's everyone,' Tarrant said, flicking ash from the cigarette. 'It leaves a little triangle of hand. Bare skin. You look next time. So you're a sneak thief, turnin' a house over. Sooner or later, if you were there more than a few minutes, you'd put your hand on a leather chair, or the wall, or the banister of the stairs. And then you'd leave a little print of that triangle of bare skin. See?'

Sandboy gazed at him and felt sick with tension, guessing the rest.

'You might as well have left your complete set of dabs, if you did that,' Tarrant said. 'No two people alike.'

'I never heard that. Dabs, yes. Not the base of the hand.'

'Don't believe me?' Tarrant picked up the phone and spoke as if he had just been laughing. 'Charley Archer, please. Charley? A moment of your valuable, if you'd be so good.'

He smoked in silence until Archer tapped on the door. The moment it opened, Tarrant was the jovial employer. 'Charley! Me and our young friend here been havin' a bit of a bet. Let's have you as the umpire, you havin' been on the force. Say I'm a villain. Say I break into a bank down the town. Say I'm wearin' kid gloves, so's not to leave fingerprints. But I don't know about that little vent at the openin' of a glove, where the button is. And let's say I leave a few prints that way, just at the base of the hand. Could they tell from those that it was me? Suppose they had a record of me?'

Archer looked at him, as if he suspected a trick. Tarrant puffed genially at an Abdullah cigarette behind the desk.

'Yes, Mr Tarrant,' Archer said cautiously, 'they could tell. All parts of the hand are individual. Distinctive. Not just fingertips.'

Tarrant beamed at him. 'Well done, Charles! You won my bet for me!' He indicated Sandboy with his thumb. 'He's a proper lad, isn't he? Takin' our bets already! That's a nod and a smile down the drinker I owe you at lunchtime, Charley, when this is over.'

Then he turned and smiled, open-mouthed, at Sandboy. 'You got a lot to learn, son,' he chuckled for Archer's benefit. 'Still, treat us right, you'll get to like it here.'

The door closed behind Archer. Tarrant turned back to Sandboy. His geniality had gone.

'There can't be any prints,' Sandboy said desperately.

'How d'you know that, if you was never there?'

'That's how! Because I was never there! Never!' It was almost a child's cry.

'Dear, oh dear!' Tarrant said humorously, as if to someone else who was in the room. 'Just 'ark at 'im! Never there! All right. You was never there? You'll want to clear your name then. Make sure the law never comes botherin' you afterwards.'

'How do you mean?'

'How do I mean? You was never there, you say. If that's true, your prints aren't there. They can't be, can they? And in poor old Pelly Pender's house, nothin's been wiped out, all the prints kept. Either where they was made or impressions taken by the law. In other words, I can pick up this phone and tell Stan Bowlett or Mr Rutter that you want a chance to clear your name. You want 'em to take a print of the base of your hand and try it all over that house. Just to eliminate you as a runner for the eight o' clock jump in a month or two. If you was never there, my son, you'd like a chance to do that, wouldn't you? I know I would, if it was my good name!'

The trap snapped shut. For the first time, Sandboy felt terror spreading like iced-water in his entrails. He was no match for Sonny Tarrant. In his stupidity, he had thought that he might hold his own, as he had done against Landis and Rutter. But this path to destruction was worse than anything he had imagined, even worse than any final split-second meeting with the two 'plain-clothes men'. He believed, with dread, in the story of the man carrying his nose in his handkerchief or his finger-tips in a trilby hat. He tried to reason with his antagonist.

'There wouldn't be anything there that they could find now. Not after all these months.' But he had to clear his throat to say it.

'You want to bet on that as well?' Tarrant asked indifferently. 'If you happen to be right, they'd still go on lookin'. If you got it wrong, you'd be danglin' in the dark under Mr Albert Pierrepoint's execution shed before summer. Neck twisted, head on one side, and your pants pissed. All the same, if you're so sure and so brave about it, you won't mind me phonin' our friend Mr Rutter to ask for a chance to clear your name.'

Sandboy said nothing. His heart was pounding and his brain deadlocked.

'You want me to lift this phone or not?' Tarrant snapped. His hand rested on the receiver, then picked it up. 'Shirley, darlin', you get me a line to Mr Jack Rutter at Scotland Yard, can you? Whitehall 1212. Apologize for interruptin' him as a busy man. Just tell him there's somethin' I think he'd like to hear.'

'No!' Sandboy sobbed the words. But in his panic and despair, he was prepared to reach across the desk and attack his tormentor.

'Hang on,' Tarrant said wearily. 'All right, Shirley girlie, not just now.'

He cradled the receiver gently, opened his rolled-silver cigarette case and chose the flattened oval of another Abdullah. 'You really think, son, if they found a cartridge case that the Walden had fired, or a fag end or matchbox, with prints like the rounds in its chambers, they wouldn't be here in five minutes to have a good feel of those soft young hands?'

Sandboy hesitated. There was nothing he could say without making matters worse. He felt himself shaking with the chill of the fear that had ambushed him.

'You got a lot to be fuckin' thankful for!' Tarrant said with quiet bitterness. 'You got a grudge because a soft old uncle like Landis clips you round the earhole? You ought to be kissin' his arse with gratitude that you was turned over to him by me and dealt with quick. All he does is take prints of your pinkie-tips. Same as the rest of us. You any idea what Scotland Yard would have done to you, if you'd been handed to them instead? You got me to thank for being turned over to Uncle Ray.'

Sandboy said nothing. He wondered if it was possible that Landis might be in Tarrant's pay.

'Don't you forget it!' Tarrant said savagely. 'And don't think of runnin' off from here, seein' you got nowhere else to go. If I was to pick up that phone and tell Mr

Rutter what I just told you, they'd nab you in ten minutes. You wouldn't live to see the spring. Still, you got that in mind now, I hope.' He looked across the desk with the first suggestion of a crooked smile of conquest.

Sandboy waited.

'But I suppose I shan't phone Mr Rutter unless I got to,' Tarrant said. 'Just keep this in mind. So long as you fetch and carry for me, you'll only answer back once. That'll be the first and last time. You don't get no second chance. And if me or Mr Archer tells you to lick spit up from the tiles, you'll dive on your knees to do it and thank you, sir. Got that? On the other hand, do as you're told and who knows, in time? You got other uses, I hear. You showed Mrs Manders some of 'em, I believe. Not too shy neither.'

Sandboy stared at him. Tarrant's ferocity had been so self-righteous that it seemed impossible he was about to demand some sexual grossness.

Tarrant blew out smoke and continued. 'Well, now. You havin' these abilities, there's Little Madam needs a moke. You like Little Madam? Yes? You know what a moke is, in the trade? No? One that never goes out of season and won't take no for an answer from the likes of her. And that's not all. A moke ain't allowed to be shy. He don't go limp when called upon, not even if some guests should happen to be watchin' the show. Savvy?'

Sandboy nodded like an automaton, scarcely listening or understanding. He felt so dizzy with the nausea of fright, after Tarrant's abortive call to Rutter, that he thought he might vomit if he tried to speak.

'Contrariwise,' Tarrant glanced at his cigarette and flicked off the ash, 'someone wants a bender, you'll grab your toes so fast you'll hardly know you done it. You could find yourself in pictures too.'

Sandboy was still not listening. Even the worst dread of the gallows had been controllable before. But the eight o'clock jump, once joked about as a professional hazard, now lay at his heels like a patient shadow. He could almost sense the pinion straps tight on his wrists, the morning light in the prison shed veiled by a canvas hood. A single telephone call would begin his protracted agony.

'Likewise,' Tarrant said, 'you lost that raincoat of yours when Gillis died, they tell me. We might even fit you out with a Burberry and a trilby hat.'

Sandboy looked at him but said nothing. Whatever spirit had been left in him after the death of Yvonne Manders, Sonny Tarrant had broken it.

Tarrant's own mood changed again with psychopathic abruptness. 'You look as if you might spew your ring, my son,' he said cheerfully. 'Not in here, if you don't mind. Go on. Clear out. But come back as soon as you done it. We haven't finished our conversation yet. You'll want to hear some of the things we'll have you doing before today's over.'

Sandboy pushed himself up from the chair and crossed the room. He had never believed literally that fear could make a man's legs give way under him but he stumbled once on his way to the door, tripping on his own foot. He turned with his hand on the doorknob. Tarrant was still watching him.

'You haven't heard it all, not by any means,' Tarrant said thoughtfully. 'Still, you can have the best bits later. Once you feel better. Ten minutes from now.'

Chapter Thirty-Three

The old woman sat in a wide padded chair. An empty wine glass was lodged neglected in her fingers. She was humming to herself, a repeated fragment of a half-remembered song. At intervals she nodded emphatically, as if the effort helped her to recall and capture the melody.

Sonny Tarrant stood at the darkened balcony window and stared out beyond the curtain lights of other apartments towards the gardens and the sea. He listened to his mother briefly and frowned into the December night.

Beyond the misted haloes of the lamps, where the muddy winter surf slapped against the pebbles, great events were moving that night. The voices on the airwaves had again spoken to him confidentially, a few hours earlier, and had put him once again at the centre of the drama.

He had heard the king's abdication broadcast only once. Yet it seemed to him that he could recite every line of it in his mind, like the confession of a friend. He heard again every emphasis and hesitation, as easily as if he had made them himself. 'But *you* must believe *me* . . . when I *tell* you that *I* have found it impossible to carry the heavy *burden* of responsibility, and to discharge my duties as *King* as *I* would wish to do without the help and support of the woman I *love* . . '

The magnificent lines of royal tragedy ran, over and over, through Tarrant's thoughts, quickening his blood each time by the thrill of their finality. The murk of the winter drizzle seemed to wall in the seaside apartment blocks. Yet the lost king was out there now, keeping a lonely vigil, the slim bows of the grey destroyer cutting the sullen tide of the Channel as it carried him away to France.

The pathos and the gallantry were irresistible, the young monarch gone into exile for the woman he loved, just like that other young king, Ivor Novello's romantic hero in *Glamorous Night*. Curious that the stage play should have opened at Drury Lane the year before Edward VIII had come to the throne. Tarrant paused in his thoughts and wondered if the composer could possibly have read some secret in the future.

Beyond the long brightly lit windows of the pavilion, the band that had been playing when the old king died moved from a waltz to a quick step arrangement. 'Champagne Charlie is my name . . . Champagne drinking is my game . . . There's no drink as good as Fizz, Fizz, Fizz . . . I'll drink every drop there is, is, is . . ' The passing of one king and the accession of another was nothing to the dancers. They moved faster in the changed rhythm, like clockwork toys newly wound. King Edward would never come back, Tarrant supposed. But that trim, spruce figure, with a hint of America in his voice, the cigarette held casually between the fingers, the nights spent dancing with his girl to the music of the band at the Embassy Club, had moved the world on.

A new age. The tall cabinet of the radiogram in the

corner of the room brought its voices to him from beyond the fog and drizzle of the Channel. It was tuned to the transmitters of Berlin, Hamburg, Budapest, Rome, Madrid ... Its music echoed the marching songs of a modern order, the hymns of the warrior legions, the leader's salute and the crowd's roar, but also the easy rhythms of night clubs and palm courts.

Even in England, Sonny Tarrant saluted the changes that were coming, new men with new ideas replacing the old gang of loons and pig breeders. Manny had been right about that, at least. The voices of the new order were closer now than Berlin or Rome. They rang out every week in London, at Olympia, at Earl's Court, at the Albert Hall. Their words promised that a good many eggs would have to be broken before the grand omelette could be made.

Tarrant thought of this and smiled at its truth.

'What you thinking about, son?'

He turned, his lip moving in its familiar smile. 'Us, Ma,' he said gently. 'Only about us.'

He walked back and stood behind her chair.

'What about us, son?' Mrs Tarrant's voice hesitated on the verge of the question.

'The future, Ma,' he said quietly, stooping to kiss the grey crown of her head, 'Our future, mostly. We got a lot to think about now. With Manny gone, and his missus too. Sad, of course, that she went off her head and did those things. But it's our chance now.'

Before she could answer him, the smart ivory-coloured telephone rang. Tarrant picked it up. The smile slipped away and his face was impassive. 'Is that so? Well, you can tell 'em from me, Foxy, to clear off and not come back. I'm in charge here and I won't have some little guttersnipe from the papers raking muck on Lady Blue. Not unless they want their arse kicked level with their Adam's apple. Drugs and drink and men? They're only trying it because they know there can't be libel once she's dead.'

He paused and listened. 'They missed out on that, Foxy. Funeral was down here last Thursday for both of 'em. What I sent was red roses from all of us. From me and Ma, the garage, the picture-house and the Garden Royal. I had 'em done up just like it was a first night on the stage. She'd have liked that all right. They put 'em on the coffin. Nice touch. Made a good show on a winter day. I sent 'em with a card. Like I always put – Red flowers for Lady Blue.'

He listened again. 'The business is settled now, Foxy. Picture-house and Brandons Garages. Garden Royal we got already. Stannie Bowlett drew up the arrangement years back. In the event of other partner's decease, surviving party has the option to foreclose on all mortgages and debts, subject to certain provisions for surviving next of kin. Nina, in other words. I did the necessary yesterday. And seein' Little Madam ain't legally of age for four more years, I suppose she'll have to come and say please to me each time she wants her pocket money.'

The voice at the other end asked a question and Tarrant laughed. 'Of course, he never thought his Lady Blue would go so soon, bein' so much younger than him. The way it is, though, I'm the one that holds the strings. I'm what you might call Little Madam's guardian for the next four years. Stannie Bowlett done the goods there all right. We ought to see him right for a drink or two. Him having put himself out by quite a bit.'

There was another question from his caller. 'Seeing

as Mrs Tarrant's here just now, Foxy, I shan't repeat what needs saying to the little guttersnipe from the papers. But you tell 'im just the same. He's safe from libel, perhaps, but not from a good bootin'. I know she was a tart. You know she was a tart. No reason it should be all over the papers. There's plenty others out there of that sort, if they want 'em, only too glad to be in their poxy newspapers.'

He put the phone down and came back to stand behind the old woman's chair.

'Your friends got a lot to be grateful to you for, son,' she said wistfully, 'You never been one to let 'em down.'

He worked her arthritic shoulders affectionately with his fingers. 'It's going to be easy now, Ma, from now on. If we can't see to Little Madam between us, we both need skinnin' alive. Bit hysterical, she is, but there's ways of curin' that. She'll learn to stop, after she sees it don't get her nowhere. We could even make somethin' of her. I been wonderin' if that young Sandboy mightn't give her a run.'

Mrs Tarrant giggled. 'You never mean to start playin' Cupid, son! Finding her a sweetheart?'

'No reason not, Ma. He's clean, I should think. Stop her frettin' and pinin'.'

The old woman nodded agreement.

'Trouble with her now,' he said confidentially, 'she'd like to think herself high strung and fancy. But what she is underneath, all said and done, is a bit common. Like you said once. A bit brass. She needs watchin', and bein' made to show herself to please, and act grateful in front of people we know. No more of this want to be alone. Who she think she is?'

He smiled at their reflections in the darkened window. 'You could manage her all right, Ma. You're twice

what she is or ever will be! Any backchat and you could
have Little Madam over your knee easy enough, in a
manner of speakin'. You'll see if I'm not right. There's
nothing special about 'er. She'll come round, once she
sees that all she gets for bein' contrary is bruises on her
bruises.'

Mrs Tarrant began to laugh at the wildness of their
secret exchanges. In her dotage, her son talked to her
with the outrageous humour of a lover. Then the laughter
made her belch a little. She stopped and began to hum
contentedly again, the tune that the band had played,
occasionally breaking into the lines she could remember
from her youth as a stage dancer.

'I'm the idol of the barmaids . . . And Champagne
Charlie is my name . . .'

Standing behind her chair, Sonny Tarrant heard the
rambling lyric and stared down at the grey nodding head.
With a sense of dismay and fascination, he wondered if
he might one day need courage of a higher order. The
courage to provide for Evelyn Tarrant that act of oblivion
which had already given rest from care to Manny and
Yvonne.